"We've got to find the murderer! I expected great things of you, Gethryn."

THE RASP

BY

Philip

MacDonald

DOVER PUBLICATIONS, INC.
NEW YORK

This Dover edition, first published in 1979, in an unabridged, slightly revised and corrected republication of the work originally published in London, in 1924, by William Collins, Sons & Co., Ltd.

International Standard Book Number: 0-486-23864-4
Library of Congress Catalog Card Number: 79-52526

Manufactured in the United States of America
Dover Publications, Inc.
180 Varick Street
New York, N.Y. 10014

TO

THE GUV'NOR

CONTENTS

THE RASP

All the Birds of the Air
  Fell a-sighin' and a-sobbin'
When they heard of the death
  Of poor Cock Robin.

. . . .

"Who'll dig his Grave?"
  "I," said the Owl,
  "With my little Trowel;
I'll dig his Grave."

. . . .

"Who *killed* Cock Robin?"
  "I," said the Sparrow,
  "With my Bow and Arrow,
I killed Cock Robin!"

CHAPTER I

TOLLING THE BELL

I

THE OWL shows its blue and gilt cover on the bookstalls every Saturday morning. Thursday nights are therefore nights of turmoil in the offices in Fleet Street. They are always wearing nights; more so, of course, in hot weather than in cold. They are nights of discomfort for the office-boy and of something worse for the editor.

Spencer Hastings edited *The Owl*, and owned a third of it; and the little paper's success showed him to possess both brains and capacity for hard work. For a man of thirty-three he had achieved much; but that capacity for work was hard tested—especially on Thursday nights. As to the brains, there was really no doubt of their quality. Take, for instance, *The Owl* "specials." After he had thought of them and given birth to the first, *The Owl*, really a weekly review, was enabled to reap harvests in the way of "scoops" without in any way degenerating into a mere purveyor of news.

The thing was worked like this: If, by the grace of God or through a member of the "special" staff or by any other channel, there came to Hastings's ears a piece of Real News which might as yet be unknown to any of the big daily or evening papers, then within a few hours, whatever the day or night of the week, there appeared a special edition of *The Owl*. It bore, in place of the blue and gold, a cover of red and black. The letterpress was sparse. The price was twopence. The public bought the first two out of curiosity, and the subsequent issues because they had discovered that when the red and black jacket was seen Something had really Happened.

The public bought the real *Owl* as well. It was always original, written by men and women as yet little known and therefore unspoilt. It was witty, exciting, soothing, biting, laudatory, ironic, and sincere—all in one breath and irreproachable taste.

And Hastings loved it. But Thursday nights, press nights, were undoubtedly Hell. And this Thursday night, hotter almost than its stifling day, was the very hell of Hells.

He ruffled his straw-colored hair, looking, as a woman once said of him, rather like a stalwart and handsome chicken. Midnight struck. He worked on, cursing at the heat, the paper, his material, and the fact that his confidential secretary, his right-hand woman, was making holiday.

He finished correcting the proofs of his leader, then reached for two over-long articles by new contributors. As he picked up a blue pencil, his door burst open.

"What in hell——" he began; then looked up. "Good God! Marga—Miss Warren!"

It was sufficiently surprising that his right-hand woman should erupt into his room at this hour in the night when he had supposed her many miles away in a holiday bed; but that she should be thus, gasping, white-faced, dust-covered, hair escaping in a shining cascade from beneath a wrecked hat, was incredible.

Never before had he seen her other than calm, scrupulously dressed, exquisitely tidy and faintly severe in her beauty.

He rose to his feet slowly. The girl, her breath coming in great sobs, sank limply into a chair. Hastings rushed for the editorial bottle, glass, and siphon. He tugged at the door of the cupboard, remembered that he had locked it, and began to fumble for his keys. They eluded him. He swore beneath his breath, and then started as a hand was laid on his shoulder. He had not heard her approach.

"Please don't worry about that." Her words came short, jerkily, as she strove for breath. "Please, please, listen to me! I've got a Story—the biggest yet! Must have a special done now, to-night, this morning!"

Hastings forgot the whisky. The editor came to the top.

"What's happened?" snapped the editor.

"Cabinet Minister dead. John Hoode's been killed—murdered! To-night. At his country house."

"You *know?*"

The efficient Miss Margaret Warren was becoming herself again. "Of course. I heard all the fuss just after eleven. I was staying in Marling, you know. My landlady's husband is the police-sergeant. So I hired a car and came straight here. I thought you'd like to know." Miss Warren was unemotional.

"Hoode killed! Phew!" said Hastings, the man, wondering what would happen to the Party.

"*What* a story!" said Hastings, the editor. "Any other papers on to it yet?"

"I don't think they can be—yet."

"Right. Now nip down to Bealby, Miss Warren. Tell him he's got to get ready for a two-page special *now*. He must threaten, bribe, shoot, do anything to keep the printers at the job. Then see Miss Halford and tell her she can't go till she's arranged for issue. Then please come back here; I shall want to dictate."

"Certainly, Mr. Hastings," said the girl, and walked quietly from the room.

Hastings looked after her, his forehead wrinkled. Sometimes he wished she were not so sufficient, so calmly adequate. Just now, for an instant, she had been trembling, white-faced, weak. Somehow the sight, even while he feared, had pleased him.

He shrugged his shoulders and turned to his desk.

"Lord!" he murmured. "Hoode murdered. *Hoode!*"

2

"That's all the detail, then," said Hastings half an hour later. Margaret Warren, neat, fresh, her golden hair smooth and shining, sat by his desk.

"Yes, Mr. Hastings."

"Er—hm. Right. Take this down. 'Cabinet Minister Assassinated. Murder at Abbotshall——' "

" 'Awful Atrocity at Abbotshall,' " suggested the girl softly.

"Yes, yes. You're right as usual," Hastings snapped. "But I always forget we have to use journalese in the specials. Right. 'John Hoode Done to Death by Unknown Hand. *The Owl* most deeply regrets to announce that at eleven o'clock last night Mr. John Hoode, Minister of Imperial Finance, was found lying dead in the study of his country residence, Abbotshall, Marling. The circumstances were such' —pity we don't know what they really were, Miss Warren—'the circumstances were such as to show immediately that this chief among England's greatest men had met his death at the hands of a murderer, though it is impossible at present to throw any light upon the identity of the criminal.' New paragraph, please. 'We understand, however, that no time was lost in communicating with Scotland Yard, who have assigned the task of tracking down the perpetrator of this terrible crime to their most able and experienced officers'—always a safe card that, Miss Warren—'No time will be lost in commencing the work of investigation.' Fresh paragraph, please. 'All England, all the Empire, the whole world will join in offering their heartfelt sympathy to Miss Laura Hoode, who, we understand, is prostrated by the shock'—another safe bet—'Miss Hoode, as all know, is the sister of the late minister and his only relative. It is known that there were two guests at Abbotshall, that brilliant leader of society, Mrs. Roland Mainwaring, and Sir Arthur Digby-Coates, the millionaire philanthropist and Parliamentary Secretary to the Board of Conciliation. Sir Arthur was an extremely close and lifelong friend of the deceased and would affirm that he had not an enemy in the world——' "

Miss Margaret Warren looked up, her eyebrows severely interrogative.

"Well?" said Hastings uneasily.

"Isn't that last sentence rather dangerous, Mr. Hastings?"

"Hm—er—I don't know—er—yes, you're right, Miss Warren. Dammit, woman, are you ever wrong about anything?" barked Hastings; then recovered himself. "I *beg* your pardon. I—I——"

There came an aloof smile. "Please don't apologize, Mr. Hastings. Shall I change the phrase?"

"Yes, yes," muttered Hastings. "Say, say—put down—say——"

" '——and are stricken aghast at the calamity which has befallen them,' " suggested the girl.

"Excellent," said Hastings, composure recovered.

"By the way, did you tell Williams to get on with that padding? That sketch of Hoode's life and work? We've got to fill up that opposite-center page."

"Yes, Mr. Williams started on it at once."

"Good. Now take this down as a separate piece. It must be marked off with heavy black rules and be in Clarendon or some conspicuous type. Ready? '*The Owl,* aghast at this dreadful tragedy, yet arises from its sorrow and issues, on behalf of the public, a solemn exhortation and warning. Let the authorities see to it that the murderer is found, and found speedily. England demands it. The author of this foul deed must be brought swiftly to justice and punished with the utmost rigor of the law. No effort must be spared.' Now a separate paragraph, please. It must be underlined and should go on the opposite page—under Williams's article. 'Aware of the tremendous interest and concern which this terrible crime will arouse, *The Owl* has made special arrangements to have bulletins (in the same form as this special edition) published at short intervals in order that the public may have full opportunity to know what progress is being made in the search for the criminal.

" 'These bulletins will be of extraordinary interest, since we are in a position to announce that a special correspondent will despatch to us (so far as is consistent with the wishes of the police, whom we wish to assist rather than compete with) at frequent intervals, from the actual locus of the crime a résumé of the latest developments.'" Hastings sighed relief and leant back in his chair. "That's all, Miss Warren. And I hope—since the thing *is* done—that the murderer'll remain a mystery for a bit. We'll look rather prize idiots if the gardener's boy or some one confesses to-morrow. Get that stuff typed and down to the printers as quick as you can, please."

The girl rose and moved to the door, but paused on the threshold.

"Mr. Hastings," she said, turning quickly, "what does that last bit mean? Are you sending one of the ordinary people down there—Mr. Sellers or Mr. Briggs?"

"Yes, yes, I suppose so. What I said was all rot, but it'll sound well. We just want reports that are a bit different from the others."

She came nearer, her eyes wide. "Mr. Hastings, please excuse me, but you must listen. Why not let *The Owl* be really useful? Oh, don't you see what it would mean if we helped to catch the murderer? Our reputation—our sales. Why——"

"But I say, Miss Warren, look here, you know! We've not got an office full of Holmeses. They're all perfectly ordinary fellers——"

"Colonel Gethryn," said the girl quietly.

"Eh, what?" Hastings was startled. "He'd never —Miss Warren, you're a wonder. But he wouldn't take it on. He's——"

"Ask him." She pointed to the telephone at his side.

"What? Now?"

"Why not?"

"But—but it's two o'clock," stammered Hastings. He met the level gaze of his secretary's blue eyes, lifted the receiver from its hook, and asked for a number.

"Hallo," he said two minutes later, "is that Colonel Gethryn's flat?"

"It is," said the telephone. It's voice was sleepy.

"Is—is Colonel Gethryn in—out—up, I mean?"

"Colonel Gethryn," said the voice, "who would infinitely prefer to be called Mr. Gethryn is in his flat, out of bed, and upon his feet. Also he is beginning to become annoyed at——"

"Good Lord—Anthony!" said Hastings. "I didn't recognize your voice."

"Now that you have, O Hastings, perhaps you'll explain why the hell you're ringing me up at this hour. I may mention that I am in execrable temper. Proceed."

Spencer Hastings proceeded. "Er—I—ah—that is —er——"

"If those are scales," said the telephone, "permit me to congratulate you."

Hastings tried again. "Something has happened," he began.

"No!" said the telephone.

"D'you think you could—I know it's an extraordinary thing to ask—er, but will you—er——"

Miss Margaret Warren rose to her feet, removed the instrument from her employer's hand, put the receiver to her ear and spoke into the transmitter.

"Mr. Gethryn," she said, "this is Margaret Warren speaking. What Mr. Hastings wished to do was to ask whether you could come down here—to the office—at once. Oh, I know it sounds mad, but we've received some amazing news, and Mr. Hastings wishes to consult you. I can't tell you any more over the phone, but Mr. Hastings is sure that you'll be willing to help. Please come; it might mean everything to the paper."

"Miss Warren," said the telephone sadly, "against my will you persuade me."

CHAPTER II

ANTHONY GETHRYN

ANTHONY RUTHVEN GETHRYN was something of an oddity. A man of action who dreamed while he acted; a dreamer who acted while he dreamed. The son of a hunting country gentleman of the old type, who was yet one of the most brilliant mathematicians of his day, and of a Spanish lady of impoverished and exiled family who had, before her marriage with Sir William Gethryn, been in turn governess, dancer, mannequin, actress, and portrait painter, it was perhaps to be expected that he should be no ordinary child. And he was not.

For even after taking into consideration the mixture of blood and talents that were rightly his, Anthony's parents soon found their only child to be possessed of far more than they had thought to give him. From his birth he proved a refutation of the adage that a Jack-of-all-Trades can be master of none.

At school and at Oxford, though appearing almost to neglect work, he covered himself with academic glory which outshone even that of his excellence at racquets and Rugby football. Not only did he follow in the mathematical tracks of his father, but also became known as an historian and man of classics.

He left Oxford in his twenty-third year; read for the bar; was called, but did not answer. He went instead round and about the world, and did not, during the three and a half years he was away, use a penny other than earnings of one sort and another.

He returned home to settle down, painted two pictures which he gave to his father, wrote a novel, which was lauded by the critics and brought him not a penny, and followed up with a book of verse which, though damned by the same critics, was yet remunerative to the extent of one hundred and fifty pounds.

Politics came next, and for some six months he filled adequately the post of private secretary to a Member of Parliament suspected of early promotion to office.

Then, in Anthony's twenty-eighth year, on top of his decision to contest a seat, came the war. On the 15th of August, 1914, he was a private in an infantry regiment; by the 1st of the following November he had taken a commission in the artillery; on the 4th of May, 1915, he was recovered from the damage caused by a rifle-bullet, an attack of trench-fever, and three pieces of shrapnel. On the 18th of July in that year he was in Germany.

That calls for an explanation. Anthony Ruthven Gethryn was in Germany because his uncle, Sir Charles Haultevieux de Courcy Gethryn, was a personage at the War Office. Uncle Charles liked and had an admiration for his nephew Anthony. Also, Uncle Charles was aware that nephew Anthony spoke German like a German, and was, when occasion demanded, a person of tact, courage, and reliability. "A boy with *guts*, sir. A boy with *guts!* And common sense, sir; in spite of all this poetry-piffle and paintin' cows in fields and girls with nothin' on. A damnation *clever* lad, sir!"

So Uncle Charles, having heard the wailings of a friend in the Secret Service division concerning the terrible dearth of the right men, let fall a few words about his nephew.

And that is how, in the year 1915, Anthony Ruthven Gethryn came to be, not as a prisoner, in the heart of Germany. He was there for eighteen long months, and when Uncle Charles next saw his nephew there were streaks of gray in the dark hair of the thirty year old head.

The results of Anthony's visit were of much value. A grateful Government patted him on the back, decorated him, gave him two months' leave, promoted him, and then worked him as few men were worked even during the war. It was queer work, funny work, work in the dark, work in strange places.

Anthony Ruthven Gethryn left the army at the end of 1919, at the age of thirty-three. To show for his service he had a limp (slight), the C. M. G., the D. S. O., a baker's dozen of other orders (foreign: various) and those thick streaks of gray in his hair. Few save his intimate friends knew either of that batch of medals or of his right to the title of Colonel.

Anthony stayed with his mother until she died, peacefully, and then, since his father—who had preceded his wife by some two years—had left him no more than a few hundreds a year, looked round for work.

He wrote another novel; the public were unmoved. He painted three pictures; they would not sell. He published another book of poems; they would not sell either. Then he turned back to his secretaryship, his M. P. being now a minor minister. The work was of a sort he did not care for, and save for meeting every now and then a man who interested him, he was bored to extinction.

Then, in July of 1921, Uncle Charles fell a victim to malignant influenza, became convalescent, developed pneumonia, and died. To Anthony he left a dreadful house in Knightsbridge and nine or ten thousand a year. Anthony sold the house, set up in a flat, and, removed from carking care, did as the fancy took him. When he wanted to write, he wrote. When he wished to paint, he painted. When pleasure called, he answered. He was very happy for a year.

But then came trouble. When he wrote, he found that, immediately, a picture would form in his head and cry aloud to be put on canvas. Did he paint, verse unprecedented, wonderful, clamored to be written. Did he leave England, his soul yearned for London.

It was when this phase was at its worst that he renewed a friendship, begun at Trinity, with that eccentric but able young journalist, Spencer Hastings. To Anthony, Hastings unbosomed his great idea—the idea which could be made fact if there were exactly twice as much money as Hastings possessed. Anthony provided the capital, and *The Owl* was born.

Anthony designed the cover, wrote a verse for the paper now and then; sometimes a bravura essay. Often he blessed Hastings for having given him one interest at least which, since the control of it was not in his own hands, could not be thrown aside altogether.

To conclude: Anthony was suffering from three disorders, lack of a definite task to perform, severe warstrain, and not having met the right woman. The first and the second, though he never spoke of them, he knew about; the third he did not even suspect.

CHAPTER III

COCK ROBIN'S HOUSE

I

THE sudden telephone message from Hastings at two o'clock on that August morning and his own subsequent acceptance of the suggestion that he should be *The Owl's* "Special Commissioner," had at least, thought Anthony, as he drove his car through Kingston four hours later, remedied that lack of something definite to do.

He had driven at once to *The Owl's* headquarters, had arranged matters with Hastings within ten minutes, and had then telephoned to a friend—an important official friend. To him Anthony had outlined, sketchily, the scheme, and had been given in reply a semi-official, "Mind you, *I* know nothing about it if anything happens, but get ahead" blessing. He had then driven back to his flat, packed a bag, left a note for his man, and set out for Marling in Surrey.

From his official friend he had gathered that once on the right side of Miss Hoode and his way was clear. As he drove he pondered. How to approach the woman? At any mention of the Press she would be bound to shy. Finally, he put the problem to one side.

The news of John Hoode's death had not moved him, save in the way of a passing amazement. Anthony had seen too much of death to shed tears over a man he had never known. And the Minister of Imperial Finance, brilliant though he had been, had never seized the affections of the people in the manner of a Joe Chamberlain.

Passing through Halsemere, Anthony, muttering happily to himself, "Now, who *did* kill Cock Robin?" was struck by a horrid thought. Suppose there should be no mystery! Suppose, as Hastings had suggested, that the murderer had already delivered himself.

Then he dismissed the idea. A Cabinet Minister murdered without a mystery? Impossible! All the canons were against it.

He took his car along at some speed. By ten minutes to eight he had reached the Bear and Key in Marling High Street, demanded a room and breakfast, and had been led upstairs by a garrulous landlord.

2

Bathed, shaved, freshly-clothed and full of breakfast, Anthony uncurled his thin length from the best chair in the inn's parlor, lit his pipe, and sought the garden.

Outside the door he encountered the landlord, made inquiry as to the shortest way to Abbotshall, and, placidly puffing at his pipe, watched with enjoyment the effect of his question.

The eyes of Mr. Josiah Syme flashed with the fire of curiosity.

" 'Scuse me, sir," he wheezed, "but 'ave you come down along o' this—along o' these *'appenings* up at the 'ouse?"

"Hardly," said Anthony.

Mr. Syme tried again. "Be you a 'tective, sir?" he asked in a conspiratorial wheeze. "If so, Joe Syme might be able to 'elp ye." He leant forward and added in yet a lower whisper: "My eldest gel, she's an 'ousemaid up along at Abbotshall."

"Is she indeed," said Anthony. "Wait here till I get my hat; then we'll walk along together. You can show me the way."

"Then—then—you are a 'tective, sir."

"What exactly I am," said Anthony, "God Himself may know. I do not. But you can make five pounds if you want it."

Mr. Syme understood enough.

As they walked, first along the white road, then through fields and finally along the bank of that rushing, fussy, barely twenty-yards wide little river, the Marle, Mr. Syme told what he knew.

Purged of repetitions, biographical meanderings, and excursions into rustic theorizing, the story was this.

Soon after eleven on the night before, Miss Laura Hoode had entered her brother's study and found him lying, dead and mutilated, on the hearth. Exactly what the wounds were, Mr. Syme could not say; but by common report they were sufficiently horrible.

Before she fainted, Miss Hoode screamed. When other members of the household arrived they found her lying across her brother's body. A search-party was at once instituted for possible murderers, and the police and a doctor notified. People were saying—Mr. Syme became confidential—that Miss Hoode's mind had been unhinged by the shock. Nothing was yet *known* as to the identity of the criminal, but (here Mr. Syme gave vent to many a dark suggestion, implicating in turn every member of the household save his daughter.)

Anthony dammed the flow with a question. "Can you tell me," he asked, "exactly who's living in the house?"

Mr. Syme grew voluble at once. Oh, yes. He knew all right. At the present moment there were Miss Hoode, two friends of the late Mr. Hoode's, and the servants and the young gent—Mr. Deacon—what had been the corpse's secretary. The names? Oh, yes, he could give the names all right. Servants—his daughter Elsie, housemaid; Mabel Smith, another housemaid; Martha Forrest, the cook; Lily Ingram, kitchenmaid; Annie Holt, parlor-maid; old Mr. Poole, the butler; Bob Belford, the other man-servant. Then there was Tom Diggle, the gardener, though he'd been in the cottage hospital for the last week and wasn't out yet. And there was the chauffeur, Harry Wright. Of course, though, now he came to think of it, the gardener and the chauffeur didn't rightly *live* in the house, they shared the lodge.

"And the two guests?" said Anthony. It is hard to believe, but he had assimilated that stream of names, had even correctly assigned to each the status and duties of its owner.

"One gent, and one lady, sir: Oh, and there's the lady's own maid, sir. Girl with some Frenchy name. Duboise, would it be?" Mr. Syme was patently proud of his infallibility. "Mrs. Mainwaring the lady's called—she's tall, 'andsome lady with goldy-like sort of 'air, sir. And the gent's Sir Arthur Digby-Coates—and a very pleasant gent he is, sir, so Elsie says."

Anthony gave a start of pleasure. Digby-Coates was an acquaintance of his private-secretarial days.

Digby-Coates might be useful. Hastings hadn't told him.

"There be Habbotshall, sir," said Mr. Syme.

Anthony looked up. On his left—they had been walking with the little Marle on their right—was a well-groomed smiling garden, whose flower-beds, paths, pergolas, and lawns stretched up to the feet of one of the strangest houses within his memory.

For it was low and rambling and shaped like a capital L pushed over on its side. Mainly, it was two stories high, but on the extreme end of the right arm of the recumbent L there had been built an additional floor. This gave it a gay, elfin humpiness that attracted Anthony strangely. Many-hued clouds of creeper spread in beautiful disorder from ground to half-hidden chimney-stacks. Through the leaves peeped leaded windows, as a wood-fairy might spy through her hair at the woodcutter's son who was really a prince. A flagged walk bordered by a low yew hedge ran before the house; up to this led a flight of stone steps from the lower level of the lawns. Opposite the head of the steps was a verandah.

"This here, sir," explained Mr. Syme unnecessarily, "is rightly the back of the 'ouse."

Anthony gave him his congé and a five pound note, hinting that his own presence at Marling should not be used as a fount for barroom gossip. Mr. Syme walked away with a gait quaintly combining the stealth of a conspirator and the alertness of a great detective.

Anthony turned in at the little gate and made for the house. At the head of the steps before the verandah he paused. Voices came to his ear. The tone of the louder induced him to walk away from the verandah and along the house to his right. He halted by the first ground-floor window and listened, peering into the room.

Inside stood two men, one a little, round-shouldered, black-coated fellow with a dead-white face and hands that twisted nervously; the other tall, burly, crimson-faced, fierce-moustached, clad in police hue with the three stripes of a sergeant on his arm.

It was the policeman's voice that had attracted Anthony's attention. Now it was raised again, more loudly than before.

"You know a blasted sight more o' this crime than you says," it roared.

The other quivered, lifted a shaking hand to his mouth, and cast a hunted look round the room. He seemed, thought Anthony, remarkably like a ferret.

"I don't, sergeant. Re-really I don't," he stammered.

The sergeant thrust his great face down into that of his victim. "I don't believe you this mornin' any more'n I did last night," he bellowed. "Now, Belford, me lad, you confess! If you 'olds out against Jack 'Iggins you'll be sorry."

Anthony leaned his arms on the window-sill and thrust head and shoulders into the room.

"Now, sergeant," he said, "this sort of thing'll never do, you know."

The effect of his intrusion tickled pleasantly his sense of the dramatic. Law and Order recovered first, advanced, big with rage, to the window and demanded what was the meaning of the unprintable intrusion.

"Why," said Anthony, "shall we call it a wish to study at close quarters the methods of the County Constabulary."

"Who the—— ——ing 'ell are you?" The face of Sergeant Higgins was black with wrath.

"I," said Anthony, "am Hawkshaw, the detective!"

Before another roar could break from outraged officialdom, the door of the room opened. A thick-set, middle-aged man of a grocerish air inquired briskly what was the trouble here.

Sergeant Higgins became on the instant a meek subordinate. "I—I didn't know you were—were about, sir." He stood stiff at attention. "Just questioning of a few witnesses, I was, sir. This er—gentleman"—he nodded in the direction of Anthony—"just pushed his 'ead——"

But Superintendent Boyd of the C. I. D. was shaking the interloper by the hand. He had recognized the head and shoulders as those of Colonel Gethryn. In 1917 he had been "lent" to Colonel Gethryn in connection with a great and secret "round-up" in and about London. For Colonel Gethryn Superintendent Boyd had a liking and a deep respect.

"Well, well, sir," he said, beaming. "Fancy seeing you. They didn't tell me you were staying here."

"I'm not," Anthony said. Then added, seeing the look of bewilderment: "I don't quite know what I am, Boyd. You may have to turn me away. I think I'd better see Miss Hoode before I commit myself any further."

He swung his long legs into the room, patted the doubtful Boyd on the shoulder, sauntered to the door, opened it and passed through. Turning to his right, he collided sharply with another man. A person this, of between forty and fifty, dressed tastefully in light gray; broad-shouldered, virile, with a kindly face marked with lines of fatigue and mental stress. Anthony recoiled from the shock of the collision. The other stared.

"Good God!" he exclaimed.

"You exaggerate, Sir Arthur," said Anthony.

Sir Arthur Digby-Coates recovered himself. "The most amazing coincidence that ever happened, Gethryn," he said. "I was just thinking of you."

"Really?" Anthony was surprised.

"Yes, yes. I suppose you've heard? You must have. Poor Hoode!"

"Of course. That's why I'm here."

"But I thought you'd left——"

"Oh, yes," said Anthony, "I've left the Service. Quite a time ago. I'm here because—look here, this'll sound rot if I try to explain in a hurry. Can we go and sit somewhere where we can talk?"

"Certainly, my boy, certainly. I'm very glad indeed to see you, Gethryn. Very glad. This is a terrible, an awful affair—and, well, I think we could do with your help. You see, I feel responsible for seeing that *everything's* done that can be. It may seem strange to you, Gethryn, the way I'm taking charge like this; but John and I were—well ever since we were children we've been more like brothers than most real ones. I don't think a week's passed, except once or twice, that we haven't seen—— This way: we can talk better in my room. I've got a sitting-room of my own here, you know. Dear old John——"

3

It was three-quarters of an hour before Anthony descended the stairs; but in that time much had been decided and arranged. So much, in fact, that Anthony marveled at his luck—a form of mental exercise unusual in him. He was always inclined to take the gifts of the gods as his due.

But this was different. Everything was being made so easy for him. First, here was dear, stolid old Boyd in charge of the case. Next, there was Sir Arthur. As yet they were the merest acquaintances, but the knight had, he knew, for some time been aware of and impressed by the war record of A. R. Gethryn, and had welcomed him to the stricken household. Through Sir Arthur, Miss Hoode—whom Anthony had not seen yet—had been persuaded to accept Anthony, despite his present aura of journalism.

Oh, most undoubtedly, everything was going very well! Now, thought Anthony, for the murderer. This in spite of its painful side, was all vastly entertaining. Who killed Cock Robin Hoode?

Anthony felt more content than for the last year. It appeared that, after all, there might be interest in life.

In the hall he found Boyd; with him Poole, the butler—a lean, shaking old man—and a burly fellow whom Anthony knew for another of Scotland Yard's Big Four.

Boyd came to meet him. The burly one picked up his hat and sought the front door. The butler vanished.

"I wish you'd tell me, colonel," Boyd asked, "exactly where you come in on this business?"

Anthony smiled. "It's no use, Boyd. I'm not the murderer. But lend me your ears and I'll explain my presence."

As the explanation ended, Boyd's heavy face broke into a smile. He showed none of the chagrin commonly attributed to police detectives when faced with the amateur who is to prove them fools at every turn.

"There's no one I'd rather have with me, colonel," he said. "Of course, it's all very unofficial——"

"That's all right, Boyd. Before I left town I rang up Mr. Lucas. He gave me his blessing, and told me to carry on—provided I was accepted by the family."

Boyd looked relieved. "That makes everything quite easy, then. I don't mind telling you that this is a regular puzzler, Colonel Gethryn."

"So I have gathered," Anthony said. "By the way, Boyd, do drop that 'Colonel,' there's a good Inspector. If you love me, call me mister, call me mister, Boydie dear."

Boyd laughed. He found Anthony refreshingly unofficial. "Very well, sir. Now, if we may, let's get down to business. I suppose you've heard roughly what happened?"

"Yes."

"Much detail?"

"A wealth. None germane."

Boyd was pleased. He knew this laconic mood of Anthony's; it meant business. He was pleased because at present he felt himself out of his depth in the case. He produced from his breast-pocket a notebook.

"Here are some notes I've made, sir," he said. "You won't be able to read 'em, so let me give you an edited version."

"Do. But let's sit down first."

They did so, on a small couch before the great fireplace.

Boyd began his tale. "I've questioned every one in the house except Miss Hoode," he said. "I'll tackle her when she's better, probably this afternoon. But beyond the fact that she was the first one to see the body, I don't think she'll be much use. Now the facts. After supp—dinner, that is, last night Mr. Hoode, Miss Hoode, Mrs. Mainwaring and Sir Arthur Digby-Coates played bridge in the drawing-room. They finished the meal at eight-thirty, began the cards at nine and finished the game at about ten. Miss Hoode then said good-night and went to her bedroom; so did the other lady. Sir Arthur went to his own sitting-room to work, and the deceased retired to his study for the same purpose."

"No originality!" said Anthony plaintively. "It's all exactly the same. Ever read detective stories, Boyd? They're always killed in their studies. Always! Ever notice that?"

Boyd—perhaps a little shocked by the apparent levity—only shook his head. He went on: "That's the study door over there, sir, the only door on the right side of the hall, you see. That little room just opposite to it—the one you climbled into this morning—is a sort of den for that old boy Poole, the butler. Poole says that from about nine-forty-five until the murder was discovered he sat in there, reading and thinking. *And* he had the door open all the time. *And* he was facing the door. *And* he swears that no one entered the study by that door during the whole of that time."

"Mr. Poole is most convenient," murmured Anthony. He was lying back, his legs stretched out before him.

Boyd looked at him curiously. But the thin face was in shadow, and the greenish eyes were veiled by their lids. A silence fell.

Anthony broke it. "Going to arrest Poole just yet?" he asked.

Boyd smiled. "No sir. I suppose you're thinking Poole knows too much. Got his story too pat, so to speak."

"Something of the sort. Never mind, though. On with the tale, my Boyd."

"No, Poole's not my man. By all accounts he was devoted to his master. That's one thing. Another is that his right arm's practically useless with rheumatism and that he's infirm—with an absolute minimum of physical strength, so to speak. That proves he's not the man, even if other things were against him, which they're not. You'll know why when I take you into that room there, sir." The detective nodded his head in the direction of the study door.

"Well," he continued, "taking Poole, for the present at any rate, as a reliable witness, we know that the murderer didn't enter by the door. The chimney's impossible because it's too small and the register's down; so he must have got in through the window."

"Which of how many?" Anthony asked, still in that sleepy tone.

"The one farthest from the door and facing the garden, sir. The room's got windows on all three sides—three on the garden side, one in the end wall, and two facing the drive; but only one of 'em—the one I said—was open."

Anthony opened his eyes. "But how sultry!" he complained.

"I know, sir. That's what I thought. And in this hot weather and all. But there's an explanation. The deceased always had them—those windows—shut all day in the hot weather, and the blinds down. He knew a thing or two, you see. But he always used to open 'em himself at night, when he went in there to work. I suppose last night he must 'ave been in a great hurry or something, and only opened one of 'em." He looked across at Anthony for approval of his reasoning, then continued: "But the queer thing is, sir, that that open window shows no traces of anything—no scratches, no marks, no nothing. Nor does the flower-bed under it either."

"Any finger-prints anywhere on anything?" said Anthony.

"None anywhere in the room but the deceased's—except on one thing. I've sent that up to the Yard—Jardine's taken it—for the experts to photograph. I'll have the prints sometime this afternoon I should think." Boyd's tone was mysterious.

Anthony looked at him. "Out with it, Boyd. You're like a boy with a surprise for daddy."

"As a matter of fact, sir," Boyd laughed, rather shamefacedly, "it's the *modus operandi,* so to speak."

"So you've found the ber-loodstained weapon. Boyd, I congratulate you. What was it? And whose are the finger-prints?"

"The weapon used, sir, was a large wood-rasp, and a very nasty weapon it must have made. As for the finger-prints, I don't know yet. And it's my firm belief we shan't be much wiser when we've got the enlargements—not even if we were to compare 'em with all the prints of all the fingers for miles round. I don't know what it is, sir, but this case has got a nasty, puzzling sort of feel about it, so to speak."

"A wood-rasp, eh?" mused Anthony. "Not very enlightening. Doesn't belong to the house, I suppose?"

"As far as I can find out, sir, most certainly not." Boyd's tone was gloomy.

"H'mm! Well, let us advance. We've absolved the aged Poole; but what about the rest of the household?" Anthony spread out his long fingers and ticked off each name as he spoke. "Miss Hoode, Mrs. Mainwaring, her maid Duboise, Sir Arthur, Elsie Syme, Mabel Smith, Maggie—no, Martha Forrest, Lily Ingram, Annie Holt, Belford, Harry Wright. Any of them do? The horticultural Mr. Diggle's in hospital and therefore out of it, I suppose."

Boyd stared amazement. "Good Lord, sir!" he exclaimed, "you've got 'em off pat enough. Have you been talking to them?"

"Preserve absolute calm, Boyd; I have not been talking to them. I got their dreadful names from an outsider. Anyhow, what about them?"

Boyd shook his head. "Nothing, sir."

"All got confused but trustworthy alibis? That it?"

"Yes, sir, more or less; some of the alibis are clear as glass. To tell you the truth, I don't suspect any one in the house. Some of the servants have got 'confused alibis' as you call it, but they're all obviously all right. That's the servants; it's the same only more so with the others. Take the secretary, Mr. Deacon; he was up there in his room the whole time. There's one, p'r'aps two witnesses to prove it. The same with Miss Hoode. And the other lady; to be sure she's got no witnesses, but that murder wasn't her job, nor any woman's. Take Sir Arthur, it's the same thing again. Even if there was anything suspicious—which there wasn't—about his relations with the deceased, you can't suspect a man who was, to the actual knowledge of five or six witnesses who saw him, sitting upstairs in his room during the only possible time when the murder can have been done.

"No sir!" Boyd shook his head with vigor. "It's no good looking in the house. Take it from me."

"I will, Boyd; for the present anyhow." Anthony rose and stretched himself. "Can I see the study?"

Boyd jumped up with alacrity. "You can, sir. We've been in there a lot, taking photos, etcetera; but it's untouched—just as it was when they found the body."

CHAPTER IV

THE STUDY

ONCE across the threshold of the dead minister's study, Anthony experienced a change of feeling, of mental attitude. Until now he had looked at the whole business in his usual detached and semi-satirical way; the reasons for his presence at Abbotshall had been two only—affection for Spencer Hastings and desire to satisfy that insistent craving for some definite and difficult task to perform. He had even felt, at intervals throughout the morning, a wish to laugh.

But, now, fairly in the room, this aloofness failed him. It was not that he felt any sudden surge of personal regret. It was rather that, for him at least, despite the sunlight which blazed incongruously in every corner, some cold, dark beastliness brooded everywhere.

The big room was gay with chintz and as yet unfaded flowers of the day before; the solid furniture was of some beauty—in fact, a charming room. Yet Anthony shivered even before he had seen the thing lying grotesque upon the hearth. When he did see it, somehow the sight shook him out of the nightmare of dark fancy. He stepped forward to look more closely.

Came the sound of a commotion from the hall. With a muttered excuse, Boyd went quickly from the room. Anthony knelt to examine the body.

It sprawled upon the hearth-rug, legs toward the window in the opposite wall. The red-tiled edge of the open grate forced up the neck. The almost hairless head was dreadfully battered; crossed and recrossed by five or six gaping gashes, each nearly half an inch wide and an inch or so deep. Of the scalp little remained but islands and peninsulas of skin and bone streaked with the dark brown of dried blood, among it ribands of gray film where the brain had oozed from the wounds.

The body was untouched, though the clothes were rumpled and twisted. The right arm was outstretched, the rigid fingers of the hand resting among the pots of fern which filled the fireplace. The left arm was doubled under the body.

Anthony, having gazed his fill, rose to his feet. As he did so, Boyd re-entered. He looked flushed and not a little annoyed.

Anthony turned to him, raising his eyebrows.

"Only a bit more trouble with some of these newspaper fellows, sir. But thank the Lord, I've got rid of 'em now. Told 'em I'd give 'em a statement to-night. What they'd say if they knew you were here—and why—God knows. There'll be a row after the case is over, but there you are. Miss Hoode's agreeable to you, and I don't blame her, but she won't hear of any of the others being let in. I don't blame her for that either." He nodded towards the body. "What d'you make of it, sir?"

"Shocking messy kill," Anthony said.

"You're right, sir. But what about—things in general, so to speak?"

Anthony looked round the room. It bore traces of disturbance. Two light chairs had been overturned.

Books and papers from the desk strewed the floor. The grandfather clock, which should have stood sentinel on the left of the door as one entered it, had fallen, though not completely. It lay face-downwards at an angle of some forty-five degrees with the floor, the upper half of its casing supported by the back of a large sofa.

"Struggle?" said Anthony.

"Yes," said Boyd.

"Queer struggle," said Anthony. He sauntered off on a tour of the room.

Boyd watched him curiously as he halted before the sofa, dropped on one knee, and peered up at the face of the reclining clock.

He looked up at Boyd. "Stopped at ten-forty-five. That makes the murder fit in with the times the people in the house have told you?"

"Yes, sir."

"When are you going to have the room tidied?"

"Any time now. We've got the photos."

"Right." Anthony got to his feet. "Let us, Boyd, unite our strength and put grand-dad on his feet."

Between them they raised the clock. Anthony opened the case and set the pendulum swinging. A steady tick-tock began at once.

Anthony looked at his watch. "Stopped exactly twelve hours ago, did grandfather," he said. "Doesn't seem to be damaged, though."

"No, sir. It takes a lot to put those old clocks out of order."

Anthony went back to the front of the sofa and stood looking down at the carpet.

"No finger-prints, you said?"

"Except on the wood-rasp, absolutely none but those

of the deceased, sir. I've dusted nearly every inch of the room with white or black. All I got for my pains were four good prints of the deceased's thumb and forefinger. They're easy enough to tell—very queer-shaped fingers and a long scar on the ball of his right thumb."

Anthony changed the subject. "What time did you get here, Boyd?"

"About four this morning. We came by car. I made some preliminary inquiries, questioned some of the people, and went down to the village at about eight."

"Who's that great red hulk of a sergeant?" said Anthony, flitting to yet another subject. "You ought to watch him, Boyd. When I came along he was indulging in a little third degree."

"I heard it, sir. That's why I came in."

"Good. Who was the timid little ferret?"

"Belford—Robert Belford, sir. He's a sort of assistant to Poole and was valet to the deceased."

"How did he answer when you questioned him?"

"Very confused he was. But his story's all right —very reasonable. I don't consider him, so to speak. He hasn't got the nerve, or the strength."

Anthony stroked his chin. "It's easy enough to see," he said, "that you don't want to be persuaded away from your idea that an outsider did this job."

"You're right, sir," Boyd smiled. "As far as I've progressed yet an outsider's my fancy. Most decidedly. Still one never knows where the next turning's going to lead to, so to speak. Of course, I've got a lot of inquiries afoot—but so far we've less than nothing to go on."

"Anything stolen?"

"Nothing."

Anthony was still gazing down at the carpet before the sofa. Again he dropped on one knee. This time he rubbed at the thick pile with his fingers. He rose, darting a look round the room.

"What's up, sir?" Boyd was watching attentively.

"A most convenient struggle that," murmured Anthony.

"What's that? What d'you mean, sir?"

"I was remarking, O Boyd, that the struggle had been, for the murderer, of an almost incredible convenience. Observe that the two chairs which were overturned are far from heavy; observe also that the carpet is very far from thin. These light chairs fell, not, mark you, on the parquet edging of the floor, but conveniently inward upon this thickest of thick carpets. Observe also, most *puissant* inspector, that the articles dislodged from the writing-table besides falling on the carpet, are nothing but light books and papers. Nothing heavy, you see. Nothing which would make a noise."

"I follow you, sir," Boyd cried. "You mean——"

" 'Ush, 'ush, I will 'ave 'ush! I would finally direct your attention to the highly convenient juxtaposition of this sofa here and our friend the clock. The sofa is a solid, stolid lump of a sofa; it's none of your trifling divans. In fact, it would require not merely a sudden jerk but a steady and lusty pull to move it, wouldn't it?"

The detective applied his considerable weight to the arm of the sofa. Nothing happened.

"You see!" continued Anthony with a gesture. "See you also then the almost magical convenience with which, in the course of the struggle, this lumping sofa was moved back toward grandfather, who stood nearly three feet from the sofa's usual position, which position can be ascertained by noting these four deep dents made in the carpet by the castors. Oh, it's all so convenient. The sofa's moved back, then grandfather falls, not with a loud crash to the floor, but quietly, softly, on to the back of the sofa. Further, those two vases on that table there beside the clock weren't upset at all by the upheaval. Those vases wobble when one walks across the room, Boyd. No, it won't do; it won't do at all."

"You're saying there wasn't any struggle at all; that the scene was set, so to speak." Boyd's tone was eager. His little gray eyes were alight with interest.

Anthony nodded. "Your inference is right."

"I had explained things to myself by saying that the carpet was thick and old Poole rather deaf," said the detective, "because he did say that he heard a noise like some one walking about. Of course, he just thought it was his master. I'll wager it wasn't, though. I'm sure you're right, sir. I hadn't noticed the sofa had been shifted. This is a very queer case, sir, very queer!"

"It is, or anyhow it feels like that. What about the body, Boyd? Aren't you going to have it moved?"

"Yes, sir, any time now. It was going to be moved before you came; then Jardine wanted to take some more photos. After that, you being here, sir—well, I thought if you *were* going to have anything to do with the case you might like to see everything in *status quo*, so to speak."

Anthony smiled. "Thanks, Boyd," he said. "You're a good chap, you know. This isn't the first job we've done together by any means; but all the same, it's most refreshing to find you devoid of the pro's righteous distrust of the amateur."

Boyd smiled grimly. "Oh, I've got that all right, sir. But I don't regard you in that light, if I may say so, though we *may* disagree before this case is over. And—well, sir, I've not forgotten what you did for me that night down at Sohlke's place in Limehouse——"

"Drop it, man, drop it," Anthony groaned.

Boyd laughed. "Very well, sir. Now I'll go and see about having the body moved upstairs."

"And I," said Anthony, "shall think—here or in the garden. By the way, when's the inquest?"

"To-morrow afternoon, here," said Boyd, and left the room.

Anthony ruminated. This study of Hoode's, he reflected, was curious, being in itself the end of the long wing of the house and having, therefore, window or windows in all three sides. As Boyd had said, only one of these windows was open, the farthest from the door of the three which looked out upon the terraced gardens and the river at their foot. All the others—two in the same wall, one in the end wall, and two overlooking the drive—were shut and latched on the inside. The open one was open top and bottom.

Anthony looked at it, then back at the writing-table. He seemed dissatisfied, for he next walked to the window, surveyed the room from there, and then crossed to the swivel-chair at the writing-table and sat down. From here he again peered at the open window, which was then in front of him and slightly to his left.

He was still in the chair when Boyd came back, bringing with him a policeman in plain clothes and a man in the leather uniform of a chauffeur. Anthony did not move; did not answer when Boyd spoke to him.

The body covered and lifted, the grim little party, Boyd leading, made for the door. As they steered carefully through it, the grandfather clock began to strike the hour. Its deep ring had, it seemed to Anthony, a note ominous and mournful.

The door clicked to behind the men and the shrouded thing they carried. The clock struck again.

"Good for you, grandfather," muttered Anthony, without turning in his chair to look. "I wish to High Heaven you could talk for a moment or two."

"Bong!" went the clock again.

Anthony pulled out his watch. The hands stood at eleven o'clock. "All right, grand-dad," he said. "You needn't say any more. I know the time. I wish you could tell me what happened last night instead of being so damned musical."

The clock went on striking. Anthony wandered to the door, paused, and went back to the writing-table. As he sat down again the clock chimed its final stroke.

He felt a vague discomfort, shook it off and continued his scrutiny of the table. It was of some age, and beautiful in spite of its solidity. The red leather covering of its top had upon it many a stain of wear and inks. Yet one of these stains seemed to Anthony to differ from the general air of the others. He rubbed it with his fingers. It was raised and faintly sticky. It was at the back of the flat part of the table-top. Immediately behind it rose two tiers of drawers and pigeon-holes. Also, its length was bisected by a crack in the wood.

He rubbed at the stain again; then cursed aloud. That vague sense of something wrong in the room, something which did not fit the essential sanity of life, had returned to his head and spoilt these new thoughts.

The door opened and shut. "What's the matter, sir? Puzzled?" Boyd came and stood behind him.

"Yes, dammit!" Anthony swung round impatiently. "This room's getting on my nerves. Either there's something *wrong* in it or I've got complex fan-tods. Never mind that, though. Boyd, I think I'm going to give you still more proof that there was no struggle. Come here."

Boyd came eagerly. Anthony twisted round to face the table again.

"Attend! The body was found over there by the fireplace. If one accepts as true the indications that a struggle took place, the natural inference is that Hoode was overpowered and struck down where he was found. But we have found certain signs that lead us to believe that the struggle was, in fact, no struggle at all, and here, I think, is another which will also show that Hoode's body was dragged over to the hearth after he had been killed."

Boyd grew excited. "How d'you mean, sir?"

"This is what I mean." Anthony pointed to the stain he had been examining. "Look at this mark here, where my finger is. Doesn't it look different from the others?"

"Can't say that it does to me sir. I had a look over that table myself and saw nothing out of the ordinary run."

"Well, I beg to differ. It not only looks different, it feels different. I notice these things. I'm *so* psychic, you know!"

Boyd grinned at the chaff, watching with keen interest as Anthony opened a penknife and inserted the blade in the lock of the table's middle drawer.

"I think," said Anthony, "that this is one of those old jump locks. Aha! it is." He pulled open the drawer. "Now, *was* that stain different? *Voilà!* It was."

Boyd peered over Anthony's shoulder. The drawer was a long one, reaching the whole width of the table. In it were notebooks, pencils, half-used scribbling pads, and, at the back, a pile of notepaper and envelopes.

On the white surface of the topmost envelope of the pile was a dark, brownish-red patch of the size, perhaps, of a half-crown. Boyd examined it eagerly.

"You're right, sir!" he cried. "It's blood right enough. I see what you were going to say. This is hardly dry. It must have dripped through that crack where the stain you pointed out was. And the position of that stain is just where the deceased's head would have fallen if he had been sitting in this chair here and had been hit from behind."

"Exactly," said Anthony. "And after the first of those pats on the head Hoode must've been unconscious—if not dead. Ergo, if he received the first blow sitting here, as this proves he did, there was no struggle. One doesn't sit down at one's desk to resist a man one thinks is going to kill one, does one? What probably happened is that the murderer—who was never suspected to be such by Hoode—got behind him as he sat here, struck one or all of the blows, and then dragged the body over to the hearth to lend a touch of naturalness to the scene of strife he was going to prepare. He must be a clever devil, Boyd. There's never a stain on the carpet between here and the fireplace.

There wouldn't have been on the table either, only he didn't happen to spot it."

The detective nodded. "I agree with you entirely, sir."

But Anthony did not hear him. That *wrong* something was troubling him again. He clutched his head, trying vainly to fix the cause of this feeling.

Boyd tried again. "Well, we know a little more now, sir, anyhow. Quite a case for premeditation, so to speak—thanks to you."

Anthony brought himself back to earth. "Yes, yes," he said. "But hearken again, Boyd. I have yet more to say. Don't wince, I have really. Here it is. Assuming the reliability, as a witness, of Poole, the old retainer, we know the murderer didn't come into this room through the door. Nor could he, as you've explained, have used the chimney. Remains the one window that was open. Observe, O Boyd, that that window is in full view of a man seated at this table. Now one cannot come through a window into a room at a distance of about two yards from a man seated therein at a table without attracting the attention of that man unless that man is asleep."

"I shouldn't think Hoode was asleep, sir."

"Exactly. It is known that Hoode was a hard worker. Further, if I'm not mistaken, he's been more than usually busy just recently—over the new Angora Agreement. I think we can take it for granted he wasn't asleep when the murderer came in through that window. That leads us to something of real importance, namely, that Hoode was not surprised by the entry of the murderer."

Boyd scratched his head. " 'Fraid I don't quite get you, as the Yanks say, sir."

Anthony looked at him with benevolence. "To make myself clearer, I'll put it like this: he either (i) expected the murderer—though not, of course, as such—and expected him to enter that way; or (ii) did not expect him to enter that way, but on looking up in surprise saw some one who, though he had entered in that unfamiliar way, was yet so familiar in himself as not to cause Hoode to remain long, if at all, out of his seat. Personally, I think he didn't leave his chair at all. Is not all this well spoken, Boyd?"

"True enough, sir. I think you're quite right again. I've been a fool." Boyd was dejected. "Of the two views you propounded, so to speak, I think the first's the right one. The murderer was an outsider, but one the deceased was expecting—and by that entrance."

"And I," said Anthony, "incline strongly toward my second theory of the unconventional entry of the familiar."

Boyd shook his head. "You'd hardly credit it, sir," he said solemnly, "but some of these big men get up to very funny games. I've had over twenty years in the C. I. D., and I know."

"The mistake you're making in this case, Boyd," Anthony said, "is thinking of it as like all your others. From what little I've seen so far of this affair it's much more like a novel than real life, which is mostly dull and hardly ever true. As I asked you before, d'you ever read real detective stories? Gaboriau, for instance?"

"Lord, no, sir!" smiled the real detective.

"You should."

"Pardon me, sir, but you're a knock-out at this game yourself and it makes me wonder, so to speak, how you can hold with all that 'tec-tale truck."

"A knock-out? Me?" Anthony laughed. "And I feel as futile as if I were Sherlock Holmes trying to solve a case of Lecoq's." He put a hand to his head. "There's something about this room that's haunting me! What is the damned thing? Boyd, there's something *wrong* about the blasted place, I tell you!"

Boyd looked bewildered. "I don't know what you mean, sir." Then, to humor this eccentric, he added: "Ah, if only this furniture could tell us what it saw last night."

"I said that to the clock," said Anthony morosely, then suddenly: "The clock, the clock! Grandpa *did* tell me something! I knew I'd seen or heard something that was utterly wrong, insane. The clock! Good God Almighty! What a fool not to think of it before!"

Boyd became alarmed. His tone was soothing. "What about the clock, sir?"

"It struck. D'you remember it beginning when you were taking the body away?"

"Yes." Boyd was all mystification.

"What time was that?"

"Why, eleven, of course, sir."

"Yes, it was, my uncanny Scot. But grandfather said twelve. I was thinking about something else. I must have counted the strokes unconsciously."

"But—but—are you *sure* it struck twelve when" —Boyd glanced up at the old clock—"when it said eleven?"

Anthony crossed the room, opened the glass casing of the clock-face, and moved the hands on fifteen minutes. They stood then at twelve.

"Bong!" went the clock.

They waited. It did not strike again.

Anthony was triumphant. "There you are, Boyd! Grandpa looks twelve and says one. There's another strand of that rope you're making for the murderer. Miss Hoode came in here at eleven-ten, to find the murder done and the murderer gone. Your time's almost fixed for you. He wasn't here at eleven-ten, but he was here after eleven, because, to put the striking of that clock out as it is, the murderer must have put back the hands after the hour—eleven, that is—had struck. If he'd done it before the striking had begun, grand-dad wouldn't be telling lies the way he is."

Boyd's expression was a mixture of elation and doubt. "I suppose that's right, sir," he said. "About the striking, I mean. Yes, of course it is; just for the moment I was a bit confused, so to speak. Couldn't work out which way the mistake would come."

"It seems to me," said Anthony, "that the whole reason he faked this elaborate struggle scene was in order that the clock could be stopped under what would seem natural circumstances. But why, having stopped the clock, did he alter it? Two reasons occur to me. One is that he merely wished to make it seem that the murder was done at any other time except when it really was. That's rather weak, and I prefer my second idea. That is, that the time to which he moved the hands has a significance and wasn't merely a chance shot. In other words, he set the thing at ten-forty-five because he had a nice clean alibi for that time. Judging by the rest of his work he's a man of brains; and that would've been a pretty little safeguard—if only he hadn't made that mistake about the striking."

"They all make bloomers—one time or another, sir. That's how we catch 'em in the main."

"I know." Anthony's tone was less sure than a moment before. "All the same it's a damn' silly mistake. Doesn't seem to fit in somehow. I'd expected better things from him."

"Oh, I don't know, sir. He'd probably got the wind up, as they say, by the time he'd got so near finishing."

Anthony shrugged. "Yes, I suppose you're right. By the way, Boyd, tell me this. How did Miss Hoode come to be downstairs at ten past eleven? I thought she was supposed to have gone to by-by after that game of cards."

"As far as I know—I haven't been able to see her yet, sir—she came down to use the telephone—not this one but the one in the hall—about some minor affair she'd forgotten during the day. After she'd finished phoning she must've wanted to speak to her brother. Probably about the same matter. That's all, sir."

"It's so weak," said Anthony, "that it might possibly be true." Then, after a pause: "I think I've had about enough of this tomb. What you going to do next, Boyd? I'm for the garden." He walked to the door. "You took the weaker end of my reasoning if you still believe in the mysterious outsider."

Boyd followed across the hall, through the verandah and down the steps which led from the flagged walk behind the house to the lawns below.

Anthony sat himself down upon a wooden seat set in the shade of a great tree. He showed little inclination for argument.

But Boyd was stubborn. "You know, sir," he said, "you're wrong in what you say about the 'insider.' You'd agree with me if you'd been here long enough to sift what evidence there is and been able the way I have to see *and* talk to all the people instead of hearing about them sketchy and second-hand as it were."

Anthony looked at him. "There's certainly something in that, Boyd. But it'll take a lot to shift me. Mind you, my predilection for the 'insider' isn't a conviction. But it's my fancy—and strong."

Boyd fumbled in his breast-pocket. "Then you just take a good look at this sir." He held out some folded sheets of foolscap. "I made that out before you got here this morning. It'll tell you better what I mean than I can talking. And I only sketched the thing to you before."

Anthony unfolded the sheet, and read:—

SUMMARY OF INFORMATION ELICITED

1. MISS LAURA HOODE.—Played cards until 10 o'clock with the deceased, Sir A. D.-C., and Mrs. Mainwaring. Then went to bed. Was seen in bed at approximately 10.30 by Annie Holt, parlormaid, who was called into room to take some order as she passed on her way to the servants' quarters. Miss Hoode remembered, at about 11.05, urgent telephone call to be made. Got up, went downstairs to phone, then thought she would consult deceased first. Entered study, at 11.10, and discovered body. [*Note.*—By no means a complete alibi; but it seems quite out of the question that this lady is in any way concerned. She is distraught at brother's death and was known to be a devoted sister. They were, as always, the best of friends during day.]
N.B.—It appears impossible for a woman to have committed this crime, since the necessary power

to inflict blows such as caused death of deceased would be that of an unusually strong man.

2. MRS. R. MAINWARING.—Retired at same time as Miss Hoode. Was seen in bed by her maid, Elsie Duboise, at 10.35. Was waked out of heavy sleep by parlor-maid, Annie Holt, after discovery of body of deceased.
3. ELSIE DUBOISE.—This girl sleeps in room communicating with Mrs. Mainwaring's. The night was hot and the door between the two rooms was left open. Mrs. Mainwaring heard the girl get into bed at about 10.40. The parlor-maid had to shake her repeatedly before she woke.
4. SIR A. DIGBY-COATES.—Went upstairs, after cards, to own sitting-room (first-floor, adjoining bedroom) to work at official papers. Pinned note on door asking not to be disturbed, but had to leave door open owing to heat. Was seen, from passage, between time he entered room until time murder was discovered, at intervals averaging a very few minutes by Martha Forrest (cook), Annie Holt (parlor-maid), R. Belford (manservant), Elsie Duboise, Mabel Smith (housemaid), and Elsie Syme (housemaid). The time during which the murder must have been committed is covered.
5. MR. A. B. T. DEACON (Private Secretary to deceased).—Went to room (adjoining that of Sir A. D.-C.) to read at approximately 10.10. Was seen entering by Mabel Smith, who was working in linen-room immediately opposite. She had had afternoon off and was consequently very busy. Stayed there till immediately (say two minutes) before murder was discovered. She

can swear Mr. Deacon never left room the whole time, having had to leave door of linen-room open owing to heat.

6. WOMEN SERVANTS.—These are Elsie Syme, Mabel Smith, Martha Forrest, Annie Holt, Lily Ingram. All except the first two account for each other over the vital times, having been in the servants' quarters (in which the rooms are inter-communicating) from 10.15 or so onwards. Elsie Syme, who was downstairs in the servants' hall until the murder was discovered, and Mabel Smith, may be disregarded. They have no one to substantiate their statements, but there is no doubt at all that they are ordinary, foolish, honest working-girls. (See also note after details re Miss Hoode.)

7. ALFRED POOLE (Butler).—Has not a shred of alibi. Was seated, as usual, in his den opposite study all the evening. After 10 spoke to no one; was seen by nobody. May, however, be disregarded as in any way connected with murder. Will be very useful witness. May (in my opinion) be trusted implicitly. Not very intelligent. Very old, infirm, but sufficiently capable to answer questions truthfully and clearly. [Has, for one point, nothing like half strength murderer must have used.] Was devoted to deceased, whose family he has served for forty-one years.

8. ROBERT BELFORD (Man-servant).—Has certain support for his own account of his actions; but not enough probably for fuller test. Nothing against him, and last man in world for crime of this type. Might possibly poison, but has neither courage nor strength enough to have murdered

deceased. Seems nervous. *May* know more than he admits, but unlikely.

9. OTHER MEN-SERVANTS.—Harry Wright, chauffeur, and Thomas Diggle, gardener. Both not concerned. Diggle is in hospital. Wright, who lives in the lodge by the big gates, was off last night and with reputable friends in Marling village. He did not return until some time after murder had been discovered. The three lads who work under Diggle live in their homes in the village. All were at home from eight o'clock onwards last night.

Anthony, having reached the end, read through the document again, more slowly this time. Boyd watched him eagerly. At last the papers were handed back to their owner.

"Well, sir," he said. "See what I mean?"

"I do, Boyd, I do. But that doesn't necessarily mean I agree, you know."

Boyd's face fell. "Ah, sir, I know what it is. You're wondering at an old hand like me trying to prove to you that nobody in the house could've done it, when all the time most of 'em haven't got what you might call sound alibis at all. But look here, sir——"

Anthony got to his feet. "Boyd, you wrong me! I like your guesses even better than your proofs. Guesses are nearly always as good as arithmetic—especially guesses by one of your experience. I didn't say I didn't agree with you, did I?"

"You didn't *say* so, sir, so to speak!"

"Nor I didn't mean it either." Anthony laughed. "My mind's open, Boyd, open. Anyhow, many thanks for letting me see that. I know a lot more detail than

I did. I suppose that's a basis for a preliminary report, what?"

Boyd nodded, and fell into step as Anthony turned in the direction of the house.

CHAPTER V

THE LADY OF THE SANDAL

I

ANTHONY was still in the garden. Anthony had found something. Clouds of pipe-smoke hung round his head in the hot, still air. Anthony was thinking.

He was alone. Boyd, indefatigable, had gone at once into the house, bent upon another orgy of shrewd questioning. This time his questions would have, in the light of what the study had told, a more definite bearing.

What Anthony had found were two sets, some eighteen inches apart, of four deep, round impressions of roughly the size of a sixpence. They were in the broad flower-bed which ran the whole length of the study wall and were directly beneath the sill of the most easterly of the three windows—the farther closed window, that is, from the open one through which it seemed that the murderer must have effected entrance to the study. The flower-bed, Anthony noticed, was unusually broad—so broad, in fact, that any person, unless he were a giant, wishing to climb into any of the three windows, would perforce tread, with one foot at least, among the flowers.

He stooped to examine his find. Whoever, in the absence of Mr. Diggle the gardener, had so lavishly watered the flower-bed on the previous day received his blessing. Had the soil not been so moist, those holes would not have been there.

Anthony thought aloud: "Finger-holes. Just where my fingers would go if I was a good deal narrower across the shoulders and squatted here and tried to look into the room without bringing either of my feet on to the bed."

He stepped deliberately on to the flower-bed and bent to examine the low sill of the window. There was a smudge on the rough stone. It might be a dried smear of earthy fingers. On the other hand, it might be almost anything else. But as he straightened his back a bluish-black gleam caught his eye.

He investigated, and found, hanging from a crevice in the rough edge of the sill, a woman's hair. It was a long hair, and jet black.

"That explains the closeness of those finger-marks," he muttered. "A woman in the case, eh? Now, why was she here, in front of the closed window? And was she here last night? Or this morning, quite innocent like? The odds are it was last night. One doesn't crouch outside a Cabinet Minister's window in daylight. Nor at all, unless one's up to no good. No, I think you were here last night, my black beauty. I love little pussy, her hair is so black, and if I don't catch her she'll never come back. Now where did you come from, Blackie dear? And have you left any other cards? O, Shades of Doyle! What a game!"

He stepped back on to the path and knelt to examine the stone edging to the flower-bed. In the position she must have been in, the woman would most probably, he argued, have been on one knee and had the foot of the other leg pressed vertically against this edging.

She had; but Anthony was doubly surprised at what he found. For why, in this dry weather, should the mark of her foot be there at all? And, as it was there, why should it look like a finger-print a hundred times enlarged?

He scratched his head. This was indeed a crazy business. Perhaps he was off the rails. Still, he'd better go on. This all *might* have something to do with the case.

More closely he examined this footprint that was like a finger-print. Now he understood. The mark had remained because the peculiar sole of this peculiar shoe had been wet and earthy. There had been no rain for a week. Why was the shoe wet? And why —he looked carefully about—were there no other such marks on the flagstones of the path? Ah, yes; that would be because in ordinary walking or running the peculiar shoes did not press hard enough to leave anything but a wet patch which would quickly dry. Whereas, in pressing the sole of the foot against that edging to the flower-bed, much more force would have to be used to retain balance—sufficient force to squeeze wet clayish earth out in a pattern from that peculiar sole.

But what about the wetness? He hadn't settled that. Suddenly his mind connected the peculiarity of that imprint with the idea of water. A rope-soled sandal. When used? Why, bathing. Here Anthony laughed aloud. "Sleuth, you surpass yourself!" he murmured. "Minister murdered by Bathing Belle— only not at the seaside! Cock Robin's murderer not Sparrow as at first believed, but one W. Wagtail! Gethryn, you're fatuous. Take to crochet."

He started for the verandah door. Half-way he

stopped, suddenly. He'd forgotten the river. But the idea was ridiculous. But, after all—well, he'd spend ten minutes on it, anyhow. Now, to begin—assuming that the woman *had* come out of the river and had wanted (strange creature!) to get back there —he would work out her most probable route and follow it. If within five minutes he had found no more signs of her, he'd stop.

After a moment's calculation he started off, going through the opening in the yew hedge, down the grass bank to his right and then crossing the rose garden at whose far side there began a pergola.

At the entrance to the pergola he found, caught round a thorny stem of the rose-creeper that fell from the first cross-piece of the archway, four long black hairs.

Anthony controlled his elation. These might not, he thought, be from the same head. But all the same it was encouraging. It fitted well. Running in the dark and a panic, she hadn't ducked low enough. He could see her tearing to free her hair. Well, he'd get on. But really this mad idea about swimming women *couldn't* be true.

From the other end of the pergola he emerged on to a lawn, its center marked by a small but active fountain. A graveled path, along which he remembered having walked up to the house, ran down at the right of the grass to the gate on the river-bank through which he had entered. He paused to consider the position; then decided that one making in a hurry for the gate would cut across the grass.

He found confirmation. Round the fountain's inadequate basin was a circle of wet grass, its deep green in refreshing contrast to the faded color of the rest. At the edge of the emerald oasis were two indistinct imprints of the sandal and its fellow, and two long smeared scars where the grass had been torn up to expose the soil beneath. Farther on, but still within the circle, were two deeper, round impressions; beyond them, just where the wet grass ended, was another long smear.

Anthony diagnosed a slip, a stagger, and a fall. Not looking for more signs—he had enough—he hurried on to the little gate. The other side of it, on the path which ran alongside the blustering pigmy of a river, he hesitated, looking about him. Again he felt doubt. Was it likely that any one would swim the Marle at night? Most decidedly it was not. In the first place there was, only some three hundred and fifty yards or so downstream to his right, a perfectly good bridge, which joined the two halves of the village of Marling. In the second place, the Marle, though here a bare twenty yards wide, seemed as uncomfortable a swim as could well be, even for a man. Always turbulent, it was at present actually dangerous, still swollen as it was by the months of heavy rain which had preceded this record-breaking August.

"No!" said Anthony aloud. "I'm mad, that's what it is. But then those *are* bathing sandals. *And* didn't I just now tell Boyd he was making a mistake in not treating this business like the goriest of 'tec-tales?"

He stood looking over the river. If only he could fit any sort of reason——

One came to him. He laughed at it; but it intrigued him. It intrigued him vastly. There was a house, just one house, on the opposite bank. It was perhaps thirty yards higher up the stream than the gate by which he was standing.

Suppose some one from that house wanted to get to Abbotshall quickly, so quickly that they could not afford to travel the quarter-mile on each side of the river which crossing by the bridge would involve. Taking that as an hypothesis, he had a reason for this Captain Webb business. The theory was insane, of course, but why not let fancy lead him a while?

The very fact that the woman was so good a swimmer as she must be, made it probable that she would be sufficiently water-wise to make use of, rather than battle helplessly against, the eight-mile-an-hour stream. Very well, then, before taking to the river, on her way back she would have run upstream along this bank to a point some way above the house she wished to return to on the opposite bank.

Still laughing at himself, Anthony turned to his left and walked upstream, his eyes on the soft clay at the river's edge. When he had passed by fifty yards the house on the other side, he found two sandal-marks. They were deep; the clay gave a perfect impression.

He was surprised but still unbelieving. Then, as he stood for a moment looking down into the dark water only a few inches below the level of his feet, a gleam of white caught his eye. Curious, he squatted, pulled up his sleeve and thrust his arm into the water, groping about the ledge which jutted out from the bank some inches below the surface. His fingers found what they sought. He rose to his feet and examined his catch.

A small canvas bathing-sandal. From its uppers dangled a broken piece of tape. The sole was of rope.

"Benjamin," said Anthony to his pipe, "I'm right. And I've never been so surprised in my life. It looks to *me*, my lad, as if A. R. Gethryn *may* have been wrong and Brother Boyd right. Where's my 'insider' now?"

2

Anthony had crossed the river. Behind him lay Marling's wooden bridge, before him the house which must shelter the swimming lady. In his hip-pocket rested the sandal, wrung free of some of its wetness and wrapped in a piece of newspaper found by the hedge.

He walked slowly, framing pretexts for gaining admission to the house. His thoughts were interrupted by a hail. He swung round to see Sir Arthur Digby-Coates coming at a fast walk from the direction of the bridge.

Sir Arthur arrived out of breath. "Hallo, my boy, hallo," he gasped. "What are you doing here? Calling on Lucia? Didn't know you knew her."

"I don't. Lucia who?"

"Mrs. Lemesurier. That's her house there. Just going there myself."

"I'll walk along to the gate with you," said Anthony. He saw a possible invitation. He began to make talk. "I wasn't going anywhere; just strolling. I wanted to get away from Abbotshall and think. After I left the study, I drifted through the garden and crossed the river without knowing I'd done it." Not even to Sir Arthur was he saying anything yet of his discoveries.

The elder man picked his remarks up eagerly. "You've hit on something to think about, then? That's more than I've done, though I've been racking my brains since midnight. That detective fellow don't seem much better off either."

"Oh, Boyd's a very good man," Anthony said. "He generally gets somewhere."

"Well, I hope so." Sir Arthur sighed. "This is a terrible business, Gethryn. Terrible! I can't talk much about it yet—poor old John. Did you know him at all?"

"No. Shook hands with him once at some feed, that's all."

"You'd have liked him, Gethryn. He—we'd best not talk about it. God! What an outcry there'll be —is already, in fact."

"Yes," said Anthony. "A blow to England and a boon to Fleet Street. Look here, don't let me keep you. I hope Mrs.—Mrs. Lemesurier appreciates the beauty of her house."

"Charming, isn't it? Gleason built it, you know." He paused, and Anthony feared his bait unswallowed.

They had arrived at the gate to the garden. Over the hedge showed lawns, flowers, and the house. Anthony had not been merely diplomatic when he had praised its beauty. It was a building in the best modern manner and in its way as good to look upon as Abbotshall.

Anthony made as if to leave.

But Sir Arthur had swallowed the bait. "Look here, Gethryn," he said, "why not come in with me? The inside's more worth seeing than the out. And I'd like you to meet Lucia and her sister. They'd be glad to see you too. They were expecting another to lunch besides me—young Deacon, John's secretary. He wouldn't come. He's very busy, and being young, I suppose he feels it'd be a sin to enjoy himself in any way to-day. Silly, but I like him for it. He don't know the necessity yet for doing anything to keep sane." He laid a hand on Anthony's arm. "Do come along."

Anthony allowed himself to be persuaded. They walked through the garden and then round the house to the front door. They were shown by a cool, delightful maid to a cool, delightful drawing-room.

Through the French-window, which opened on to the garden they had approached by, there burst a girl. Anthony noted slim ankles, a slight figure, and a pretty enough face. But he was disappointed. The hair was of a deep reddish-gold.

Sir Arthur presented Mr. Anthony Gethryn—he knew of Anthony's dislike of the "Colonel"—to Miss Dora Masterson.

The girl turned to the man she knew. "But—but where's Archie? Isn't he coming, too?"

Sir Arthur's face lost its conventional smile. "No, my dear. I'm afraid he's not. He—he's very busy." He hesitated. "You will have heard—about Mr. Hoode?"

The girl caught her breath. "Yes. But only just now. You must think it awful of me not to have asked you at once; but—but I hardly believed it. It wasn't in any of the papers we had this morning. And I've only just got up; I was so tired yesterday. Travers, the parlor-maid, told me. Loo doesn't know yet. I think she's got up—or only just; she stayed in bed this morning too." The girl grew agitated. "Why are you looking like that? Has—is Archie in—in trouble?"

Sir Arthur laughed, and then grew grave again. "Lord, no, child! It's only that he's busy. You see, there are detectives and—and things to see to. I'm rather a deserter, I suppose, but I thought I'd better come along and bring Mr. Gethryn with me. He arrived this morning, very fortunately. He's helping the police, being—well, a most useful person to have about." He paused. Anthony, to conceal his annoyance at this innocent betrayal, became engrossed in examination of a water-color of some merit.

Sir Arthur continued: "It is a terrible tragedy, my dear——"

"What! What is it?" came a cry from the doorway behind them.

The voice would have been soft, golden, save for that harsh note of terror or hysteria.

Sir Arthur and the girl Dora whipped round. Anthony turned more slowly. What he saw he will never forget.

"A woman tall and most superbly dark," he said to himself later. Tall she was, though not so tall as her carriage made her seem. And dark she was, but with the splendor of a flame: dark with something of a Latin darkness. Night-black hair dressed simply, almost severely, but with art; great eyes that seemed, though they were not, even darker than the hair; a scarlet, passionate mouth in which, for all its present grimness, Anthony could discern humor and a gracious sensuality; and a body which fulfilled the promise of the face. Anthony looked his fill.

Dora was beside her. "Loo darling! Lucia!" she was saying. "It—it's terrible, but—but it's nothing to do with us. What's upset you so? What's the matter, darling?"

Sir Arthur came forward. Simply, straightforwardly, he told of Hoode's death. "It's an awful blow for me," he concluded, "but I wouldn't have frightened you for worlds, Lucia."

From where he stood discreetly in the background, Anthony saw a pale half-smile flit across her face. She was seated now, the young sister hovering solicitous about her, but he noted the tension of all the muscles that preceded that smile.

"I—I don't know what made me so—so foolish," she said. And this time her voice, that golden voice, was under control. Anthony was strangely moved.

She became suddenly aware of the presence of a stranger. Anthony was presented. The touch of her hand sent a thrill up his arm and thence through his body, a thrill which first sent the blood madly to his head and then left him pale. He kept his face from the light. He reproached himself for possessing, in the thirties, the sudden emotions of sixteen.

The two sisters withdrew. Lunch, they said, would be ready in five minutes.

Sir Arthur dropped into a chair and looked across at Anthony with raised eyebrows.

"A little overwrought," said Anthony.

"Yes. She can't be well. Most unusual for Lucia to be anything but mistress of herself. Except she was feeling cheap and then got scared by my sepulchral voice." He fell silent for a moment; then a smile broke across the tired sadness of his face. "Well, what impression has she made on you, Gethryn?"

"My feelings," Anthony said, "are concerned with Mr. Lemesurier. I wonder is he worthy of his luck?"

Sir Arthur smiled again. "You'll have a job to find out, my boy. Jack Lemesurier's been dead for four years."

A gong announced lunch. At the foot of the stairs Mrs. Lemesurier encountered her sister.

Dora was still solicitous. "Feeling better, Loo darling?" she asked.

Lucia grasped her sister's arm. "Dot, who—who was that man with Sir Arthur?" Her voice rose. "Who is he? Dot, tell me!"

Dora looked up in amazement. "What *is* the matter, dear? I've never known you to behave like this before."

Lucia leant against the balusters. "I—I don't know exactly. I—I'm not feeling well. And then this—this murder——" Again she clutched at her sister's arm. "Dot, you must tell me! They say Mr. Hoode was killed last night. But how? Who—who shot him?"

The door of the drawing-room opened behind her. Anthony emerged. His poker-playing is still famous; not a sign did he give of having heard the last remark of his hostess.

But he admired her courage, the way she took command of herself, almost as much as her beauty.

3

If that lunch was a success it was due to Anthony Gethryn. Until he came to the rescue there was an alternation of small-talk and silence so uncomfortable as to destroy the savor of good food and better wine. Sir Arthur was sinking deep into the toils of sorrow—one could see it—Miss Masterson was anxious about her sister and her absent lover, and the hostess was plainly discomposed.

So Anthony took command. The situation suited him well enough. He talked without stint. Against their desire he interested them. It must be believed that he had what is known as "a way with him." Soon he extorted questions, questions which he turned to discussion. From discussion to smiles was an easy step. Sir Arthur's face lost some of its gloom. Dora frankly beamed.

Only the woman at the head of the table remained aloof. Anthony took covert glances at her. He could not help it. Her pallor made him uncomfortable. He blamed himself. He saw that she was keeping herself under an iron control, and fell to wondering, as he talked to the others, how much more beautiful she would be were this fear or anxiety lifted from her shoulders.

But was she beautiful? He stole another look, purely analytical. No, she was not: not, at least, if beauty were merely perfection of feature. The eyes were too far apart. The mouth was too big. No, she was better than beautiful. She was herself, and therefore——

Anthony reproved himself for the recurrence of these adolescent emotions. His thoughts took a grimmer turn. He thought of that spongelike mess that had been a man's head. It was time he got to work.

He slid into another story. The silence which fell was flattering. It was a good story. Whether it was true is no matter.

It was a tale of Constantinople, which Anthony knew as his listeners knew London. He had, it seemed, been there, almost penniless, in nineteen hundred and twelve. It was a tale of A Prosperous Merchant, A Secret Service Man, A Flower of the Harem, and A Globe-Trotter. Its ramifications were amusing, thrilling, pathetic, and it was at all times enthralling. Its conclusion was sad, for the Flower of the Harem was drowned. She could not swim the distance she had set herself. And the Secret Service Man went back to his Secret Service Duties.

Sir Arthur cleared his throat. Dora Masterson's eyes held tears. At the head of the table her sister sat rigid, her white hands gripping the arms of her chair. Anthony noted her attitude with quickened pulse: she had shown no interest until the end of the story.

"Of course," he said, "she was a little fool to try it. Think of the distance. And the tide was strong. It'd be impossible even for an athletic Englishwoman." He is to be congratulated upon making so ridiculous a statement in so natural a tone.

"Oh! Mr. Gethryn, surely not," cried Dora excitedly. "Why Loo——"

A spurt of flame and a crash of breaking china interrupted her sentence. Mrs. Lemesurier had overturned spirit-lamp and coffee-pot. Much damage had resulted to cups and saucers. The tablecloth was burning.

"Not bad at all," thought Anthony, as he rose to help. "But you won't get off quite so easily."

Order was restored; fresh coffee made and drunk. The party moved to the drawing-room and thence to garden.

Anthony lingered in the pleasant room before joining the others on the lawn.

At last he took a seat beside his hostess. The deck-chairs were in the shade of one of the three great cedars.

"A delightful room, your drawing-room, if I may say so." His tone was harmlessly affable.

The reply was icy . "I am glad it pleases you, Mr.—Mr. Gethryn."

Anthony beamed. "Yes, charming, charming. It

has an air, a grace only too rare nowadays. I admired that sideboard thing immensely; Chippendale, I think. And how the silver of those cups shows up the polish of the wood!"

With this speech he did not get the effect for which he had wished. Beyond a pulse in the white throat that leapt into startled throbbing, there was no sign of alarm. She remained silent.

Half his mind applauded her and reviled himself. But the other half, ruthless, urged him on. "Have another try; you must," it whispered. "Get to the bottom of this business. Don't behave like a schoolboy!"

"I'm afraid I was so interested that I had to examine those cups and their inscriptions," he murmured. "Very rude of me. But to have won all those! You must be a wonderful swimmer, Mrs. Lemesurier."

The little pulse in her throat beat heavily. "I have given it up—long ago," she said simply. Her eyes—those eyes—looked at him steadily.

Anthony spurred himself. "Of course," he said, smiling, "there's no opportunity for pleasure swimming about here, is there? Except the Marle. And one would hardly tackle that for pleasure, what? The motive would have to be sterner than that."

The blood surged to the pale face, and then as suddenly left it. Anthony was seized with remorse. His mind hunted wildly for words to ease the strain, but he could find none. The sandal in his pocket seemed to be scorching his flesh.

She rose slowly to her feet, crossed to where her sister sat with Sir Arthur some yards away, said something in a low voice, and walked slowly across the grass toward the house. Though Anthony could see that she only attained movement by a great effort of will, the grace of her carriage gave him a swift sensation—half pleasure, half pain—which was like a clutch at his throat. The clinging yellow gown she wore seemed a golden mist about her.

He turned to join the other two, deep in conversation. A little cry came to their ears. They swung round to see a limp body sink huddled to the gravel of the path before the windows of the drawing-room.

Anthony reached her side before the girl or the elder man had moved. As they came up,

"Dead faint," he said. "Nothing to be frightened about, Miss Masterson. Shall I carry her in?" He waved a hand toward the open French-windows.

"Oh, please do." Dora picked nervously at her dress. "It—it *is* only a faint, isn't it?"

She was reassured. Anthony gathered the still body in his arms and bore it into the room.

He withdrew to the background while Sir Arthur and the girl ministered. Had he wished he could not have helped them. He had held Her in his arms. His heart hammered at his ribs. He felt—though he would not have acknowledged it—actually giddy. Only by an effort did he manage to mask his face with its usual impassivity. His one desire for the moment was to get away and think; to leave this house before he did more harm. Reason; thought; his sense of justice—all deserted him.

Sir Arthur stepped back from the couch. Color had come back to the cheeks of the woman. The lids of the eyes had flickered. Sir Arthur turned.

Anthony touched him on the arm. "I think we're superfluous, you know," he said.

The other nodded. "You're right. I've told Dora

I'd send a doctor, but she doesn't seem to think it's necessary. Come on."

They slipped from the room, and in two minutes were walking back along the river-bank toward the bridge.

CHAPTER VI

THE SECRETARY AND THE SISTER

I

THEY had walked for perhaps two hundred yards before the elder man broke the silence.

"I hope Lucia will be all right," he said. "Probably it was the heat. It's a scorcher to-day."

Anthony nodded. He was in no mood for talk.

"Dora was telling me," continued Sir Arthur, "that Lucia had been feeling queer since last night. They hardly saw her after dinner. She vanished to her room and locked herself in. But apparently she'd been all right this morning until lunch-time."

Anthony began to take notice. Here was more confirmation—though it was hardly needed.

They were drawing near the bridge now. Another silence fell. Again it was Sir Arthur who broke it.

"You're very silent, my boy," he said. "Perhaps you've got something to think about, though. Something definite, I mean." His tone changed. "God! What I would give to get my hands on the—the animal that killed John! I shan't sleep till he's caught. It's torture he needs! Torture!" The kindly face was distorted.

Anthony looked at him curiously. "The great difficulty so far," he said, "is failure to find any indication of motive. I mean, you can't do anything in a complicated case unless you can do *some* work from that end. A motiveless murder's like a child without a father—damn' hard to bring home to any one. Suppose I suddenly felt that life wouldn't be worth living any longer unless I stabbed a fat man in the stomach; and I accordingly went to Wanstead and assuaged that craving on the darkest part of the Flats, and after that took the first train home and went to bed. They'd never find me out. The fat man and I would have no connection in the minds of the police. No, motive's the key, and so far it's hidden. Whether the lock can be picked remains to discover."

Sir Arthur smiled. "You're a curious feller, Gethryn. You amuse while you expound." He grew grave again. "I quite see what you mean: it's difficult, very difficult. And I can't imagine any one having a grudge against John."

Anthony went on: "Another thing; the messiness of the business indicates madness on the part of the murderer. With homicidal mania there might be no motive other than to kill. Myself, I don't think the murderer was as mad as all that. Look at the care he took, for all his untidiness. No, the murderer was no more mad than the rest of the affair. It's all mad if you look at it—in a way. Mad as a Hatter on the first of April. And so am I, by God!" His voice trailed off into silence.

They had crossed the bridge now. Sir Arthur, instead of turning directly to his right to return to Abbotshall by the riverside path, chose the way which led to the village. Anthony drifted along beside him in unheeding silence. He was thinking.

Yes, "mad" had been the right word to use. There didn't seem to be any common sense about the thing.

Even She was mad! Why swim to Abbotshall? The saving in time, he calculated, could have only been a matter of ten minutes or so. And she couldn't—well, she must have been in hell's own hurry. But the sandals indicated a bathing-dress, and surely the time taken to change into that might have been spent in covering the distance on dry land. And what had she been there for, outside that window of the study? She—surely She had nothing to do with the messy crime—must be interrogated. Oh, yes! His heart beat faster at the thought of seeing her again.

He rebuked himself for thus early and immorally losing interest in his task, and returned to consciousness of his surroundings. He found himself in Marling High Street.

Sir Arthur disappeared, suddenly, into a low-browed little shop, whose owner seemed, from his wares, to be an incongruous combination of grocer, tobacconist, draper and news-agent. Anthony stood looking about him. The narrow street, which should have been drowsing away that blazing August afternoon, carried an air of tension. Clumps of people stood about on its cobbles. Women leaned from the windows of its quaint houses. The shop outside which he waited, and two others across the road, flaunted shrieking news placards.

" 'Orrible Murder of a Cabinet Minister!" Anthony quoted with a wry face. "Poor devil, poor devil. He's made more stir by dying than he ever did in his life."

Sir Arthur emerged, a packet of tobacco in one hand, a sheaf of newspapers in the other. With fleeting amusement Anthony noticed the red and black cover of an *Owl* "special." They walked on.

The elder man glanced down at the papers in his

hand. "It's a queer thing, Gethryn," he said, "but I somehow can't keep away from the sordid side of this awful, terrible tragedy. Up at the house I keep feeling that I must get into that study—that room of all places! And I came this way really to buy newspapers, though I cheated myself into thinking it was tobacco I wanted. And I can't help nosing about while the detectives are working. I expect I shall bother you." His voice was lowered. "Gethryn, do you think you'll succeed? He was my best friend—I—my nerves are on edge, I'm afraid. I——"

"Great strain." Anthony was laconic. Conversation did not appeal to him.

He tried to map out a course of action, and decided on one thing only. He must see and talk with the Lady of the Sandal again. For the rest, he did not know. He must wait.

They walked on to the house in silence. At the front door was a car. Boyd was climbing into it. He paused at the sight of Anthony. Sir Arthur passed into the house.

Boyd was excited, respectably excited. "Where've you been, sir? You've missed all the fun."

"Really?" Anthony was skeptical.

"Yes. I don't mind telling you, sir, that the case is over, so to speak."

"Is it now?"

"It is. You were quite right, sir. It *was* some one belonging to the house. I can't tell you more now. I'm off back to town. I'll see you later, sir."

Anthony raised his eyebrows. Things were going too fast. Had Boyd found out anything about Her?

"Shalt not leave me, Boyd." He raised a protesting hand. " 'The time has come, the Walrus said——'

You're too mysterious. Be lucid, Boyd, be doosid lucid."

The detective glanced at his watch with anxiety. He seemed torn between the call of duty and desire to be frank with the man who had helped him.

"I'll have to be very short, then, sir," he said, pushing the watch back into his pocket. "Ought to have started ten minutes ago. This is very unofficial on my part. I'm afraid I must ask you——"

"Don't be superfluous, Boyd."

"Very well, sir. After I left you in the garden this morning, I asked them all—the household—some more questions, and elicited the fact that one of what you called the 'cast-iron' alibis was a dud, so to speak. It was like this, sir: one of the maids had told me she'd seen Mr. Deacon—that's the deceased's secretary—go to his room just after ten. That coincided with what he told me himself, and also with what Sir Arthur Digby-Coates said. Now, this girl spent the time from ten until about a minute before the murder was discovered working—arranging things and what not, I take it—in the linen-room. Apparently it took her so long because she'd been behindhand, so to speak, and was doing two evenings' jobs in one. This linen-room's just opposite Mr. Deacon's room, and the girl said last night that she knew he hadn't come out because, having the door of this linen-room open all the time, she couldn't have helped but see him if he had.

"But she told a different tale this morning, sir, when I talked to her after you'd left me. I wasn't thinking about Deacon at all, to tell you the truth, when out she comes with something about having made a mistake. 'What's that?' I said, and told her not to be nervous. Then she tells me that she hadn't been in the linen-room all that time after all. She'd left it for about ten minutes to go downstairs. She was very upset—seemed to think we'd think she was a criminal for having made a slip in her memory." Boyd laughed.

Anthony did not. "What time was this excursion from the linen-closet?" he asked.

"As near as the girl can remember, it was ten minutes or so after she saw Deacon go into his room, sir."

"And I suppose, according to you, that this Deacon left his room while the girl was away, slipped out of the house, waited, climbed into the study window, killed his employer, climbed out again, hid somewhere till the fuss was over, got back unseen to his room, and then pretended he hadn't ever left it."

Boyd looked reproach. "You're being sarcastic, sir, I know; but as a matter of fact that's very nearly exactly what he did do."

"Is it? You know, Boyd, it doesn't sound at all right to me."

"You won't think that way, sir, when I tell you that we *know* Deacon's our man." Boyd lowered his voice. "Colonel Gethryn, those finger-prints on the weapon—the wood-rasp—are Deacon's!"

"Are they now?" said Anthony irritably. "How d'you know? What did you compare 'em with?"

Boyd looked at him almost with pity. "Got every one's marks this morning, sir." He smiled happily. "Handed each one of 'em—when I was alone with 'em, of course—a bit of white paper. Very mysterious I was about it too, asking 'em if they recognized it. They didn't: very natural when you come to think each sheet was out of my note-book." He looked again at his watch.

"One moment," said Anthony. "Found anything like a motive?"

The watch went back into his pocket. "We have, sir. Yes, you may well look surprised—but we have. And the motive's a nice little piece of evidence in itself. A chance remark Sir Arthur made when I was talking to him before luncheon-time put me on to it. Yesterday morning he happened to walk with the deceased into the village. The deceased went into the bank, and, luckily, Sir Arthur went in with him. Mr. Hoode drew out a hundred of the best, so to speak—all in ten-pound notes. We didn't know of this before, because Sir Arthur had mentioned it to the Chief Constable—Sir Richard Morley—last night, and Sir Richard had somehow not thought it important enough information to pass on." Boyd's tone conveyed his opinion of the Chief Constable of the county. "Well, sir, I had a search made. That hundred was missing. But we found it!"

Anthony ground his heel savagely into the gravel.

"I suppose it was secreted behind the sliding panel in Deacon's room, all according to Cocker?"

"Don't know anything about any sliding panel, sir; nor any Mr. Cocker. But Deacon's room is just where we did find it. I verified the numbers of the notes from the bank."

"What's Deacon say about it?"

The detective barked scornfully. "Said Mr. Hoode gave it to him for a birthday present. Lord, a birthday present! So probable, isn't it, sir?"

"Why the withering irony, Boyd? It's so improbable that it's probably true."

Boyd snorted. "Now, sir, just think about it! Turn it over in your mind, so to speak. Deacon's alibi turns out all wrong. His movements last night fit the time of the murder. A hundred pounds drawn from the bank by the deceased are found stuffed into a collar-box in Deacon's room—a good hiding-place, but not one to put a 'birthday-present' in. *And,* sir, Deacon's finger-prints are found on the weapon which the murder was done with! Why! it's a case in a million, so to speak. Wish they were all as easy."

"All right, Boyd; all right. I'll admit you've some justification. Yes—I suppose—queer about those finger-prints! Very queer!"

Boyd smiled. "In fact, they settle the business by themselves, as you might say." His kindly face grew grave. "It's quite clear, sir, I think. That murder—one of the worst in my experience—was done for the sake of a paltry hundred pounds!"

Anthony was not moved. "And your culprit, I presume," he said, "languishes in Marling's jail."

"If you mean have we arrested Deacon, sir, we have not. He doesn't know anything about us having found the prints of his fingers. And I'm afraid I must ask you, sir, officially, to say nothing to him about what I've told you. You see, this is one of those cases where contrary to the general rule we should like the coroner's jury to pass a verdict against our man and then arrest him. I'm having him watched until the inquest to-morrow, and we'll nab him after." Out came the watch again; a look of horror crossed its owner's face. "I must really get off now, sir. I'm terrible late as it is. Got to report up at the Yard. Good-day, sir, I'll see you to-morrow if you're still here. And thank you for your help. It was you and what you said in your study about it being an 'insider,' so to speak, that put me on the right track, though

I did take your other view at first. Now I see—as I've done in the past, sir—that you generally know."

Anthony concealed a smile at this attempt to gild the pill. "So I put you on the right track, did I?" he said softly. "Or the wrong, my friend; or the wrong! I don't like it. I don't like it a little bit. It's too rule-of-thumb. The Profligate Secretary, the Missing Bank-Notes, the Finger-Printed Blunt Instrument! It's not even a good shilling shocker. It's too damnation ordinary, that's what it is!"

If Boyd heard him he gave no sign, but hurried back to the waiting car.

Anthony watched it out of sight. He communed with himself. No, he didn't like it. And where did She come in? And why, in the name of a name, had she said: "Who shot him?" when the poor devil had had his head battered in?

"That rather lets her out as regards the actual bashing," he said, half-aloud. "That's a comfort, anyhow. But, it's perplexing, very perplexing. 'Do I sleep, do I dream, or is Visions about?' I think, yes, I think a little talk with the murderous secretary would do me good—always remembering the official injunction not to tell him he's going to be hanged soon."

2

Archibald Basil Travers Deacon—his parents have much to answer for—was in the drawing-room. He sprawled in an easy-chair beside the open windows. A book lay face-downwards upon his knees.

Anthony, entering softly, had difficulty in persuading himself that this was the man he sought. He had expected the conventional private secretary; he found a man in the late twenties with the face of a battered but pleasant prize-fighter, the eyes of a lawyer, and the body of Heracles.

Anthony coughed. The secretary heaved himself to his feet. The process took a long time. The unfolding complete, he looked down upon Anthony's six feet from a height superior by five inches. He stretched out a hand and engulfed Anthony's. A tremendous smile split his face.

He boomed softly: "You must be Gethryn. Heard a lot about you. So you're here disguised as a bloodhound, what? Stout fellah!"

They sat, and Anthony produced cigars. When these were well alight,

"Queer show, this," said Deacon.

"Very," Anthony agreed.

Silence fell. Openly they studied each other. Deacon spoke first.

"Boyd," he said, settling a cushion behind his great shoulders, "is quite wrong."

"Eh?" Anthony was startled.

"I remarked, brother, that your Wesleyan-lookin' detective friend was shinning up the wrong shrub."

"Indeed," said Anthony. "How?"

"Your caution, brother, is commendable; but I think you know what I mean. Chief Detective Inspector, or whatever he is, W. B. Boyd of Scotland Yard's Criminal Investigation Department—bless his fluffy little bed-socks—is laborin' under the delusion that I, to wit Archibald Etcetera Deacon, am the man who killed John Hoode. You apprehend me, Stephen?"

Anthony raised his eyebrows. "How much do you know, I wonder?"

"All depends on your meanin'. If you're asking

whether I know anything about how the chief was done in, the answer's 'nothing.' But if you mean how much do I know of Scotland Yard's suspicion of me, that's a different story."

"Number two's right," said Anthony. "Fire ahead."

"Comrade Boyd," said the secretary, "is a tenacious, an indefatigable old bird, and he's found out some funny things. But what he doesn't see is that they're only funny and no more. First, I didn't contradict him—very foolish of me, that—when it was obvious that he thought I'd been in my room last night from ten until after they found the chief done in in his study. I didn't contradict him because the mistake seemed as if it would get me out of a very compromising position. You see, at about a quarter-past ten I left my room, went downstairs, out of the front door, and enjoyed a cheery stroll on my lonesome. When I came back I found the whole damn' place in an uproar, the murder having been already discovered. There was such a general shemozzle that nobody noticed me come in until I got there, what! My—what's the officialese for it?—'suppression of the truth' gave Boyd clue number one.

"Clue number two was the money. And the money was what had made me seize on an alibi when it was handed to me on a plate—the alibi, I mean. You see, it was so hellish awkward, this money business, and I let old Bloodhound Boyd fog himself because I wanted time to think. It was like this: the chief and I really were very good friends indeed—he was a damn' good fellah—though we did growl at each other occasional-like; and I believe the poor old lad was really attached to me; anyhow the money made it seem like that. He was a very canny old Haggis, you know, but he was subject to fits of extraordinary generosity. I mentioned some days ago—forget how it came up—that Wednesday was my birthday. Well, last night, or rather yesterday afternoon about five—when I took some papers in to him in the study, he wished me many happy returns of the day before, apologized for having forgotten the ceremony, and shoved an envelope into my mit: in that envelope were ten crisp little tenners, all nice and new and crumply-lookin'. Of course I did the hummin' and haain' act, but he'd have none of it.

" 'No, my boy,' he says, 'you keep it. Must let an old fellah like me do what I want.' So I scraped at the old forelock and salaamed. Thought it was damned decent of him, you know. As I was clearin' out, though, he stopped me coughin' and hum-hummin' and lookin' all embarrassed. 'Deacon,' he said, 'er-um-er-um—don't you mention that little memento to—to any one, will you?' ' Not if you'd rather I didn't, sir,' says I. He gave a sickly sort of grin and muttered. But I understood him all right. He meant his sister. She's one of those holy terrors that's not a bad sort really. I always knew she kept a pretty tight fist on the purse-ropes, though. P'r'aps that's why he didn't give me a cheque."

Anthony took the cigar from his mouth. "And Boyd," he said, "finds out that Hoode had this money in the house, institutes a search, and finds it in your collar-box, which looks like an ingenious hiding-place but was really just an accidental safe. He also finds out that you weren't in your room last night during all the time that you let him think you were, and that you entered the house—probably by the verandah door—just after the body was found. He looks at you and connects your obvious strength with the ruts in Hoode's skull. He sees your titanic length of leg and argues that you're the only person in the house likely to be able to step through that open study-window without marking the flower-bed by treading on the flowers. He does a sum, and the answer is: x equals the murderer and Archibald Deacon equals x. That's what you know, isn't it?"

"You have it all, old thing, all! *Quel lucidité!*"

"But you haven't," said Anthony, thinking of the finger-prints and his promise to Boyd. "There's more in it than that, I'm afraid." He puffed at his cigar. "By the way, you didn't do it, did you?"

"No," said Deacon, and laughed.

Anthony smiled. "I shouldn't have believed you if you'd said yes. You can't give me a line, I suppose? Any private suspicions of your own? I've a bag of data, but nothing to hang it on."

"The answer, old thing, is a lemon. Nary suspicion. But what's all this about data? Found anythin' fresh?"

"Oh, well, you know"—Anthony waved vague hands. "Possibly yes, possibly no, if you follow me. I mean, you never can tell."

Deacon smiled. "Kamerad!" he said. "Served me right. But that's me all over, I'm afraid. Damn nosey! But you must admit I'm an interested party."

"I do," Anthony said; then suddenly leaned forward. "Have you told me *all* you know?" he asked. "And are you going to tell me anything you don't *know*, but merely feel?"

Deacon was silent for perhaps a minute. "I can't tell you anything more than I *know*," he said at last and slowly. "And as to the other, what exactly are you driving at? D'you mean: do I definitely suspect any one as being the murderer?"

Anthony nodded. "Just that."

"Then the answer's no. But I'll tell you what I do feel very strongly, and that's that it isn't any one belonging to the house."

"So you think that, do you?" said Anthony. "You know, I've heard that before about this affair."

Deacon sat up. "Oh! And what do *you* think? The reverse?"

Anthony shrugged non-committal shoulders.

"But it's absurb," said the secretary. "Quite utterly imposs' my dear feller!"

"Is it?" Anthony raised his eyebrows. "Ever read detective stories, Deacon? Good ones, I mean. Gaboriau's, for instance. If you do, you'll know that the 'It' is very often found among a bunch of 'unlikely and impossibles.' And one of my chief stays in life is my well-proved theory that Fiction is Truth. The trouble is that the stories are often more true than the real thing. And that's just where one goes wrong, and sometimes gets left quite as badly off the mark as the others. I'm beginning to think I may be doing that here."

Deacon scratched his head. "I think you're ahead of me," he said.

"Never mind, I'm ahead of myself. A long way ahead."

"Well, says I, I hope you catches yourself up soon."

"Thanks." Anthony got to his feet. "Is it possible for me to see Miss Hoode this afternoon?"

" 'Fraid not. Our Mr. Boyd saw her this morning, and she's given orders that that was enough."

"Well, I prowl," said Anthony, and walked to the

door. "By the way, on that walk of yours last night, that awkward walk, did you meet any one? or even see any one?"

"No. And that's awkward, too, isn't it? Nary human being did I pass."

Anthony opened the door. "Any time you think I'd be useful, let me know," he said, and passed into the passage.

Deacon's voice followed him. "Thanks. When you're wanted I'll make a noise like a murderer. Stout fellah!"

Walking down the passage which led to the great square hall, Anthony pondered. It seemed impossible that this gigantic imperturbability was a murderer. But how to explain the finger-prints? And Deacon did not know of those prints. What would he do when told of them?

"The man's in a mess," he said to himself. "This week's problem: how to extricate him? The solution will be published in our next week's issue—per-haps!"

He came out into the hall. The utter silence of the house oppressed him. Any sound, he thought, would be welcome, would make things seem less like a nightmare.

He turned to his left, making for the verandah door. His fingers on its handle, he paused. Behind him, to his right, was the door of the study. His ears had caught a sound, a rustling sound, from that direction. He looked about him. No one was near, in sight even. The two men Boyd had left on duty had disappeared.

Quietly, he crossed to the study door. He laid his ear against it. He heard the click of a lock, a light lock, then a rustle of paper, then soft footsteps.

He crossed the hall to the foot of the stairs in three jumps. A barometer and a clock hung on the wall. He studied them.

He heard the study door open, slowly, as if the one who opened were anxious not to be noisy. Then came a rustle of skirts. He stepped out from the shadow.

Half-way between the study and where he stood by the foot of the stairs was a woman. Her hand which had been at the bosom of her dress, fell to her side.

Anthony moved towards her. Closer, he saw her more plainly—a tall, square-shouldered grenadier of a woman, with a sexless, high-cheekboned, long-nosed face. The features, the sand-colored hair, were reminiscent of the dead minister.

"Miss Hoode?" Anthony bowed. "My name is Gethryn. I believe that Sir Arthur Digby-Coates has explained my presence."

"Yes." The woman's tones were flat, lifeless as her face. She essayed cordiality. "Yes, indeed. I told him I was glad, very glad, to have your help. I need to apologize for not having spoken to you before, but—I—but——"

Anthony raised a hand. "Believe me, madam, I quite understand. I would like, if it is not an impertinence, to express my condolence."

The woman bowed her head. "Thank you," she said; pressing a hand to her heart. "I—I must leave you. Give orders for anything you may want."

Anthony watched her mount the stairs and disappear. "My good woman—if you really are a woman—what's your trouble? Sorrow? Or fear? Or both?" he thought. "And why were you in the study? And why were you so secret about it? And above all, what did you hide in your flat bosom when you saw me? Two whats and two whys."

He stood filling his pipe. Assuredly this fresh mystery must be investigated. And so must that of the lady that swam rivers in the night and blinded her pursuer's eyes and assaulted his heart in the morning. If it had not been for Her all this would have been great fun; but now—well, it was anything but amusing. She must know something, and since Boyd had seen fit to suspect the one obviously innocent person, it was Anthony Ruthven Gethryn's business to find out what she knew. What was so disturbing was the unreasonableness of the affair. Nothing seemed to have motive behind it. Of course, there was reason for everything—the Lady of the Sandal's swim over the river, the secret ravishing of the study by the bosomless, sexless sister of the corpse, even the appearance of an innocent man's finger-prints on the murderer's weapon—but were they sane reasons? At present it seemed as if they could not be, and what could be more hopeless than the search of a sane man for the motives of lunatics!

Anthony shook himself, chided and took himself in hand. "Gethryn," he murmured, " do something, man! Don't stand here saying how difficult everything is. Well, what shall I do? Have a look at the study? All right."

He still had the hall to himself. Quietly, he entered the study and closed the door behind him.

He surveyed the room. He stroved for memory of the sounds he had heard just now when Laura Hoode had been there and he outside.

There had been a fumbling, a click, a pause and then the rustling of paper. The writing-table was the most likely place. The drawers, he knew, were all locked, but perhaps the gaunt sister had duplicate keys. The originals were in Boyd's official possession.

But it was unlikely that sister would have keys. He looked thoughtfully at the table. Something of a connoisseur, he judged it as belonging to the adolescence of the last century.

A desk more than a hundred years old! A mysterious, sinister woman searching in it! "A hundred to one on Secret Drawer!" thought Anthony, and probed among the pigeon-holes. He met with no success, and felt cheated. His theory of the essential reality of story-books had played him false, it seemed.

Loath to let it go, he tried again; this time pulling out from their sheaths the six small, shallow drawers which balanced the pigeon-holes on the other side of the alcove containing the ink-well. The top drawer, he noticed with joy, was shorter by over an inch than its five companions. He felt in its recess with long, sensitive fingers. He felt a thin rim of wood. He pressed, and nothing happened. He pulled, and it came easily away. The Great Story-book Theory was vindicated. He peered into the unveiled hollow. It was filled with papers, from their looks recently tossed and crumpled.

"Naughty, naughty Laura!" said Anthony happily, and pulled them out.

There were letters, a small leather-covered memorandum-book, a large note-book and a bunch of newspaper-cuttings.

He pulled a chair up to the table and began to read. When he had finished, he replaced the two little books and the letters. They were, he judged, unimportant. The newspaper-cuttings he retained, slipping them into his wallet. The illegality of the proceeding did not apparently distress him.

He replaced the little drawers, careful to leave things as he had found them. On his way to the door, he paused to examine the little polished rosewood table which stood beside the grandfather clock and was the fellow of that which supported the two tall vases he had spoken of to Boyd. A blemish upon its glossy surface had caught his eye.

On close inspection he found a faint scar some twelve inches long and two wide. This scar was compounded of a series of tiny dents occurring at frequent and regular intervals along its length and breadth.

Anthony became displeased with himself. He ought to have noticed this on his first visit to the room. Not that it seemed important—the wood-rasp had obviously been laid there, probably by the murderer, possibly by some one else—but, he ought, he considered, to have noticed it.

He left the room, passed through the still empty hall and so into the garden. Here, pacing up and down the flagged walk outside the study, he became aware of fatigue. The lack of a night's sleep and the energies of the day were having their effect.

To keep himself awake, he walked. He also thought. Presently he halted and stood glaring at the wall above the windows of the study. As he glared, he muttered to himself: "That bit of dead creeper, now. It's untidy. Very untidy! And it doesn't fit!"

Ten minutes later Sir Arthur found him, heavy-eyed, hands in pockets, still looking up at the wall, heavy-eyed, and swaying ever so little on his feet.

"Hallo, Gethryn, hallo!" Sir Arthur looked at him keenly. "You look fagged out, my boy. This won't do. I prescribe a whisky and soda." He caught Anthony's arm. "Come along."

Anthony rubbed his eyes. "Well, I grow old, I grow old," he said. "Did you say a drink? Forward!"

CHAPTER VII

THE PREJUDICED DETECTIVE

THORNTON, Mrs. Lemesurier's parlor-maid, was enjoying her evening out. To Mrs. Lemesurier and her sister, drinking their coffee after dinner, came Thornton's second-in-command.

"Please, ma'am," she said, "there is a gentleman."

"What? Who?" Lucia pushed back her chair.

"There is a gentleman, ma'am. In the drawing-room. He says might he see you. Very important, he said it was. Please, ma'am, he wouldn't give no name." The girl twisted her apron-strings nervously.

"Shall I go, dear?" Dora asked placidly. Inwardly she was frightened. She had thought her sister recovered from her attack of the afternoon, but here she was getting ill again. White-faced! Nervy! Not at all like the usual Lucia.

Mrs. Lemesurier rose to her feet. "No, no. I'd better see him. Elsie, what name—oh, you said he wouldn't give one. All right. The drawing-room, you said?" She walked slowly from the room.

Outside the drawing-room door she paused, fought for composure, gained it, and entered. Anthony came forward to meet her.

Her hand went to her naked throat. "You!" she whispered.

Anthony bowed. "You are right, madam."

"What do you want? What have you come here for, again?" So low was her voice that he could barely catch the words.

"You know," said Anthony, "we're growing melodramatic. Please sit down." He placed a chair.

Mechanically she sank into it, one hand still at the white throat. The great eyes, wide with fear, never left his face.

"Now," said Anthony, "let us clear the atmosphere. First, please understand, that I have no object here except to serve you. I wasn't quite clear about that this morning, hence my clumsy methods. The next move's up to you. Suppose you tell me all about it."

Her eyes fell from his. "All about what? Really, Mr.—Mr. Gethryn, do you always behave in this extraordinary way?"

"Good! Quite good!" Anthony approved. "But it won't do, you know. It won't do. I repeat, suppose you tell me all about it."

She essayed escape by another way. She looked up into his face, a light almost tender in her eyes.

"Did you—do you—really mean that about—about serving? Is it true that you want to help me?" she asked. And still her voice was soft; but with how different a softness!

"Most certainly."

"Then I assure you, Mr. Gethryn, most honestly and sincerely, that you will help me best by—by"—she hovered on the brink of admission—"by not asking me anything, by not trying any more to—to——" She broke down. Her voice died away.

Anthony shook his head. "No. You're wrong, quite wrong. I'll show you why. Last night John Hoode was murdered. During the night you swam across the river, crept up to the house, and crouched outside the window of the room in which the murder was done. Why did you do all this? Certainly not for amusement or exercise. Then, unless a coincidence occurred greater than any ever invented by a novelist in difficulties, your visit was in some way connected with the murder. Or, at any rate, some of the circumstances of the murder are known to you."

"No! No!" Lucia shrank back into her chair.

"There you are, you see." Anthony made a gesture. "I was putting the point of view of the police and public—what they would say if they knew—not giving my own opinion.

"The sleuth-hounds of fiction," he went on, "are divinely impartial. The minions of Scotland Yard are instructed to be. But I, madam, am that *rarissima avis,* a prejudiced detective. Ever since this case began I've been prejudiced. I've been picking up new prejudices at every corner. And the strongest, healthiest, and most unshakable prejudice of them all is the one in favor of you. Now, suppose you tell me all about it."

"I—I don't understand," she murmured, and looked up at him wide-eyed. "You're so—so bewildering!"

"I'll go further, then. If I say that even if you killed Hoode and tell me so, I won't move in any way except to help you, will—you—tell—me—all—about—it?"

Those eyes blazed at him. "Do you dare to suggest that I——"

"Oh, woman, Illogicality should be thy name," Anthony groaned. "I was merely endeavoring, madam, to show how safe you'd be in telling me all that you know. Listen. I'm in this business privately. I oblige a friend. If I don't like my own conclusions, I shall say nothing about them. I seek neither Fame nor Honorarium. I have, thank God, more money than is good for me." He was silent for a moment, and then added: "Now, suppose you tell me all about it."

She half rose, then sank back into her chair. Her eyes were full on his. For a moment that seemed an hour he lost consciousness of all else. He saw nothing, felt nothing, but those dark twin pools and the little golden lights that danced deep down in the darkness.

"I believe you," she said at last. "I *will* tell you"—she laughed a little—"all about it."

Anthony bowed. "May I sit?" he asked.

"Oh! Please, please forgive me!" She sprang to her feet. "You look *so* tired—and I've kept you standing all this time. And while I've been so melodramatic, too. Is there anything you——"

"Only your story." Anthony had discovered a need to keep a hold upon himself. Contrition had made her, impossibly, yet more beautiful. He pulled up a chair and sat facing her.

The white hands twisted in her lap. She began: "I—I hardly know where to begin. It's all so—it doesn't seem real, only it's too dreadful to be anything else——"

"Why did you go to Abbotshall last night? And why, in Heaven's name, since you did go there, did you choose to swim?" Anthony conceived that questions would help.

"There wasn't time to do anything else," she said, seeming to gather confidence. She went on, the words tumbling over each other: "We'd been out all day—Dora and I and some friends. I—when we got back

—Dora and I—there was only just time to change for dinner. As I came in I saw some letters in the hall, and remembered I'd not read them in the morning—we'd been in such a hurry to start. Then I went and forgot them again till after dinner.

"It wasn't till after half-past ten that I thought of them. And then, when—when I read the one from Jimmy, I—I—oh, God!—" She covered her face with her hands.

"Who," said Anthony sharply, "is Jimmy?"

With an effort so great that it hurt him to watch, she recovered. The hands dropped to her lap again. He saw the long fingers twist about each other.

"Jimmy," she said, "is my brother. I'm most awfully fond of him, you know. He *is* such a darling! Only—only he's not been quite the same since he got back from Germany. He—he's ill—and he's—he's been d-drinking—and—he was a prisoner there for three years! When they got him he was wounded in the head and they never even—the beasts! The beasts! Oh, Jim, darling——"

"That letter, madam," Anthony was firm.

"Yes—yes, the letter." She choked back a sob. "I—I read it. I read it, and I thought I should go mad! He said he was going—going to sh-shoot Hoode—that night!"

"Your brother? What had he to do with Hoode?" Anthony was at once relieved and bewildered. He knew why she had said, 'Who shot him?' But why should Brother want to shoot?

She seemed not to have heard his question. "I tried hard—ever so hard—to persuade myself that the letter was all nonsense, that it was a practical joke, or that Jimmy was ill or—or anything. But I couldn't.

He—he was so precise. The train he was coming by —and everything. The——"

"What had your brother to do with Hoode?" Anthony interrupted. He felt that unless she were kept severely to the point her self-control would vanish altogether.

"He was his secretary until Archie took his place—about six months ago. I—I never knew why Jimmy left, he wouldn't tell me. He wouldn't tell me, I say!"

Anthony shifted uneasily in his chair. There had been a note of hysteria in those last words.

Suddenly she was on her feet. "He did it! He did it!" she wailed, her hands flung above her head. "Oh, Christ! he'll be—oh, Jimmy, Jimmy!" And then she began to laugh.

Anthony jumped at her, took her by the shoulders, and shook. The ivory-white flesh seemed at once to chill and burn his clutching fingers. With every movement of his arms her head lolled helplessly. Knowing himself right, he yet detested himself.

The dreadful laughter changed to sobbing; the sobbing to silence.

"I'm s-sorry, p-please," she said.

Anthony's hands fell to his sides. "I," he said, "am a brute. Please sit down again."

They sat. A silence fell.

At last he broke it. "Then you were so impressed by the sincerity of your brother's letter that you determined you must try to stop him. Is that right?"

She nodded.

"But why, in God's name, didn't you walk or run, or do anything rather than swim?"

"There wasn't time. You see, it—it was so late—as I explained—before I read the—the l-letter that

I knew th-that Jimmy was probably almost there. There wasn't time to—to—to——"

"I see. Judging that you'd save at least ten minutes by crossing the river here, you pretended you were going to bed, probably removed the more clinging of your garments—if you didn't put on a bathing-dress—put on a pair of bathing-sandals to make running easy without hindering swimming, slipped out of the house quietly and beat all previous records to Abbotshall by at least ten minutes. That right?"

"Yes." Besides other emotions there was wonder in her tones.

"Good. Now, when you were kneeling outside the window of Hoode's study, what did you see? You'll understand that if I am to be allowed to help you I must find out all I can and as quickly as I can."

Their lids veiled the great eyes. A convulsive movement of the white throat told of the strain she was under. When she spoke it was without feeling, without emphasis, like a dull child repeating a lesson memorized but not understood.

"I saw a man lying face-downwards by the fireplace. There was blood on his head. It was a bald head. I saw a clock half-fallen over; and chairs too. And I came away. I ran to the river."

"Do you know," Anthony asked slowly, "what time it was when you got back here?"

"No," said the lifeless ghost of the voice that had thrilled him.

He was disappointed, and fell silent. Nothing new here, except, of course, the brother. And of this business of Brother James he did not yet know what to think.

With this silence, Lucia's cloak of impassivity left

her. "What shall we do?" she whispered. "What shall we do? They'll find out that Jimmy—they'll find out. I *know* they will, I——"

"The police know nothing about your brother, Mrs. Lemesurier." Anthony's tone was soothing. "And if they did, they wouldn't worry their heads about him. You see, they've found a man they're sure is the murderer. There's quite a good *prima facie* case against him, too."

Relief flooded her face with color. For a moment she lay relaxed in her chair; then suddenly sat bolt upright again, her hands clutching at its arms.

"But—but if they're accusing some one else, they—we must tell them about—about—Jimmy." Her face was white, dead white, again.

"You go too fast, you know," said Anthony. "Don't you think we'd better find out a few people who didn't do it before we unburden ourselves to the Law?"

She laid eager hands on his arm. "You mean—you think Jim didn't—didn't do it?"

Anthony nodded. "More prejudice, you see. And I know the man the bobbies have got hold of had nothing to do with it either. Again prejudice. Bias, lady, bias! There's nothing like it to clear the head, nothing! Now, have you a telephone?"

"Yes, yes," she said eagerly. Hope, trust and other emotions showed in the velvet darkness of her eyes.

"And your brother's address?"

Unhesitatingly she gave it; then added: "The phone's in here." She pointed to a writing-table at the far end of the room.

As he turned to go to it, she clutched again at his arm. "Damn it!" thought Anthony. "I *wish* she wouldn't keep doing that. So disturbing!" But he smiled down at her.

"Isn't it dangerous to use the telephone?" she whispered. "Isn't it? The girls at the exchange—if you use his name——"

"Credit me with guile," smiled Anthony.

He crossed the room, sat by the table and pulled the instrument toward him. She stood beside him, her fingers gripping the back of his chair. He lifted the receiver and asked for a city number.

"Is it a trunk-call?" he added. "No? Good!"

To Lucia, her heart in her mouth, it seemed hours before he spoke again. Then—

"Hallo. That *The Owl* office?" he said. "It is? Well, put me on to Mr. Hastings, please. At once. You can't? My child, if I'm not put through *at once* you'll go to-morrow! Understand?" A pause. To Lucia it seemed that the heavy thudding of her heart must be filling the room with sound. She pressed a hand to her breast.

Then Anthony's voice again. "Ah, that you, Spencer? Oh, it's the unerring Miss Warren, is it? Yes, Gethryn speaking. He is, is he? When'll he be back? Or won't he? Oh, you're all always there until after midnight, are you? Well, when he comes in, will you please tell him—this is important—that I've run across some one who knows where our old friend Masterson, Jimmy Masterson, is. Hastings will want to see him at once, I know. He and I have been trying to find Masterson for years. And say that I want to find out what Jimmy was doing last night. Tell Hastings to ask him or find out somehow where he was. It's a great joke.

"The address is 14, Forest Road, N. W. 5. Now, Miss Warren, if you wouldn't mind repeating the message?" A pause. Then: "That's exactly right, Miss Warren, thanks. You never make mistakes, do you? Don't forget to tell Hastings he simply must go there this evening, whether the work'll allow him or not. And he's got to ring me up here—Greyne 23—and tell me how he got on. And, by the way, ask him from me if he remembers his Cicero, and tell him I said: *Haec res maxim est: statim pare.* Got it? I won't insult you by offering to spell it.

"Thanks so much, Miss Warren. Good-night."

He replaced the receiver and rose from his chair. He turned to find the face of his hostess within an inch of his own. The color had fled again from her cheeks; the eyes again held fear in them. It seemed as if this passing-on of her brother's name had revived her terror.

"Preserve absolute calm," said Anthony softly. "The cry of the moment is 'dinna fash.'" Gently, he forced her into a chair.

The eyes were piteous now. "I don't—I don't understand *anything!*" she gasped. "What was that message? What will it do? What am I to—to do? Oh, don't go! Please don't go!"

"The message," Anthony said, "was to a great friend whose discretion is second only to mine own. Don't you think it was a nice message? Nothing there any long ears at the exchange could make use of, was there? All so nice and aboveboard, I thought. And I liked the very canine Latin labeled libelously 'Cicero.' That was to make sure he understood that the affair was urgent. The need for discretion he'll gather from the way the message was wrapped up. Oh, I'm undoubtedly a one, I am!

"And as for going, I'm not until I've had an answer from Hastings. That ought to be about midnight. At least, I won't go unless you ask me to." He sat down, heavily, upon a sofa.

Something—his calmness, perhaps—succeeded. He saw the fear leave the face, that face of his dreams. For a moment, he closed his eyes. He was thirsty for sleep, yet desired wakefulness. She glanced at him, timidly almost, and saw the deep lines of fatigue in the thin face, the shadows under the eyes.

"Mr. Gethryn," she said softly.

"Yes?" Anthony's eyes opened.

"You look *so* tired? I feel responsible. I've been so very difficult, haven't I? But I'm not going to be silly any more. And—and isn't there anything I can do? You *are* tired, you know."

Anthony smiled and shook his head.

Suddenly: "Fool that I am!" she exclaimed; and was gone from the room.

Anthony blinked wonderingly. He found consecutive thought difficult. This sudden recurrence of fatigue was a nuisance. "Haven't seen her laugh yet," he murmured. "Must make her laugh. Want to hear. Now, what in hell do we do if Brother James turns out to be the dastardly assassin after all? But I don't believe he is. It wouldn't fit. No, not at all!"

His eyes closed. With an effort, he opened them. To hold sleep at bay he picked up a book that lay beside him on the couch. He found it to be a collection of essays, seemingly written in pleasant and even scholarly fashion. He flicked over the leaves. A passage caught his eye. "And so it is with the romantic. He is as a woman enslaved by drugs. From that first little sniff grows the craving, from the craving the necessity, from the necessity—*facilis descensus Averno. . . .*"

The quotation set his mind working lazily. So unusual to find that dative case; they nearly all used the almost-as-correct but less pleasant *'Averni.'* But he seemed to have seen *'Averni'* somewhere else, quite recently, too. Funny coincidence.

The book slipped from his hand to the floor. In a soft wave, sleep came over him again. His eyes closed.

He opened them to hear the door of the room closed softly. From behind him came a pleasant sound. He sat upright, turning to investigate.

Beside a small, tray-laden table stood his hostess. She was pouring whisky from decanter to tumbler with a grave preoccupation which lent an added charm to her beauty. Anthony, barely awake, exclaimed aloud.

She turned in a flash. "You were asleep," she said, and blushed under the stare of the green eyes.

"I'm so psychic, you know," sighed Anthony. "I always know when spirits are about."

She laughed; and the sound gave him more pleasure even than he had anticipated. Like her voice, it was low and soft and golden.

She lifted the decanter again. "Say when," she said, and when he had said it: "Soda?"

"Please—a little." He took the glass from her hand and tasted. "Mrs. Lemesurier, I have spent my day in ever-increasing admiration of you. But now you surpass yourself. This whisky—prewar, I think?"

"Yes." She nodded absently, then burst out: "Tell me, why are you doing all this for me—taking all this trouble? Tell me!"

To-night Anthony's mind was running in a Latin groove. *"Veni, vidi, vicisti!"* he said, and drained his glass.

CHAPTER VIII

THE INEFFICIENCY OF MARGARET

I

Miss Margaret Warren, severely exquisite as to dress, golden hair as sleek as if she were about to begin rather than finish the day's work, sat at her table in Hastings's room.

Before her was the pad on which, ten minutes ago, she had written Anthony's message. She knew it by heart. As the minutes passed she grew more troubled at her employer's absence. Here—it was obvious—was something which ought to be done without waste of time; and time had already been wasted. She knew Colonel Gethryn well enough to be sure that the talk about a "great joke" had been camouflage. No, this was all something to do with the murder. Had he not said with emphasis that Ja—Mr. Hastings was to ring him up as soon as he had found this man Masterson? He had, and all had to know, it seemed, where this man Masterson had been on Thursday night, the night Hoode had been killed. . . .

"I don't believe," thought Margaret, "that either of them know this man Masterson at all. That's all part of the camouflage, that is. And then there's that bit of terrible Latin. I thought better of Colonel Gethryn, I did. Still, there it is: 'This matter is of the greatest importance. Obey immediately.' Cicero indeed!"

She glanced at her watch. A quarter of an hour wasted already!

An idea came to her. Hastings had gone out for food. In that case he might, if he had indeed gone there, still be at that pseudo-Johnsonian haunt, The Cock. Thither she sent a messenger, hot-foot. He was back within five minutes. No, the boss wasn't there.

"Damn!" said Miss Warren.

She looked again at her watch. Twenty past ten. She put on her hat—the little black hat which played such havoc with the emotions of the editor. The copy of Anthony's message she placed on Hasting's table, together with another hastily scribbled note. Then she went down the stairs and out into Fleet Street.

After three attempts, she found a taxi whose driver was willing to take her so far afield as Forest Road, N. W. 5.

The journey, the driver said, would take 'arfenar or thereabouts. Margaret employed it in constructing two stories, one to be used if this man Masterson turned out to be over fifty, the other if he were under. They were good tales, and she was pleased with them. The "under-fifty" one involved an Old Mother, Mistaken Identity, and an ailing Fiancée. The "over-fifty" one was, if anything, better, dealing as it did with A Maiden from Canada, A *Times* "Agony," Tears, A Lost Kitten, and A Railway Journey. Both tales were ingeniously devised to provide ample opportunity for innocently questioning this man Masterson as to his whereabouts on the night of Thursday.

The taxi pulled up. The driver opened the door. " 'Ere y'are, miss. Number fourteen."

As she paid the fare, Miss Warren discovered her

heart to be misbehaving. This annoyed her. She strove to master this perturbation, but met with little enough success.

The taxi jolted away down the hill. The road was quiet; too quiet, Margaret thought. Also it was dismal, too dismal. There were too few lamps. There was not even a moon. There didn't seem to be any lighted windows. A nasty, inhospitable road.

She perceived No. 14 to be a "converted" house. A great black building that might once have housed a merchant prince, but was now the warren of retired grocers, oddities, solicitors, and divorcees.

Margaret mounted the steps, slowly. The porter's lobby in the hall was empty. From one of a series of brass plates she divined that flat 6B was the burrow of one James Masterson. Flat 6B, it seemed, was on the first floor. The lift was unattended. She walked up the stairs.

Frantically she reviewed her stories, testing them at every point. She wished she hadn't come, had waited till Hastings had got back!

Facing the door of Flat 6B, Miss Margaret Warren took herself in hand, addressed rude remarks to herself, and applied firm pressure to the bell-push.

There was no sound of footsteps; there was no hand on the latch—but the door swung open.

Margaret fell back, stifling a scream. A small squeak broke from her lips. It was such a funny squeak that it made her laugh.

"Don't be a fool, Margaret," she told herself sternly. "Haven't you heard of contraptions to open doors? Hundred per cent labor-saving."

But her heart was thudding violently as she entered

the little hall. From a room on her right came a man's voice, querulous, high-pitched.

"Who's that," it said. "Come in, damn you! Come in!"

She turned the handle, and entered a bedroom well furnished but in a state of appalling disorder. A dying fire—the temperature that day had been over ninety in the shade—belched out from the littered grate occasional puffs of black smoke. The bed-clothes were tossed and rumpled; half of them on the floor. A small table sprawled on its side in the middle of the room. Crumpled newspapers were everywhere, everywhere. Huddled in an arm-chair by the fireplace was a man.

His hair was wild, his eyes bright, burning with fever. A stubble of black beard was over the thin face. Over his cheek-bones was spread a brilliant flush. A man obviously ill, with temperature running high.

One must sympathize with Margaret. She had expected any scene but this. Again fear seized her. What a fool she had been to come! What a fool! This man Masterson was ill; yet she couldn't feel sorry for him. Those over-bright eyes fixed on hers were so malevolent somehow.

She stammered something. Her mouth was so dry that coherent speech seemed impossible.

Then the man got out of his chair. Dully, she noticed how great was the tax on his strength. He clutched at the mantel for support. Dislodged by his elbow, a bottle crashed down and splintered on the tiles of the hearth. The smell of whisky, which always made her feel sick, combined with apprehension and the heat of the room, to set Margaret's senses dancing a fantastic reel.

Clutching the mantelpiece, the man attempted a bow. "You must pardon my appearance," he said, and his voice made the girl shrink back, "but I am—am at your service. Oh, yes, believe me. What can I have the great pleasure of—of doing for you? Eh?"

He started to move toward her, aiding his trembling legs by scrabbling at the wall. Margaret felt a desire to scream; choked the scream back. She tried to burst into speech, to say something, anything, to tell one of her stories that she had been so proud of. She failed utterly.

The man continued his spider-like approach.

"Go back! Go back!" Margaret whispered. She was shaking, shaking all over.

But the man had left the wall, and without its support had fallen to his knees. His head lolling with every movement, he crawled to the overturned table and searched among the litter of newspaper beside it.

Margaret cast longing eyes at the door. She tried to move, but her legs would not obey her. Fascinated by the horror of the thing, she looked down at the man. Her eye caught heavy headlines on the tumbled papers.

"Abbotshall Murder! Cabinet Minister Assassinated! Horrible Atrocity! Is it Bolshevism?" they shrieked in letters two inches high.

And the man—this man Masterson—had found what he wanted. He sat grotesquely on the carpet, holding in both hands the butt of a heavy automatic pistol. The barrel pointed straight at Margaret's head. A queer, sick feeling came over her. She felt her knees grow weak beneath her.

"Sit down. Sit down, will you!" The man's tones were harsh, cracked—the voice of one ill to the point of collapse.

2

Spencer Hastings stood disconsolate on the threshold of the editorial chamber. He had supped with a friend who was an artist. The artist had talked. Spencer Hastings had been later than he had intended in returning to the office. When he did—she had gone.

"Damn it! Oh, damn it!" he said fervently.

One must sympathize with him. He was ashamed, bitterly ashamed, of himself. For the ten thousandth time he thought it all over. Hell! He was badly in love with the woman, why didn't he grab hold of her and tell her so? Why was it that he couldn't? Because he was afraid. Afraid of her aloof beauty, her completeness, her thrice-to-be-damned efficiency—how he loathed that word beloved of Babbits! If only she weren't quite so—so infernally and perpetually equal to the situation!

Yes, he was afraid, that's what it was! He, Spencer Sutherland Hastings, sometime the fastest three-quarter in England, sometime something of an ace in the Flying Corps, renowned in old days for his easy conquest of Woman, he was afraid! Afraid forsooth of a little slip of a thing he could almost hang on his watch-chain! Disgusting, he found himself!

He flitted dejectedly about the room. Should he go home? No, he'd better do some work; there'd be an easy time coming soon.

He crossed the room and sat down at his table. Two slips of paper, both covered with Margaret's clear, decisive handwriting, stared up at him.

He read and re-read. Here was more Efficiency! Undoubtedly she had put its real meaning to Anthony's message. In his mind alarm replaced that mixture of irritation and reverence. "I thought this should be attended to at once, so have gone to the address given by Colonel Gethryn," she had written. Aloud, Hastings heaped curses upon the loquacity of the artist with whom he had supped.

He read the message and the note a third time, then jumped to his feet. That little white darling to go, alone and at such a time, to the house of a man who might be—well, a murderer! Of course, Anthony might only be after a possible witness, but——

He seized his hat and made for the stairs and Fleet Street.

3

Margaret lay huddled in the uncomfortable chair. For perhaps the hundredth time she choked back the scream which persisted in rising to her lips. Every suppression was more difficult than its predecessor.

Still, though she seemed to have been looking down it for an eternity, the black ring which was the muzzle of the automatic stared straight into her eyes.

The man had not moved. He was crouched upon the floor, no part of him steady save the hands which held the pistol. And he went on talking. Margaret felt that the rest of her life was a dream; that always, in reality, he had been talking and she listening.

And the talk—always the same story. "You're clever, aren't you? Very clever, eh? 'Who killed Hoode?' you said to yourselves—you and your friends. I don't know you, but you're Scotland Yard, that's what you are. Well, if you want to know ***I did!*** See?

But, my golden child, I'm not going to tell any one! Oh, no! Oh, no!"

There was much more of words but none of sense. He went on talking, and always the burden of his whispering, his half-shouting, his mumbling, was the same. "I killed Hoode! But I'm not going to tell any one, oh, no! Thought he could play about with me, did he? Get rid of the man who was helping him eh? Fool!"

Once she had tried to rise, intending a wild dash for the front door she knew had not shut behind her. But the pistol had been thrust forward with such menace that ever since she had been as still as stone. Her right leg, twisted beneath her, was agony. Her head seemed bursting.

At last there came a pause in the babbling talk. The man began to struggle to his feet. Margaret shrank back still farther into her chair. Even as he heaved himself upright the gun never wavered from her.

Another scream rose in her throat, only to be fought back. He was up now, and coming towards her with wavering steps. Even in her terror she could see that his fever had increased. She prayed for his collapse as she had never prayed before.

He was close, close! Margaret shut her eyes, screwing up the lids.

She heard a rush of feet outside the door. Some one burst into the room. Slowly, unbelieving, she opened the blue eyes. Hastings stood in the doorway.

A black mist flickered before her. Through it, as if she were looking through smoked glass, she saw him walk swiftly, his right hand outstretched as if in greeting, up to the unsteady, malevolent figure in the dressing-gown.

The mist before her eyes grew thicker, darker. When it had cleared again, Hastings had the pistol in his hand. As she watched, the numbness of fear still upon her, the man Masterson crumpled to the floor.

With a great effort she rose from the chair. On her feet, she stumbled. She felt herself falling, gave a piteous little cry, and was caught up in Hastings's arms.

Now that safety had come she broke down. Her body shook with sobs. Then came tears and more tears. She burrowed her face into Hastings's shoulder, rubbing her cheek up and down against the smooth cloth of his coat.

Hastings, his heart beating too fast for comfort, looked down. All he could see was the little black hat. The shaking of her body in his arms, the very fact that in his arms she was, deprived him of speech. They remained locked together. From the floor behind them came a hoarse, delirious babbling. Neither man nor woman heard it.

The sobbing grew quieter. A great resolve swelled in Hastings's bosom.

"I w-want a—a hanky," said a small voice from his shoulder.

From his breast pocket he whipped a square foot of white silk. A little hand snatched at it. Its work completed, she smiled up at him, then endeavored to withdraw from his arms. Hastings held on.

"Please," said the small voice, "will you let me go?"

"No!" roared Hastings. "No! Never any more!"

Slowly, she raised her head to look at him again. Immediately, thoroughly, satisfying, he kissed her. For a moment, a fleeting fraction of time, it seemed to him that the soft lips had answered the pressure of his.

But then she broke free. *"Mr. Hastings!"* She stamped her foot. "How dare——"

A grin of delight was on his face. " 'Sno use," he murmured. " 'Sno use any more. I'm not frightened of you now, you *darling!"* He snatched at her again.

From the floor there came again that hoarse mutter. Again they didn't hear it.

"And you know you've been in love with me for years," said Hastings.

"Oh! I have *not!"* She was all indignation. Suddenly it went. "Yes, I have, though—for months, anyway. Oh, Jack, Jack, why didn't you do this before?"

"Frightened," said Hastings. "Wind up."

"But—but whatever of?"

"You—and your damned sufficient efficiency. Yesterday I swore to myself I'd pluck up the nerve to tell you as soon as I caught you, red-handed, making a mistake. And you see I have——"

Her eyes flashed. "What d'you mean? *Mistake!* I like that! When I've caught the murderer——"

They both swung round, remembrance flooding back. The owner of the flat lay beside the overturned table, a shapeless heap in the dark dressing-gown.

Margaret shivered. "Mistake, indeed!" she began.

"Well, you did. This is a man's job. You ought to've waited till I came back. God! how you frightened me! Suppose this outer door here hadn't been ajar."

"But, Jack——"

Hastings forgot murders. "Why d'you call me that?" he asked.

" 'Cause I couldn't always be saying 'Spencer.' I'd

feel like a heroine in a serial. And don't interrupt. I was going to say: Never mind, we've got the man. Won't Colonel Gethryn be pleased?"

Hastings came back to earth. "By God!" he said. "So that's the murderer, is it? So it was that Gethryn was after. Well, he's a very ill criminal. How d'you know he is one, by the way?"

"He confessed. He was sort of delirious. Kept saying he'd done it, but wasn't going to tell any one. Horrid it was!"

Hastings rubbed his chin. "I wonder," he said. "I wonder. Come on, we're going to have a nice diplomatic talk with that porter I saw downstairs. And don't forget we mustn't let him get a line on what we're after."

4

The hands of the clock in Mrs. Lemesurier's drawing-room stood at five minutes to midnight.

There came a lull in the conversation which Anthony had kept flowing since he had sent his message to Hastings. A wandering talk it had been, but he had achieved his object. Save for the harassed look about her eyes, there was now nothing to tell of the strain the woman had been under. She had even laughed, not once but many times. She was, in fact, almost normal. And Anthony rejoiced, for he had found her to possess humor, wit and wisdom to support her beauty. She was, he thought sleepily to himself, almost too good to be true.

For a moment his eyes closed. Behind the lids there rose a picture of her face—a picture strangely more clear than any given by actual sight.

"You," said Lucia, "ought to be asleep. Yes, you

ought! Not tiring yourself out to make conversation for an hysterical woman that can't keep her emotions under control."

"The closing of the eyes," Anthony said, opening them, "merely indicates that the great detective is what we call thrashing out a knotty problem. He always closes his eyes, you know. He couldn't do anything with 'em open."

She smiled. "I'm afraid I don't believe you, you know. I think you've done so much to-day that you're simply tired out."

"Really, I assure you, no. We never sleep until a case is finished. Never. It's rather sad in this one, because I can see it going on for ever." He saw her mouth contract with the pain of fear, and went on: "I mean, I don't believe we're ever going to catch the Sparrow."

"The Sparrow?"

"Yes. Don't you remember 'Who killed Cock Robin'? It must have been the first detective story you ever read. You know, it was the Sparrow who did the dirty work. 'And here, in a manner of speaking, we all are.' All at sixes and sevens, that is. Here am I, come to the decision that either A. R. Gethryn or the rest of the world is mad. There are the police with entirely the wrong bird.

"The only real bit of work I've done to-day," he went on, "has led me to find, not an answer, but another problem. The question is: was a certain thing done genuinely or was it done to look as if it had been done genuinely, or was it done in the way it was on purpose to look ungenuine? The answer, at present, is a lemon."

Again she smiled. "It sounds awful," she said.

Then, with a change of tone: "But—but my brother? You were saying——"

Piercing, blaring, came the angry ring of the telephone.

Lucia leapt to her feet with a cry. Before she could move again Anthony was at the instrument. As he lifted the receiver she reached his side, pleading with eyes and hands for permission to use the extra earpiece.

"Carry on," he said; and into the transmitter: "Hallo!"

She snatched at the black disk, to hear: "That you, Gethryn?"

"Yes. Hastings?"

"Yes. I've done that job——"

"What did you find?" Anthony snapped, laying a reassuring hand on the white shoulder beside him. He felt that her whole body was shaking.

The telephone made meaningless cackles.

"What?"

"I said," came a squeak of a voice, "that the man your message referred to—er—said that it was he who had pulled off that deal you were asking about."

Anthony flashed a glance at the woman beside him. With surprise and admiration he saw that there were no signs of collapse. The hand which held the extra receiver was steady as his own, the head was held erect. Only the pallor of the face, extending even to the lips, told of the shock.

The telephone had again relapsed into mere cackling and buzzing.

Anthony gave vent to his feelings. "Blast you! Speak more clearly. Go on from where he said that it was his deal."

"And blast ye, too, scum!" came in a hilarious wheeze. "I said that the extraordinary part of the business was that I found out that the merchant must have—cackle—cackle—bahk-bahk——"

"Hell! Repeat! *What* did you find out?"

"I said that the chap must have dreamed it all. I found out that he couldn't possibly have had anything to do with the thing. Why on earth he thought *he'd* —er—put his deal through, I can't say—unless the explanation is that he got the idea that he would do it when he began to be so ill, put in a goodish bit of brooding, and then, when it *was* done and he heard about it, got all mixed and thought he was really the—er—manipulator of the business. Anyway, it's certain he couldn't've had anything to do with it at all. Take it from me."

Lucia staggered, then sank weakly into a chair, still clasping the black disk to her ear. Anthony glanced at her; saw that the color had come flooding back to her face.

"You're sure about this?" he asked the telephone.

"See it wet, see it dry. The man lives by himself. He's been ill for five days. I got that from the porter of the flats. This porter told me that J.M. hasn't been outside his front door for a week. The story's right enough. You've only got to look at the chap to see he's too ill to have been trotting about. There's not a doubt. You disappointed?"

"God no! Hastings, my brother, I kiss your hands. And I congratulate you. From what I know, your explanation of why J.M. thought what he did is right. But tell me, how ill is he?"

"Baddish, but by no means dying. Er—as a matter of fact, the doctor's with him now. Severe flu, I think it is, plus old-standing shell-shock or something like that probably."

Lucia stirred uneasily in her chair.

"Oh, the doctor's with him, is he? Now, what doctor?" Anthony said.

"Well—er—as a matter of fact—er"—bubbled the telephone in embarrassed accents—"I—we—have taken him back to my place. D'you know the man?"

"I'm well, interested in him."

"Well, he's all right now, you know. You see, we —I felt rather sorry—fellow's seedy and no one to look after him. We felt rather that we owed him something for false suspicion, what? Hope you don't mind my taking charge."

"Mind? I'm very grateful! You're an excellent man. But why the hesitancy, the embarrassment? Why all this we—I—us—we? I become aware of a rat."

"Because I've done it!" roared the telephone ecstatically. "I've asked her. I'm going to be married. She——"

"One moment. Miss Warren, I gather?"

"Yes!" cried the telephone. "Congratulate me!"

"I pound your spirit on the back. Tell Miss Warren this is the only mistake I've ever known her to make. I'll offer my felicitations in person to-morrow. Now, listen."

"Right."

"I want you," said Anthony, "to come down here—you'll find it best to do it by car—to-morrow and attend the inquest. It's being held at the house—Abbotshall—and it begins at eleven o'clock in the morning. If you bring Miss Warren with you, please ask her whether she will take a complete shorthand note of the proceedings. If she can't come, get an ordinary shorthand person. I'd rather she did it, of course. After the inquest go to the Bear and Key in Marling and ask for me. I shall want to pump you. Got that?"

"Very good, sergeant."

"If you see me at the house during the inquest don't speak to me or do anything to attract attention to me. Got it?"

"Yes."

"Right. Good-by, and again congratulations." Anthony hung up the receiver.

He turned to Lucia. She lay limply in the chair. After the first wild surge of relief had come reaction.

The spare receiver had fallen from her hand. Her breast heaved as if she fought for breath.

Anthony poured whisky into a tumbler; added a little soda-water. He forced the glass into her hand. "Drink that," he said.

Obediently, like a child, she drank, looking up at him over the rim of the glass.

When she had finished, "Feeling better?" he asked.

Her eyes flashed gratitude. "Ever so much. Oh! you don't know how—what a horrible, *awful* day I've had!"

"I can guess," Anthony said.

"Oh, I know; I know you can! I didn't mean that you—— How can I ever thank you enough?"

"Thank me? Why, you know, it seems I've done nothing much yet except make a fool of myself running down blind alleys."

She sprang to her feet. "Done nothing! Done nothing!" she blazed at him. "How dare you say such a thing! Why, if it hadn't been for you and—and your cleverness I would never have known Jimmy was safe. I'd just have gone on and on thinking horrors to myself." Suddenly all the fire died out of her. "And I think I should have died," she added quietly.

Anthony said: "You overwhelm me. You can reward me best by allowing me to hope our acquaintance isn't ended."

Her eyes opened in amazement. "Why, *of course!*" she said. "But we're friends already, aren't we? At least, I am."

Anthony was silent. The only answers he wanted to make were best unsaid. He rose to his feet.

"I must go," he said. "May I suggest that I get my friend Hastings to drive you up to town to-morrow to see your brother. That'll be some time in the afternoon, after the inquest."

"Mr. Gethryn, you think of everything, everything! May I? I love Mr. Hastings already—for taking such care of Jimmy, poor darling, when he didn't know him from Adam." She smiled; and Anthony caught his breath.

He made a move in the direction of the door; then paused. "Mrs. Lemesurier," he said, "you can't, I suppose, tell me anything I haven't already picked up about the Abbotshall *ménage?*" Business seemed safer ground when his emotions were so hard to repress.

She shook her head. "I'm sorry; I can't. Except Sir Arthur—and he's only a guest—I hardly know anything about them. Mr. Hoode I met twice. I've never seen his sister. I dare say I should have known them quite well by this time if Jim hadn't left Mr. Hoode in that funny way. But after that—well, it was rather awkward somehow, and we just haven't mixed."

"D'you know this Mrs. Mainwaring at all?"

"Not at all except from the illustrated papers."

"Oh. So she's what Zenith might call a Society Snake, is she? Well, well. Not a tennis champion or a plus-four person as well, is she?"

"Oh, no. I'm sure she isn't. Mr. Gethryn, why all this curiosity?"

Anthony smiled. "Now don't get scenting murderers in everything I say, will you. Merely my 'satiable curtiosity. I shall be punished for it one day. 'And his tall aunt the ostrich spanked him with her hard, hard claw.' That was for 'satiable curtiosity, you remember." He turned to the door. "I really must go now."

She stopped him, laying a hand on his arm. "Mr. Gethryn, one minute. Now that—owing to you—I'm happy again, I'm like the elephant's child, too, simply bursting with curiosity. Who *did* do it?"

Anthony laughed. "I haven't the faintest idea—yet. On the subject of who didn't do it I could talk for hours. 'But whose the dastard hand that held the knife I know not; nor the reason for the strife.' "

"But you're going to find out, aren't you?"

"I have hope, lady."

The black eyes held the green ones for a long moment. "I think," she said at last, "that you're the most extraordinary man I've ever met. Some day, you must tell me how you knew everything I did last night. I believe you were watching me; only you couldn't have been."

"I," said Anthony, opening the door, "I am Dupont, I am Lecoq, I'm Fortune, Holmes and Rouletabille. Good-night."

She was left staring at the closed door. When she opened it to peer into the hall, he had gone.

CHAPTER IX

THE INQUEST

I

At ten o'clock the next morning they brought a note to Lucia, radiant from a nine hours' sleep.

"My Dear Mrs. Lemesurier"—she read—"Hastings's car, its owner and I will call for you at some time between four and five this afternoon.

"Do not attend the inquest this morning, and above all prevent your sister from doing so. No doubt this warning is unnecessary, but I thought safer to issue it. For it is highly probable that the coroner's jury will return a verdict of murder against Archibald Deacon.

"Do not worry about this. Deacon had nothing to do with this messy business. (The great god Bias again, you see.) At the moment, however, things look bad for him. But I repeat: do not worry. Also, prevent your sister (I understand there is an alliance) from doing so more than is unavoidable. I promise things shall be straightened out.

"Yours optimistically,

"Anthony Gethryn."

"P.S.—I find that yesterday I omitted to return to you a bathing-sandal which I found. I ought to have sent it with this letter; but have decided to keep it."

Lucia, after the first shock, obeyed orders. Fond as she was of her sister and her sister's titanic lover, she found worry, for this morning at least, impossible. After the events of yesterday, she somehow discovered herself possessed of a childlike faith in the power of Anthony Gethryn to work necessary miracles.

She told Dora; then spent the morning to such purpose that the girl's fears were in some measure allayed.

2

At ten minutes to eleven Anthony left the Bear and Key and walked slowly in the direction of Abbotshall. He was tired and very tired. In spite of his fatigue he had barely slept. There had been so much to think about. And also so much which, though nothing to do with this work of his, had yet insisted on being thought about.

He entered the house at five minutes past the hour. Proceedings were being opened. The coroner and his jury had just seated themselves round the long table set for them in the study.

All about was an air of drama, heightened by the intensity of public feeling and the fact that the court was set on the actual scene of the crime. Marling felt the eyes and ears of the world bent in its direction. It rather enjoyed the feeling, but nevertheless went sternly, and with due solemnity, about its duty.

Anthony nodded to Boyd, shook hands with Deacon, ignored Hastings and Margaret Warren, already seated at the press table, and ran an eye over the jury.

The sight depressed him. "Mutton!" he murmured.

The coroner rapped the table, cleared his throat, and opened the court.

Five minutes later Superintendent Boyd turned to address a remark to Colonel Gethryn. But Colonel Gethryn was no longer there. Nor, apparently, was he anywhere else in the room. Boyd shrugged his shoulders.

Anthony was in the hall. In the far corner, by the front door, stood a knot of servants. They were clearly absorbed in their talk. On the steps were two policemen, their blue backs toward him. Slowly, Anthony mounted the wide, curving staircase. Once out of sight from below, his pace quickened to a run.

On the first floor he found his hopes realized. It was depopulated. As he had calculated, the whole household was downstairs.

3

The court adjourned at fifteen minutes to two. Hastings and a different, softer, more charming than ever Margaret Warren were given lunch by Anthony in his sitting-room at the Bear and Key.

The meal over, Margaret was given the one comfortable chair, Hastings sat on the table, and Anthony leaned against the mantelpiece.

"Now, my children," he said, "I have congratulated you, I have filled your stomachs. To work. What of the crowner's quest?"

"Adjourned till three-thirty," said Hastings, "when, after a quarter of an hours' cosy talk, they'll bring in a red-hot verdict of wilful murder against the hulking private secretary. We needn't go back, I think. There's one of our men there. He'll take the rest of the report; and it's all over except the shouting."

Anthony nodded. "No, you needn't stay."

"*I*," said Margaret, "don't think the secretary had

anything to do with it. Not with those sort of eyes—he couldn't."

Hastings guffawed.

"I agree with you, Miss Warren," Anthony said. "And it was the eyes which made me think that way."

Hastings exploded. "Oh! I say! But——"

"Quiet, dog!" Anthony waved him to silence. "I am Richard on the Spot. The case is mine, and I say that Archibald Deacon's a non-starter. Children, I am about to question you. Make ready."

Hastings cast his smile. Margaret produced a note-book.

Anthony said: "So far, the case against Deacon is, I assume: one, that in his possession were found bank-notes for a hundred pounds proved as having been drawn by Hoode from his bank on the morning of the murder; two, that his explanation that this money was given to him by Hoode as a birthday present was neither regarded as at all probable nor supported by any witness; three, that his explanation as to his where-about during the time within which the murder was committed was both unsatisfactory and entirely un-corroborated; four, that he attempted to mislead officers of the law by means of an alibi which he knew to be false; five, that in view of his size, strength, length of leg, and the fact that every one else for miles round appears to be accounted for, he seems the most likely person; and six, that his finger-prints were found on the wood-rasp with which the deed was done."

"Look here," said Hastings, "if you were at the inquest, what's all the palaver about?"

"I wasn't, and you'll see. Some of this I knew already, some I guessed. Wonderful, isn't it?"

Margaret leaned forward. "But who do you think did do it, Mr. Gethryn? Do you suspect any one?"

"Every one in the world," said Anthony. "Except Deacon, you, James Masterson, and one other. But I look first at the household; just as a matter of interest like." He ticked off names on his fingers. "The butler Poole, the chauffeur Wright, Martha Forest the cook, Robert Belford the other man-servant; Elsie Syme, Mabel Smith, housemaids; Lily Ingram the kitchenmaid, and one Thomas Diggle, gardener. Also the sister of the corpse, Sir Arthur Digby-Coates, and Mrs. Mainwaring. And there we have the ' 'ole ruddy issue, incloodin' the 'eads.' "

"Shades of Pelman!" Hastings was moved to exclaim.

"And," said Anthony benignantly, "what about 'em all? Their stories, their behavior?"

Margaret consulted the notebook. "The servants," she said, "were all right. Most obviously all right—except the man Belford. The girls no one could accuse of murder, they're too timid and their stories were all connected enough. In most cases they fitted in with each other naturally enough. The cook was in bed before ten-thirty, and slept through the whole thing. The chauffeur was talking to friends outside the lodge. The butler was apparently in his little room all the evening. He can't prove it by witnesses, but you couldn't suspect an old man like that. He's not strong enough for one thing; and he's obviously dreadfully upset by the death of his master. Mrs. Mainwaring seemed all right. She went to bed early, and was seen there by both Miss Hoode and the maid Smith—the one that was afterward in the linen-room. After the murder was discovered she was found fast asleep. Sir Arthur Digby-Coates is quite all right. He was in his own sitting-room—it has his bedroom on one side of it and the secretary's on the other, apparently—from ten-fifteen until the body was found by Miss Hoode and the old butler rushed up and fetched him. During that time he was seen by various people, including Deacon, at very short intervals. As for Miss Hoode, she deposed—that's the word, isn't it?—that she was in bed by half-past ten, reading. At about eleven she suddenly remembered something about an invitation to some one—she wasn't very clear in her evidence—and went downstairs to use the telephone and to speak to her brother. After that, well, you know what happened. That's all."

Anthony smiled. "And very good, too. I congratulate you, Miss Warren. 'So there, in a manner of speaking, they all are.' Of course, it's all very untidy, this evidence. Very untidy! Not at all neat!"

"I know, Mr. Gethryn. But then, you see, it wasn't as if they were all on trial. I mean, all this about where they were and that sort of thing came out mixed up with other things. It wasn't cross-examination with everything on the point and nowhere else. And if people don't know there's going to be a murder, they can't very well all get up nice, smooth alibis, can they?"

Anthony laughed. "Just what I said, Miss Warren. They can't. Now, about ferret-face—Belford, I mean. You seem to think his evidence wasn't as good as the others'. What did he do? Or say?"

Hastings took up the tale. "Nothing very unusual in itself. But his manner was all wrong. Too wrong, I thought, to be merely natural nervousness. Margaret thinks the same. It wasn't that he said anything one could catch hold of; he was just fishy. He made rather a bad impression on the court too. In fact, I think there'd have been a lot more of him later if the case against your limpid-eyed pet hadn't come out so strong.

"Damn it all!" he went on, after a moment's silence, "in any other circumstances I'd be quite willing to bow to your vastly greater experience, Gethryn. And to Margaret's womanly intuition and all that sort of thing. But this is a bit too much. When you get such a lot of circumstantial and presumptive evidence as there is against this man Deacon and then add to it the fact that his finger-prints were the only ones on the weapon the other feller was killed with, it does seem insane to blither: '*He* couldn't have done it! Just look at his *sweet* expression!' and things like that!"

"I dare say," Anthony said. "But then Miss Warren and I are *so* psychic, you see."

"But the finger-prints, man! They——"

Anthony became sardonic. "Ah, yes! Those eternal finger-prints. Hastings, you're an incorrigible journalist. Somebody says 'finger-print' to you, you shrug—and the case is over. The blunt instrument bears the thumb-mark of Jasper Standish, *ergo,* Jasper's was the hand which struck down the old squire. It's so simple! why trouble any more? Hang Jasper! Hang him, damn him, hang him!"

"But look here, that's not——"

Anthony lifted his hand. "Oh, yes, yes. I know what you're going to say. And I know I'm talking like a fool. The finger-print system is wonderful; but its chief use is tracing old-established criminals. If you consider the ingenuity exercised by this murderer in everything else, doesn't it strike you as queer that he should leave the damning evidence of finger-marks on only one thing, and that the actual weapon? Why, he might as well have stuck his card on Hoode's shirt-front!"

Hastings looked doubtful. "I see what you're driving at," he said, "but I'm not convinced. Not yet, anyhow. And we've rather got away from Belford. Not that there's any more to say, really. He merely struck us as being rather too scared."

"What you really mean, I think," said Anthony, "is that in your opinion Belford was very likely in it with Deacon."

Margaret laughed. "That's got you, Jack. You shouldn't funk."

Anthony said: "Let us leave ferret-face for the moment. Was there no one else you thought behaved suspicious-like?"

Margaret fingered the notebook in her lap. Hastings looked at her.

"You shouldn't funk, Maggie," he said.

"Pig!" said Margaret. "And *don't* call me Maggie! It's disgusting!"

"What is all this, my children?" Anthony asked.

Margaret looked up at him. "It's only that I told this person that Miss Hoode made me uncomfortable."

"You've watered it down a good bit," Hastings laughed.

"Well, all I meant was that she seemed so contradictory. Not in what she said, you know, but in the way she looked and—and behaved. It was funny, that feeling I had. At first I thought she wasn't suffering over her brother's death, but was just worn out with fear and with trying to—to hide something. And then after that I began to think she was sorry after all, and that all the queer things about her were due to grief. And then after that again I sort of half went back to my first ideas. That's all. You must think I'm mad, Mr. Gethryn."

"I think," said Anthony, "that you're a remarkable young woman. You ought to set up in the street of Baker or Harley, or both." His tone was more serious than his words; Margaret blushed.

"Did they," asked Anthony, after a pause, "exhibit the wood-rasp at the 'quest?"

Hastings nodded. "And a nasty weapon it must have made, too."

"I must get a look at it somehow," Anthony said. Then added, half-aloud: "Now, why does that mark worry me?"

"What's that?"

"Nothing, nothing." Anthony stretched himself. "Enough for to-day, children. Hastings, there is a lovely lady who wishes to visit your flat, and this to-night. She is the sister of our old friend J. Masterson. I promised she could see him if she went up to town this evening."

"Of course. J. Masterson, by the way, is all right. Temperature much lower; though he's very weak still, of course. Does nothing but sleep. Doctor saw him again this morning, and says his trouble is really nothing worse than 'flu, aggravated by inattention and complicated nervous thingumitights due probably to shell-shock."

"I see. It'll be all right about his sister seeing him this evening?"

"Of course." Hastings's smile was replaced by a blank sort of look. "Er—by the way, if this lady lives down here, perhaps I had—could drive her up now, what?"

"I was going to ask whether you would," Anthony said, after a pause, "but I've changed my mind. Don't look too relieved." His reasons for this sudden change of plan were mixed; it is certain they were not purely philanthropic.

"I gather, then," said Hastings, "that having left a competent subordinate to take down the dregs of the inquest, the lady Margaret and I may now get back to town."

They descended to the waiting car. Before it began to move,

"Miss Warren," said Anthony, "would you be so kind as to have that report of this morning's proceedings typed by some one and sent down to me here to-morrow; it'll be so much better than the public ones."

"I'll do it myself at once," said Margaret.

The car moved forward. Anthony waved his thanks, turned on his heel and re-entered the inn.

4

Within half an hour he was in Lucia's drawing-room. Outside the gate was his big red car.

Lucia kept him waiting barely two minutes. When she came he noticed with irritation the schoolboyish unruliness of his heart. There was for him some new, subtle quality in her beauty to-day. Something dark and wonderful and rather wild.

She gave him her hand. "I heard the car. I haven't kept you waiting, have I?" she asked.

Anthony shook his head. She glanced curiously round the room.

"No," he said. "Hastings hasn't come. He had

to get back. That's my car outside. If you'll allow me to, I'll take you up to town now. If you're ready, shall we start?" He turned to the door.

"I'm sorry," she said as he opened it, "that Mr. Hastings couldn't come. I wanted to have time to thank him properly."

Anthony, jarred, cheered himself with the thought that there had been a laugh in her voice. He glanced at her face. It told him nothing.

Her traveling-bag was carried out and placed in the car.

"I'm driving myself," said Anthony. "Will you sit in front?"

She smiled at him and took the seat beside the driver's. Annoyed with the disturbance aroused in his breast by that smile, Anthony drove out of the gate and down the narrow road to the bridge at a speed quite illegal. Then he slowed down, feeling not a little ashamed. Another new sensation for Anthony Ruthven Gethryn.

"I'm sorry," he said. "Pace frighten you?"

She turned to him not the tense, white face he had expected, but a joyous one, vivid with life under the enchanting veil.

"Not a little bit," she said; and laughter peeped through her words. "You see, after yesterday—and all that you did—I feel quite safe with you. As if you couldn't make a mistake. Not possibly!"

Anthony glowed.

"Yes," she said. "Absolutely safe, that's what I feel." A pause. "Just as a tiny girl feels if her father takes her out, say, in a tandem."

Anthony fell from heaven with a crash. Good God! "Father!" So he had aroused an emotion akin to filial, had he? Unfortunately for him, to drive a car a man must keep his eyes on the road: he had not seen the little half-smile of joyous mockery that had accompanied that last thrust.

He drove on in silence, unbroken until Guildford was reached. Here he had to slow to a crawl.

"Were you at Abbotshall this morning?" came in a small meek voice from beside him.

He nodded.

"How did the inquest go? You see, I've heard nothing, nothing! Was it—was it as bad as you said it might be?"

"I wasn't there myself," said Anthony, keeping his eyes on the road ahead, "but from what I've been told, I'm afraid it was."

"But you said you *were* there."

"At the house, yes. At the inquest, no."

The small voice mocked him. "You do so love being mysterious, don't you?"

"*Touché!* I believe I do, you know. I've been discovering a lot of youthful traits lately very ill in accord with my age." Something in his tone made her look up at him from under the rakish brim of the little hat. His profile showed grim; it seemed leaner than ever.

"I'm sorry if I was inquisitive." The small voice was smaller and very meek.

Anthony started. "Good God! No! I didn't mean that. Look here, I'll tell you. I went to Abbotshall because I wanted to play burglars on the first floor. And the best time to do it was when everybody was downstairs at the inquest. See?"

"Of course. But how thrilling! Do go on. I won't tell a soul!"

"If I hadn't known that," said Anthony, "I wouldn't have said anything at all."

"Thank you. Did you find anything—that you expected to find?"

"I found. Some of what I found I had expected to find; some not." His tone was final and silence fell again. The big car's speed increased. Soon they were among London's outskirts.

"Where are you going to stay?" Anthony asked.

"Brown's Hotel. May I go there first, please?"

To Brown's he took her, and waited with the car till she reappeared. During the journey to Hastings's flat in Kensington there was little opportunity for conversation. Once, threading skilfully through a press of traffic, he began to whistle, under his breath, the dirge of Cock Robin.

Then Hastings's flat was reached. Introductions over, they were left alone in Hastings's study while Hastings went to prepare the invalid.

Anthony picked up his hat. "I must go," he said.

"Where?"

"Back to Marling."

"Oh, Mr. Gethryn!" Lucia cried. "Did you only come up to bring me?"

"Yes," he said, after a pause.

"How awfully nice of you! But ought you to have wasted all that time?"

"All pleasure," Anthony said oracularly, "is gain. Did you warn your sister that Deacon would probably be arrested after the inquest?"

"I did. And I tried to persuade her not to worry. So I obeyed orders, you see."

"Did you believe there was no cause for worry?"

The great dark eyes met his. In their great depths he saw little golden fires dancing.

"Yes," she said.

Anthony bowed. "Good-night," he said, and was gone.

CHAPTER X

BIRDS OF THE AIR

I

It was a few minutes after half-past four when Anthony descended to the street and re-entered his car. Through London he drove fast; clear of it, terrifically. Always, when he found himself disturbed, he sought consolation in speed. It was preferable to be on a horse; but the car was better than nothing. Besides, was there not work to be done?

On the journey he thought much. One half of his mind was occupied with a problem of x and y; the other with a quantity more obscure even than x. It was that second half of his mind which conceived doubts of the worthiness of Anthony Ruthven Gethryn. The sensation was new.

As he drove through the great gates of Abbotshall and up the drive, the clock over the stables struck. A quarter to six! If the distance from Kensington to Marling is what they say it is, the word "terrifically" was not misused.

He stopped the car. Round the corner of the house, running, came Sir Arthur Digby-Coates. Though the thick, gray-flecked hair was unruffled by the wind of his speed, there was yet an agitation, a wildness about him, his fluttering tie, his clothes, most unusual.

He panted up to the car. "Gethryn, Gethryn! Just the man I was wanting! Where've you been?"

"London." Anthony was almost surly. He had been dreaming a dream.

"My God!" Sir Arthur pulled at his collar as if he were choking. "Look here! I must talk to you. But not here. Not here! Come in! Come in! My room'll be best. Come on!"

Anthony was dragged into the house and up the stairs and into Sir Arthur's room. They sat, in chairs drawn up to the window. In his, Anthony lay back, but the elder man hunched himself like a nervous schoolboy, sitting on the edge of his chair with his feet thrust backwards and then outwards until they protruded behind and beside each of the front legs. It was an old trick of his when preoccupied, and never ceased to amuse Anthony.

It was some time before Sir Arthur spoke. He seemed in his agitation to have difficulty in finding words. His hands twisted about each other.

"God!" he burst out at last. "What *are* we to do?"

"About what?"

"About this awful, this horrible mistake." Suddenly he jumped to his feet and stood over Anthony. "Why—is it possible—haven't you heard? About Deacon?"

Anthony shook his head.

"Why, man they've arrested him! The coroner's jury passed a verdict against him. And the police have arrested him. Arrested him!"

"Quite natural, when you think of it," said Anthony.

Sir Arthur stared at him. "D'you mean you think he did it?" he roared. "That boy!"

"No. I'm sure he didn't."

Sir Arthur sighed loud relief. "Thank the Lord for that! But, Gethryn, how was it you hadn't heard about this? And if you hadn't, how was it you weren't surprised? Weren't you at the inquest?"

"Only roughly speaking," said Anthony. "And I wasn't surprised because I knew on what evidence the police were working. Pardon me if I seem flippant—I'm not really—but what we've got to do is to find out who really did kill Cock Robin. That's the only way of getting Deacon off. The police take Deacon to be the Sparrow. You and I believe that he isn't; but we've got to admit that the case against him is good, extraordinarily good. His size and strength fit the part of the murderer. And above all his finger-marks were found on the Bow and Arrow. That last will want a deal of explaining, especially to an English jury, who don't, as a rule, know that real life's more like a fairy story than Hans Andersen."

"I know, I know," Sir Arthur groaned. "Those finger-prints. He must have touched the—the—what do they call the thing?"

"Wood-rasp. A file for wood."

"Ah, yes. He—I suppose he *must* have touched it. Must have. But I'll swear the boy had nothing to do with—with John's death. And he said he'd never seen the thing. And I believe him!"

"So he'd never even seen the thing," Anthony said. "Now that's interesting. Most interesting!"

But Sir Arthur was not listening. "What I'm feeling so—so damnably," he burst out, "is that my evidence helped to make things look worse for the boy."

"How."

"Because they took mine first; and in describing that awful night I mentioned, like the idiot I am, that Deacon had come into my room at a quarter to eleven. You see, he'd asked me the time, and I'd told him:

that's what made me remember. Then later it all came out about the clock in the study, and now every one says the boy put the hands back because he knew he had an alibi. Oh! It's all a ghastly, horrible mistake!"

"It is; and we shan't mend it by sitting here and talking." Anthony got to his feet. "By the way, before I go, tell me: what is Mrs. Mainwaring, who is she, that this poor swine don't see her? If it comes to that, why is she here at all?"

Sir Arthur made a wry face. "Why you haven't seen her I can't tell. Why she's staying here is, I'm sorry to say, for the notoriety. Any decent person would have left the house at once. I'm disgusted; I used almost to like the woman. I would have left, but Laura wished me to stay. And she's so apathetic that she won't get rid of the Mainwaring."

"I must see the lady," said Anthony.

Sir Arthur looked at him with curiosity, but found no enlightenment.

"In fact," said Anthony, "I must see both ladies."

Sir Arthur looked at him again, with no result.

"A last question," Anthony said: "what—without prejudice—do you think of the man-servant, Robert Belford of the ferret face?"

"I wondered whether you'd ask about him," Sir Arthur said eagerly. "I didn't like to say anything because I really know nothing against him at all. Never had anything to do with him, in fact. He used to valet John, and would have me, only I don't use valets. It's simply that I can't bear the fellow; his looks are enough to make any one suspicious. And he's been more furtive than ever—since the—the murder."

"H'm," grunted Anthony.

"It's really very ungrateful of me," said Sir Arthur, "to say anything against the man. He was one—or really two—of the witnesses to the fact that I was sitting here in this chair from ten until after—until poor old John was found. But still, joking aside, I have a very real feeling that Mr. Belford at least knows more than he has told."

"H'm. Yes," Anthony said. "And now for Miss Hoode. Where can I find her?"

"I think she's downstairs somewhere, but I'm not sure. I say, Gethryn, you're not going to—to cross-examine her, are you? I mean I don't think she'll want a lot of talk about——"

"No," Anthony said, crossing the room, "probably she won't."

Sir Arthur opened his mouth to speak; but was left staring at the closed door.

As he shut it behind him, Anthony caught sight of a black-clad figure disappearing round the corner by the stairhead. It was a back he had seen before. It wore an air of stealthy discomfort; and the speed with which it had vanished was in itself suspicious.

Anthony laughed. "Belford, my friend," he thought, "if you have done anything naughty, you're simply asking to be found out." He went on and down the stairs.

2

This evening, thought Anthony, as he stood facing her by the open windows of the drawing-room, Laura Hoode was even less prepossessing than she had seemed on the day before. She had risen at his entry, and though the thin, sharp-featured face was calm, he somehow felt her perturbation.

She waved him to a chair. He sank into it, draping one long leg over its fellow.

"What do you want of me, Mr. Gethryn?" The voice was lifeless as the woman, and Anthony shivered. The sexless always alarmed him.

"A great deal, Miss Hoode." In spite of his aversion his tone was blandly courteous.

"I cannot imagine——"

"Please—one moment," said Anthony. "As you know, I came down here to Marling to find out, if possible, who killed your brother. A——"

"That task," said the woman, "has already been performed."

"Not quite, I think. In my opinion, young Deacon had no more to do with the murder than I. Each minute I spend in this house increases my certainty. This morning I found something I had been looking for, something that may throw a light where one is badly needed, something which you must tell me about."

She drew herself yet more upright on her straight-backed chair.

"Mr. Gethryn," she said, "I like neither your manner nor your manners."

"Unfortunately," said Anthony grimly, "neither manner nor manners matter just now. Miss Hoode, I started on this business half out of boredom, half because a friend asked me to; but now—well, I'm going to finish it."

"But—but I don't understand at all what you are talking about." The woman was plainly bewildered, yet there seemed in her tone to be an uneasiness not born of bewilderment alone.

Anthony took from his breast-pocket a thick packet of letters. The paper was a deep mauve, the envelopes covered with heavy, sprawling characters. The bundle was held together by a broad ribbon, this too of deep mauve. He balanced the little bundle in the palm of his hand; then looked up to see white rage on the bony, dull face of the woman. The rage, he thought, was not unmixed with fear; but not the kind of fear he had expected.

"These," he said, "are what I want you to explain. To explain, that is, who they are from, and why you took them from your brother's desk and hid them again in your own room."

She rose to her feet; moved a step forward. "You—you——" she began, and choked on the words.

Anthony stood up. "Oh, I know I'm a filthy spy. Don't imagine that I think this private inquiry agent game is anything but noisome. It has been nasty, it will be nasty, and it is nasty, in spite of the cachet of Conan Doyle. I know, none better, that to rifle your room while you were at the inquest this morning was a filthy thing to do. I know that brow-beating you now is filthier—but I'm going to find out who killed your brother."

"It was that boy," said the woman, white-lipped. She had fallen back into her chair.

"It was not that boy. And that's why I shall go on thinking and spying and crawling and bullying until I find out who it really was. Now, tell me why you stole those letters." He moved forward and stood looking down at her.

An ugly, dull flush spread over her face. She sat erect. Her colorless eyes flamed.

"You think—you *dare* to think I killed *him?*" she cried in a dreadful whisper.

Anthony shook his head. "Not necessarily. I shall know better what I think when you've told me what I want to know."

"But what have those foul scratchings to do with —with John's death?" She pointed a shaking finger at the little package in his hands.

"Nothing, everything, or just enough," said Anthony. "You're asking me the very questions which I want you, indirectly, to answer."

She said: "I refuse," and closed tightly the thin-lipped mouth.

"Must I force your hand?" he asked. "Very well. You must tell me what I want to know, because, if you don't, I shall go to Scotland Yard, where I have some small influence, and lay these letters and the story of how I found them before the authorities. You must tell me because, if you don't, you will lead me to believe that you do, in fact, know something of how your brother met his death. You must tell me because, if you don't"—he paused, and looked at her until she felt the gaze of the greenish eyes set in the swarthy face to be unbearable—"because, if you don't," he repeated, "the contents of these letters and their implication are bound to become known to others besides you and me. You will tell me because to keep that last from happening you would do anything."

Even as he finished speaking he knew that last shot had told, fired though it had been in the dark. The woman crumpled. And in her terror Anthony found her more human than before.

"No, no, no!" she whispered. "I'll tell. I'll tell."

Anthony stood, waiting.

"Did you read those—those letters?" The words came tumbling from her lips in almost unseemly haste.

Anthony nodded assent.

"Then you must know that this *woman*—the *Thing* that wrote them was John's—John's—mistress."

Again he nodded, watching curiously the emotions that supplanted each other in the nondescript face of his victim. Fear he had seen and anxiety; but now there were both these with horror, indignation, tenderness for the dead, and a fervor of distaste for anything which savored of "loose living." He remembered what he had been told of the lady's rigid dissentingness, and understood.

She went on, more confidently now that she had once brought herself to speak of "unpleasantnesses" to this strange man who watched her with the strange eyes.

"You see," she said, "nearly a year ago I found out that John was—was associating with this—this woman. I will not tell you how I found out—it is too long a story—but my discovery was accidental. I taxed my brother with his wickedness; but he was so—strange and abrupt—his manner was violent—that I had to leave him with my protest barely voiced.

"Afterward I tried again and again to make him see the folly, the horror of the sin he was committing—but he would never listen. He would not listen to me, to me who had looked after him since he left school! And I was weak—sinfully weak—and I gave up trying to influence him and—and tried to forget what I had learnt. But those letters kept coming and then John would go away, and I—oh! what is the use—" She broke off, covering her face with her hands.

Anthony felt a growing pity; a pity irrationally the stronger for his own feeling of sympathy with the dead man in what must have been a sordid enough struggle against colorless Puritanism.

She dabbed at the red-rimmed eyes with a handkerchief and struggled on.

"There is not much more to tell you except—except that I—stole those letters for the very reason which you used to—to force me to tell you about them. It is wicked of me, but though John did sin, had been living a life of sin, I determined to keep him clean in the eyes of the world; to keep the knowledge of the evil that he did from the sordid newspapers which would delight in making public the sins of the man they are lamenting as a loss to the nation. And he *is* a loss to the nation. My poor brother—my poor little brother—" She leant her head against the back of her chair and wept, wept hopelessly, bitterly. The tears rolled slowly, unheeded, down the thin cheeks.

Anthony felt himself despicable. A great surge of pity—almost of tenderness—swept over him. Yet the thought of the great-bodied, great-hearted, cleanly-sane man who was like to be hanged held him to his work.

"Do you know," he asked, leaning forward, "the name of this woman?"

"Yes." Her tone was drab, hopeless; she seemed broken. "At least, I know that which she goes by."

Anthony waited in some bewilderment.

"She is a dancer," said the woman, "and shameless. They call her Vanda."

"Good God!" Anthony was startled into surprise. He was a fervent admirer, from this side the footlights, of the beautiful Russian. He reflected that politicians were not always unlucky.

He got to his feet. The woman started into life.

"The letters!" she cried. "Give me the letters!"

He handed them to her. "My only stipulation," he said, "is that they're not to be destroyed until I give the word." He looked at her searchingly. "I know that you won't attempt to be rid of them until then. And please believe, Miss Hoode, that you have my sincere sympathy, and that there will be no idle talk of what we two know."

"Oh, I believe you," she said wearily. "And now, I suppose you are happy. Though what good you have done Heaven alone knows!"

Anthony looked down at her. "The good I have done is this: I have added to my knowledge. I know, now, that you had nothing to do with your brother's death. And I know there is a woman in the business and who she is. She may not be concerned either directly or indirectly, but the hackneyed French saying is often a useful principle to work on."

The pale eyes of Laura Hoode regarded him with curiosity. He felt with surprise that she seemed every minute to grow more human.

"You are an unusual person, Mr. Gethryn," she said. "You spy upon me and torture me—and yet I feel that I like you." She paused; then went on: "You tell me that you know that the young man Deacon did not kill my brother; you tell me that although I have behaved so suspiciously you know also that I had nothing to do with—with the crime. How do you know these things?"

Anthony smiled. "I know," he said, "because you both told me. I know that neither of you did it as you would know, after talking to him, that the bishop hadn't really stolen the little girl's sixpence, even though all the newspapers had said he did. Now I must go. Good-night."

He left Laura Hoode smiling, smiling as she had not for many months.

As he entered the hall from the passage, a woman rushed at him. She was tall, and suspiciously beautiful. She drooped and made eyes. She was shy and daring and coy.

"Oh!" she gasped. "Is it Colonel Gethryn? *Is* it? Oh, you *must* be? Oh, Colonel, how *thrilling* to meet you! How *too* thrilling!"

Mrs. Roland Mainwaring pleased Anthony not at all. It is to be deplored that he was at no pains to conceal his distaste.

"Mrs. Mainwaring?" he said. "Madam, the thrill is yours."

She stood blocking his path. Perforce he stood still.

"Oh, colonel, *do* tell me you don't think that *sweet* boy—oh! the beastly police—it's all *too,* too horrible and *awful!"*

Anthony laughed. The thought of Deacon as a "*sweet boy*" amused him. The lady regarded his mirth with suspicion.

Anthony became ponderously official. "Your questions, madam, are embarrassing. But my opinions are—my opinions; and I keep them"—he tapped his forehead solemnly—"here."

Awestricken eyes were rolled at him. "Oh, colonel," she whispered. "Oh, colonel! How *won-derful!"*

Then, coyly: "How lucky for little me that I'm a poor weak woman!"

"I have always," said Anthony gravely, "believed in equal rights for women. They occupy an equal footing with men in my—opinions." He bowed and brushed past her, crossing the hall.

CHAPTER XI

THE BOW AND ARROW

WITHOUT a glance behind him at the beautiful lady, Anthony made for the study, entered it, and closed the door behind him.

The great room bore an aspect widely different from that of his first visit. Down the center ran the long trestle table of the coroner's court. Two smaller ones were ranged along the walls. The far end of the room was blocked with rows of chairs.

Anthony realized, with something of surprise, what a vast room it was. Then he banished from his mind everything save his immediate purpose, and turned to the little rosewood table which stood between the door and the grandfather clock.

He bent to see more clearly the scar on the table-top, the scar which he had noticed on his second visit to the room and which had, in some vague way he could not define, been persistently worrying him during the day. It was an even more perfect impression of the wood-rasp than he had remembered it to be, an orderly series of indentations which made a mark two inches wide and nearly a foot in length.

That something kept jogging in his mind; something about the mark that was indefinably wrong because the mark itself was so undoubtedly right.

Beside him the door opened. He straightened his back and turned to see Sir Arthur.

"Hallo, Gethryn. Can I come in? Thought you might be in here. Turn me out if you'd rather be alone."

"No, no," said Anthony. "Come in. I'm here because I wanted to look at something and because it was the best way to escape. What sweetness! I feel quite sticky, I do!"

Sir Arthur smiled. "Dodo Mainwaring, eh? I caught a glimpse of her. What d'you think?"

Anthony raised one eyebrow.

"Exactly," said Sir Arthur. "If that woman doesn't go soon I won't wait for Laura, I'll pack her off myself."

"Ah, yes," Anthony said vaguely, looking down at the table. "I say, have you seen the Bow and Arrow?"

"Eh? What?"

"The wood-rasp."

Sir Arthur shivered. "Oh, yes. Yes, I have. It was an exhibit at the inquest."

"What was the size of it?"

"Well, I believe it's about the biggest made. Usual short, thick handle with a blade of about a foot long and perhaps two inches wide."

Anthony pointed to the table. "Did it make this mark?" he asked.

"Of course. Why, all that came out at the inquest. Weren't——"

"I've got it!" cried Anthony, and slapped his thigh.

"What's that? What's that? Have you thought—found something?"

"I have and I have. Now, another thing: was the handle of the thing old and battered and worn at the edges and filthy and split?"

Sir Arthur smiled. "No; I'm afraid you're wrong there, Gethryn. It was almost brand-new."

"Exactly!" said Anthony. "Exactly. All polished

and convenient. Oh, ours is a nice case, our is!"

"My dear boy, I'm afraid you go too fast for me." Sir Arthur was puzzled.

"That's nothing," Anthony said. "I go a damn sight too fast for myself sometimes."

"But what are you driving at? What's all this about the wood-rasp?"

"I won't give you a direct answer—it's against the rules of the Detectives' Union—but I invite you to bring your intellect to bear on the position of this scar here. You'll see that it's roughly twelve inches by two and lies ten inches from all four edges of the table—right in the middle, in fact. Then think of the nice new handle on the wood-rasp." Anthony appeared well pleased. " 'O frabjous day, Calloo callay!' Rappings from Doyle!"

Sir Arthur shook his head. "I suppose you're not mad?" he said, smiling.

" 'No, not mad, said the monkey.' "

There fell a long silence, broken at last by the elder man.

"God!" he cried in a whisper. "Let's get out of this room. Gethryn, it's horrible! Horrible! Where poor old John was killed—and here we are cracking jokes and laughing!" He took Anthony by the arm and pulled him to the door.

They went into the garden through the verandah. By the windows of the study Anthony stopped and stood staring at the creeper-covered wall; staring as he had stared on the afternoon before. Sir Arthur stood at his elbow.

"Splendid sight, that creeper," said Anthony, "*Ampelopsis Veitchii,* isn't it?"

"So you're a botanist? It may be what you say. I'm afraid it's just creeper to me."

Anthony, turning, saw Boyd walking toward them, and waved a hand.

"Damn!" Sir Arthur growled. "The Scotland Yard man. He arrested the boy. Officious fool!"

"Oh, Boyd's a good chap. I like Boyd. He's done his best. On the evidence he couldn't do anything but take Deacon."

"I know, I know," said Sir Arthur impatiently. "But all the same, he——" He broke off, turning to go.

Boyd came up to them. "Good evening, gentlemen."

"Evening, Boyd," said Anthony.

Suddenly, "By Gad!" Sir Arthur cried, and turned a bewildered face upon them. "I didn't think of that before!"

"Think of what, sir?" asked Boyd.

"Why, something that may change everything! Look here, that's the window of my sitting-room up there—the one over the window of the study which you say the murderer must have got in by!"

Anthony was silent. Boyd said stolidly: "Well, sir?"

"But don't you see, man? Don't *you* see, Gethryn? I was sitting up in my room, by that window, all the time. I should have been bound to hear something. Bound to!"

"But you didn't, sir," said Boyd.

"Ach!" Sir Arthur turned on his heel and flung away from them and into the house.

"He's very upset because he thinks you've taken the wrong man, Boyd," said Anthony.

"I know, sir. Do you?"

Anthony laughed. "I do, I do. By the way, can I see him?"

"You can, sir. He asked for you. That's really what I came up for. That and the walk."

"Thanks. I'll take you down in the car. How long before Deacon's moved to the county jail?"

"He'll be going to-morrow sometime, sir. Afternoon or evening."

They walked in silence to the car. Anthony drove out of the gates and down the hill very slowly. Boyd sighed relief: he knew "the colonel's" driving of old.

"I'm afraid, sir," he said at last, "that this case has been a disappointment to you, so to speak."

Anthony looked round at him. "Why so fast, Boyd? Why so fast?" After a moment he added: "Pumps not working too well to-day, are they?"

The detective gave a rumbling chuckle. "I suppose it was a bit obvious, sir," he said. "But you're puzzling me, that you are."

"What am I that I should flummox one of the Big Four? Oh, Fame! Oh, Glory! I stand within your gates."

Boyd reddened. "Oh, don't josh, sir. What I mean is, here are we with as clear a case as ever there was, and yet there are you, a gentleman who's no amateur, still searching around and—and trying to *make* another criminal, so to speak."

"It's not a bit of good trying to get me to explain what I'm doing, Boyd, because I don't know myself. I'm groping—and it's devilish dark. There is a little light, but I don't know where it's coming from—yet. But I will." He fell silent; then added in a different tone: "Look here: we'll take it that I'm mad and that the law is sane. But will you help me in my madness? Just one or two little things?"

"As far as I can, sir," Boyd said solemnly, "of course I will."

"You're a good fellow, Boyd," said Anthony warmly, "and you can start now." He stopped the car and turned in his seat. "Where's the Bow—I mean the wood-rasp?"

"At present it's at the station. Where we're going. To-morrow it'll be taken up to the Yard."

"Can I see it this evening?"

"You can, sir, seeing that you're an old friend, if I may say so."

"Excellent man!"

"Look here, sir," Boyd took a wallet from his pocket; from the wallet some photographs. "You might care to see these. Enlargements of the finger-prints."

Anthony took the six pieces of thin pasteboard and bent eagerly to examine them. They had been taken, these photographs, from three points of view. They showed that the handle of the rasp had been marked by a thumb and two fingers—all pointing downwards toward the blade.

"And these were the only marks?" Anthony said.

"Enough, aren't they, sir?"

"Yes," murmured Anthony. "Oh, yes. What lovely little marks! How kind of Archibald!"

"What's that, sir?"

"I was remarking, Boyd, on the kindly forethought which Mr. Deacon showed for Scotland Yard. He couldn't bear to think of you wasting your time detecting all the wrong people, so he left his card for you."

"I don't know what you're getting at at all, sir." Boyd shook his head sadly.

Anthony handed back the photographs and started the car. In less than a minute they had finished the descent and turned the corner into the village of Marling. Boyd caught his breath and clung to his seat. The High Street streamed by them. At its far end Anthony pulled up, outside the little police station. Marling was proud of its police station, an offensive affair of pinkish brick. To Anthony, coming upon it in the midst of the little leaning houses, the low-browed shops and thatched cottages, it was like finding a comic postcard of the Mother-in-law school in an exhibition of pleasing miniatures.

He shivered, and dragged Boyd inside. Here he was received by the local inspector. At a word from Boyd the inspector produced keys, opened locks and at last laid on the table the wood-rasp.

It was, as Sir Arthur had said, the biggest of its kind—a foot-long bar of serrated iron, looking like a file whose roughnesses have been ten times magnified. To the points of these roughnesses clung little scraps of stained and withered flesh, while in the corresponding hollows were dark encrustations of dried blood. The handle was new, of some light-colored wood, and was perhaps four inches long and three and a half in circumference.

"Now that's not at all pretty," said Anthony, with a grimace. "Can I pick it up? Or would that spoil the marks?"

Boyd said: "Oh, that's all right, sir. The coroner's jury have passed it about. And we've got the official record and the photos."

Anthony took it from the table; peered at it; shook it; weighed it in his hand.

Boyd pointed to the blade. "Not much doubt that's what did the trick, is there, C—Mr. Gethryn?"

"Never a doubt," said Anthony, and shook the thing with vigor.

There was a sudden clatter. The blade had flown off, struck the table, and fallen to the floor.

"Bit loose," said Anthony, looking at the handle in his fingers.

He stooped and picked up the blade, holding it gingerly.

"Those blows that broke in the deceased's skull," said Boyd, "must've been hard enough to loosen anything, so to speak."

"Possibly." Anthony's tone was not one of conviction. "Aha! Now what are *you* doing here, little friends?" He picked, from a notch in the thin iron tongue upon which the handle had been fitted, two threads of white linen. "And you, too, what are you?" He stopped and picked up from the floor a small, thin wedge of darkish wood. "There should be another of you somewhere," he murmured, and peered into the handle. He shook it, and there dropped out of the hollow where the tongue of the blade had been another slip of wood, identical with the first.

He turned to the two men watching him. "Boyd, I give these, the threads and the woods, into your official keeping. You and the inspector saw where they came from." He took an envelope from his pocket, slipped his discoveries into it and laid it upon the table beside the dismembered rasp.

The inspector looked at the man from Scotland Yard, and scratched his head.

"That's all, I think," Anthony said. "Can I see the prisoner now?"

CHAPTER XII

EXHIBITS

THE door of the cell clanged to behind Boyd. From a chair, Deacon unfolded his bulk to greet Anthony. They shook hands.

"Wasn't long before I yelled for you," the criminal grinned. "Take the chair. I'll squat on the gent's bedding."

Anthony sat, running his eye over the cell. There was the chair he sat on, the truckle bed, a tinware wash-stand, a shelf, a dressing-case of Deacon's, and, in one corner, a large brown-paper parcel.

"Pretty snug, brother, isn't it?" Deacon smiled. "I languish in comfort. 'D've been pretty glad of this at times during the recent fracas in France. I say, wouldn't you like to write the story of my life? *Some Criminals I have Known: Number One—The Abbotshall Murderer*. You know the sort of thing."

Anthony laughed. "Well, you take it easily enough. I'm afraid I should alternate fury and depression."

For a moment Deacon's blue eyes met his; and in them Anthony saw a kind of despairing horror. But only for the half of a second. And then the old laughing look was in them again. More than ever, Anthony felt admiration and a desperate desire to get this large man out of this small cell; to make him free again—as free as the hot, gleaming streak of the setting sun which pierced the little barred window and painted a broad line of gold upon the drab floor. But to get him out one must work.

"What about those finger-prints?" he asked suddenly.

"You have me," said Deacon, "on the hip. That's *the* most amazing bit of jiggery pokery about all this hocus pocus. What about 'em to you?"

"They certainly savor," Anthony said, "of hanky panky. In fact, since I know they're yours and that you didn't kill Hoode, I know they must be. Now, have you seen that wood-rasp?"

"Yes. At the inquest."

"Never before?"

"Not as I knows on, guv'nor. In fact, I'd almost swear to 'never.' But then I'm the most amazing ass about tools. A fret-saw or a pile-driver, they're all one to me."

"Did you notice the handle?" Anthony asked.

"With interest; because they said it had my paw-marks on it."

"Ever seen that before? By itself, I mean."

Deacon shook his head. "Never." He fell silent, then said: "I suppose those prints *couldn't* be any one else's, could they?"

"I'm afraid they couldn't," said Anthony. "You see, it's as near proved as a thing like that can be that no two men have the same markings on the fingers. They compared those on the wood with those on the bit of paper Boyd got you to hold, and their experts don't make mistakes. By the way, I suppose you realized at the inquest how you'd been caught?"

Deacon smiled. "Not at the inquest, brother, but at the time. I've read too many spot-the-murderer serials in my time not to know what a sleuth's up to when he hands me a bit of paper and asks me whether I ever saw it before. But I didn't mind at the time, you see, not knowing about that blasted file thing. I say, Gethryn, are we mad? Or is this all a bloody nightmare? I tell you, I didn't kill the boss, and yet the thing he's killed with is all over the marks of my fingers! And as far as I know I never even saw the gadget before! It doesn't work out, does it?"

"It's got to," Anthony said. "I'll damned well make it. Now, what d'you know about the incomparable Vanda?"

Deacon whistled. "How did you get hold of that?" he asked, wonderingly.

"You know my methods, my dear Deacon. But what d'you know about Vanda? Beyond the fact that she's the most wonderful dancer of all time."

"I don't really *know* anything; but I've a shrewd little suspish that she was the boss's mistress."

"She was. But as you didn't actually know anything, I gather you can't help me further there."

" 'Fraid not. For one thing my suspicion was founded on something that happened by accident, and for another I've not the foggiest idea of what you're driving at."

"They *will* all say that!" Anthony sighed. "And it's just what I want some one to tell *me*. Never mind, we'll get on with the exhibits. Have you ever seen this?" He took from a swollen hip pocket a small paper package, unfolded it, and handed the contents to Deacon.

They were a coil of filthy, black-smeared silk cord. Curiously, the prisoner shook it out, letting one end fall to the floor. He saw now that it was knotted at regular intervals along its length, which was a full sixteen feet.

"Never saw it in my natural." He looked up at Anthony. "What is it?"

"Obviously a length of silk cord," Anthony said, "with, as you would probably say, knobs on."

"I mean, where did you find it? What bearing's it got?"

"I found it," said Anthony slowly, "in your bedroom at Abbotshall."

"What?"

"In your room. On a ledge inside that wonderful old chimney; about six inches higher than the mantelpiece. That accounts for the filth. You can see the rope was white once, and not so long ago."

Deacon frowned at the floor. "Well, it's either been there up in the chimney since I went to the house—last May, that is—or else it's been planted there. I never set eyes on it before."

"Good!" Anthony coiled up the cord, wrapped it up in the paper, and returned the parcel to his pocket.

"But what's the beastly bit of string *mean?* What's it got to do with me or you or anything in this business? Tell me that!"

"Shan't," said Anthony. "I'm not sure yet myself. You'll have to wait."

Deacon shrugged his great shoulders. "Right-o. Next, please."

Anthony's hand went to his breast pocket. From a leather wallet he took a bunch of newspaper cuttings.

"These," he said, "I found in a really-truly secret drawer in your late chief's desk. Know anything about 'em? Or why they were there?"

In silence, Deacon read each slip. When he had finished,

"Well?" Anthony said.

"They mean nothing in my young life. These three rags—*The Searchlight, The St. Stephen's Gazette,* and the weekly one, *Vox Populi*—always were dead agin the boss. I can't make head or tail of what you're driving at, Gethryn, I can't really!"

Anthony groaned. "There you go again. Never mind that, but tell me, did you know Hoode was keeping these cuttings?"

"No."

"Did he ever mention the persistent attacks of these three papers?"

"No."

"No? Pity." Anthony got to his feet. "I must move. Anything you want? Books? Food? Tobacco?"

Deacon smiled. "Nothing, thanks awfully. Our Arthur—old Digby-Coates, you know—has done all that. Brought me down a sack of books, a box of cigars, and arranged for decidedly improved victuals to be brought over from the White Horse by quite a neat line in barmaidings. Also, he's fixed up the solicitors and trimmings. They're going to try to get Marshall, K. C."

"Excellent! Marshall's about the best counsel there is. There's nothing you want, then."

"Nothing. Shall I see you to-morrow?"

Anthony nodded. "You will. Early afternoon, probably, as I hear they're moving you later. Good-night; and don't forget I'm going to get you out of this—somehow."

They shook hands. A minute later Anthony was

walking slowly back toward his inn up the cobbled street. The sun was sinking behind the gables of a twisted house at the top of the rise, and the road which had been gold was splashed with blood-red blotches.

He shivered. In all this morass of doubt and wilderness of evil—a wilderness wherein innocent men had obviously committed crimes they had nothing to do with, where every one was sure except Anthony Ruthven Gethryn—he felt alone. Not even the golden-dark background to his thoughts which was the perpetual image of the Lady of the Sandal could compensate for the blackness of bewilderment—the blackness through which he could see light but not yet the way to light.

Then his thoughts turned to Deacon, his cheerfulness, his ease of manner, his courage which surely masked a hell of distress. Suddenly the admiration which he felt somehow cheered him. His step quickened.

"By God!" he muttered, "that's a man and a half——" and broke off sharply. He had collided with something softly hard. A girl, running. A girl with wild, red-rimmed eyes and hatless, disheveled, golden head.

Before he could voice apology; almost before he was aware of the collision, she had passed him and was stumbling down the uneven little road with its splashes of crimson painted by the dying sun. From a doorway a slatternly woman peered out, curious with the brutal, impersonal curiosity of the yokel.

Anthony struggled to adjust his memory. Ah, yes! It was the sister. Her sister. Dora Masterson. He turned; caught up with four long strides; laid a hand upon the girl's shoulder. She shook it off, turning to him a face disfigured by desire for more tears, tears that would not come.

"You were going to the police-station, Miss Masterson?" Anthony asked.

She nodded.

"You mustn't—not like this." He took her gently by the arm. "You could do nothing—and you'd make him feel as if things were unbearable."

"I must see him." She spoke dully, an unnatural pause between each word.

"Not now," said Anthony firmly. "Not when I want your help." He wondered if the lie showed through his words; cursed that he should have to hamper himself with an hysterical girl.

She swallowed the bait. "Help you?" she asked eagerly. "About—about Archie? How can *I* do that?

"I can't tell you here. You must come up to the inn." He led her back up the hill.

CHAPTER XIII

IRONS IN THE FIRE

I

Up in his little, low-ceilinged, oak-paneled sitting-room in the Bear and Key, Anthony sat the girl in the one arm-chair. She refused whisky so pleadingly that he ordered tea. When it had come and the bearer departed, he sat on the table and watched her drink.

"Now," he said, "suppose you tell me about it," and was immediately smitten with very fragrant memories of another occasion when he had used that phrase.

Dora Masterson said simply: "I was frightened. Oh, so horribly, *horribly* frightened!"

Anthony was puzzled. "But why just now? Surely you must have felt like this as soon as you heard?"

"N-no. Of course it was—terrible! But Lucia told me what you said, Mr. Gethryn—and she—she seemed to so absolutely *believe* that you would make everything all right that I—I tried to believe too."

Anthony's heart gave a leap that startled him.

The girl went on, struggling for control. "But—but it was when I heard about the end of the inquest—that he was actually in—— Oh, it's too awful! It's too *terrible!*" She swayed about in the big chair, hands hiding her face, the slim shoulders twisting as if her pain were bodily.

Again was Anthony puzzled. Something in the tone

told him that here was something he had not heard of. And this tendency to hysteria must be stopped.

"What d'you mean? Explain!" he said sharply.

She sat upright at that, her face working. "I mean that—that—if only I hadn't been a senseless, vicious little fool; if—if only I hadn't be-behaved like a b-beastly schoolgirl, Archie wouldn't—wouldn't be in that awful place! Oh! why was I ever born!" She pressed her hands to her face and doubled up in the chair until her forehead rested on her knees.

"I'm afraid I don't understand yet," said Anthony.

She raised her head. "Weren't you at the inquest?" she asked, dabbing at her swollen eyes with the back of a hand like the schoolgirl she had named herself.

"Not exactly," said Anthony, and wondered how many more times he would have to answer this question.

"Why, then you—you don't know that—that Archie s-said he went out for a walk during the time when the —the Thing must have been done. And the *beasts* d-don't believe him because nobody at all saw him while he was out!"

"I still don't——"

She broke in on his sentence with a flood of speech, springing to her feet.

"Oh, you fool, you fool!" she cried. "*I* ought to have seen him! *I, I, I!* *I* was to have met him down there on the bank, this side, by the bridge. We'd arranged a walk! And then, because *I* thought *I* was some one; because *I* thought he had been rude to *me* that afternoon, I must needs think *I* would punish *him!* And I didn't go! I didn't meet him! I stayed at home! Christ help me, I stayed at home!"

Anthony was shocked into sympathy. "My *dear*

chap," he said. "My *dear* chap!" He went to her and dropped a hand on her shoulder. "You poor child!"

Wearily, she sank against him. The reddish-golden head fell on his shoulder. But she made no sound. She was past tears.

For a moment they stood thus, while he patted the slim shoulder. Then she drew herself upright and away from him.

"You must sit down," he said.

She looked up at him. "Please forgive me," she said. "I didn't mean to—to make such a fool of myself. And I was very rude." She sat down.

Anthony waved aside apology. "What we've got to do," he said, smiling down at her, "is to do something."

"Yes, yes, I know. But what, what? Oh, you said I could help, but I believe you only did it out of kindness. But if I could really help—how much less—less filthy I should feel!"

Anthony conceived a liking for this girl; a liking born not altogether of sympathy. But he wondered, with half-humorous desperation, how he was to provide the cleanser and yet not waste much time.

"Consoler-in-Chief to the Birds of the Air, I am," he said to himself; then aloud: "You can help, Miss Masterson, by listening to me think. In this business, I'm like a mad poet without hands or tongue. I mean, I've found out more than the other fellows—the police—but it's all odds and ends and tangles—little things, queer in themselves, that men would tell me might be found anywhere if one only troubled to look for 'em. But I say they're not; that they fit!"

The girl was sitting upright now, alert, gazing at him intently. "Think, then," she whispered.

"Now for it," thought Anthony, "and God send it'll take her in—and quickly."

Aloud, he began: "Reconcile for me—put these things into order and make 'em mean something—if you can. Innocent finger-prints on a weapon which performed a murder. An innocent person—not the one of the finger-prints—stealing letters from the corpse to hide the fact that the corpse had a mistress. An attempt to make a clock give an alibi, the attempt being so clumsily carried out that it seems very ill in accord with other indications of the murderer's ingenuity. Secret drawer in corpse's desk full of newspaper-cuttings, all of 'em vicious attacks on corpse when alive. Finger-prints——"

"Mr. Gethryn!" the girl interrupted harshly; "you're making fun of me! No, that's not fair; you're just playing with me to make me think I can help. No doubt you mean to be kind—but I *hate* it!"

Anthony for once was crestfallen. The truth of the accusation was so complete as to make an answer impossible. He found himself in the indefensible position of one "who means well." He groped wildly for words, but was saved; for, suddenly, Dora sprang to her feet.

"Those cuttings!" she cried. "Did you mean—do you *really* want to know anything about them?"

Anthony was surprised. "Most certainly I do. I don't know exactly what I want to know, but that means I want to know everything."

"Well, go and see Jim—my brother—now, at once!" She stamped her foot at him in her excitement. "When he was secretary to Mr. Hoode he was full of those attacks in the press. I remember we thought he was rather silly about them. He used to say there was something more than mere—what did he call it?—policy behind them, and swore he'd make Mr. Hoode take notice of them. I *think* it was what they eventually quarreled about, but I'm not sure, because he'd never tell me. He wouldn't even tell Loo—my sister. But if you want to know anything about those papers, Mr. Gethryn, Jimmie's more likely to be able to tell you than any one else!"

Anthony looked at her and said: "The best apology I can make to you is to go up to town now. Your brother ought to be well enough by this time. He's got to be!" He paused; then added with a smile: "You know you wouldn't have found me out if I'd been less preoccupied. I'm a bit tired, too."

Dora, forgetting herself, looked at him closely. "Why—why, you look almost *ill!*" she cried, "p'r'aps you—oughtn't to go to-night."

"Oh, I'm going right enough," Anthony said; "and now. And I'm not ill; that's only my interesting pallor. You must go home—and don't worry."

She cried: "How can I *help* worrying? Worrying till I wish I'd never been born! Unless there's a miracle——"

"Chesterton once wrote," Anthony interrupted her, "that 'the most wonderful thing about miracles is that they sometimes happen.' And he's a great and wise man."

The girl flashed a tremulous smile at him and passed out of the door.

2

At ten minutes past ten the great red Mercedes drew up outside the block of flats where Spencer Hastings lived. Anthony had broken his own record of that afternoon for the Kensington-Marling journey.

Stiffly, he clambered to the pavement, noted with curiosity that his hands were shaking, and ran up the steps. As he went he wondered would he see Her. He arrived at the door of No. 15 more out of breath than the climb should have made him.

Wonderfully, it was She who opened it, and at her smile the shortness of his breath was foolishly increased. For the smile was one, it seemed, of open delight at seeing him.

Hastings, she told him, was out, being at his office. His housekeeper, too, was out, being on holiday. But wasn't Mr. Hastings a dear? Wasn't Mr. Hastings's betrothed a charming betrothed? The invalid was ever so much better; temperature down; sleeping; in fact, almost all right. And she hadn't forgotten how everything, everything was due to the sagacity, kindliness, and general wonderfulness of Mr. Gethryn!

They were by this time in the little drawing-room; and as yet Anthony had done nothing save stare with all his eyes. She finished speaking, and he realized that he must say something. But what? He wanted to shout to Heaven that he hadn't seen her for hours longer than years. He wanted to catch her hands—those long, slim hands—and cover them with kisses. He wanted to tell her that she was most glorious of women and he the vainglorious fool who dared to love her. He wanted—oh, what did he not want?

He said: "Er—good evening. Hastings out?"

She opened her eyes at him. "But—but, Mr. Gethryn, I've just told you that Mr. Hastings is at his office!"

"Of course. Ah, yes," said Anthony.

"Did you want to see him?"

Anthony recovered himself; remembered that he had work to do, and that by attending to it he could save himself from behaving foolishly.

"No," he said shortly. "Mrs. Lemesurier, I must see your brother." It was, he thinks now, the great fatigue which had accumulated during the past days and the strain of that flying drive which led him to speak with such curtness.

"To see Jim? Oh, but you can't," Lucia said. Her tone was gentle and rather aloof and very firm.

"Oh, but I must," Anthony said. His loss of temper is regrettable, and was inexplicable to himself even at the time.

The dark eyes blazed at him. "You can't," she said.

Anthony said with brutal clearness: "Mrs. Lemesurier, I am, as best I know how, trying to clear of the charge of murder a man I believe innocent. I've got to a point where a five minutes' conversation with your brother will help me. Your brother—you have told me yourself—cannot be considered as seriously ill. I must see him."

This time it was her eyes that fell. Anthony was angry—with himself. And a man angry with himself is invincible.

With a grace that burned a picture into his mind she crossed the room, to stand with her back to the door.

Anthony picked his hat from the table and walked slowly toward her, smiling as he walked. It was not a nice smile. It was a smile which crept up on one side of his face and stopped before it reached his eyes. A black smile. There are men in odd corners of the world who would counsel, out of personal experience, that when one sees that smile one had better get out.

He came close to her, still smiling. For a moment she faced him; then faltered; then stood to one side and let him pass.

He closed the door softly behind him and began his search for the sick-room. He found it at once. He entered, closing this door even more softly.

A shaded lamp arranged to leave the bed in shadow was the only light. In the bed lay a man. Peering at his face, Anthony could trace a certain faint resemblance. He sat on the chair by the bed and waited.

"What the devil are you?" said a weak voice.

Clearly, but with rapidity, Anthony explained his presence.

"I'm sorry," he said in conclusion, "to disturb a sick man, and I'll get the business over as quickly as possible. But I've got to find out all I can, you see."

"Quite, quite." Masterson's voice was stronger now. Free of fever, shaven, clean, he was vastly different from Margaret's bogey.

"How can I help?" he asked after a silence.

Anthony told him. Bored at first, Masterson woke to sudden interest at the mention of the newspaper-cuttings.

"So he *did* keep 'em!" He lifted himself in the bed to rest on one elbow.

Anthony pushed the little bundle of slips into the thin hands. Eagerly, the sick man read each.

"Some of these are new," he said. "After my time with Hoode, I mean. But these three—and this one—I remember well. Dammit, I ought to! These are what we had that infernal row about."

"How?"

"Well, you see, I'd been watching these three papers for a long time, and I'd come to a definite conclusion that there was one man behind all the attacks. I told Hoode so, and he laughed at the idea! That made me as mad as hell. I've always had a foul temper, but since the war, y'know, it's really uncontrollable. I mean I actually can't help it."

"I know," Anthony nodded.

"That's all. I cursed him for a blind, pig-headed, big-headed fool, and he sacked me. He couldn't very well do anything else. I still feel very bitter about it; though not quite so much now he's dead. He was such a brilliant cove in some ways, but so blasted silly in others. Simply wouldn't listen to what I had to say—and I was sweating to benefit him!"

"'Zeal, all zeal, Mr. Easy!'" said Anthony.

"Exactly; but zeal's a damn good thing at times, 'specially in private secretaries, and being turned down like that made me brood. I really couldn't help it, you know. After I got the sack I brooded to such an extent that I simply went to pieces. Drank too much. Made an idiot of myself. I say, Lucia's told me all about things, and I want to thank——"

"You can do that best," Anthony interrupted, "by keeping on about Hoode and these press-cuttings. I've made some conclusions about 'em myself, but you know more."

A slight flush rose to the sallow cheeks of the man in bed. He turned restlessly.

"When I come to think of it," he said nervously, "I don't know a great deal. Mostly surmise, and from what I've heard of you I should say you're better at the game than I am."

Anthony grew grim. "Some one's been exaggerating. You fire ahead. The sooner you do, the sooner I'll be able to get away and leave you in peace."

Masterson said hesitantly: "All right. When I first saw the things coming out one by one I didn't think anything about 'em. But after a week or so—it may have been a month—something queer struck me. At first I couldn't place it. Then after collecting a few of the articles, I tumbled. It seemed to me that one man was behind 'em. More, that one man was writing 'em—and for three papers of widely different politics and apparently belonging to different people!"

Anthony was pleased. "You support me. I thought the author seemed to be one man, though I've not had time to study the things carefully. I went so far as to think—the authorship being the same and the papers so different in views—that one man controlled all three." He fell silent a moment, then added slowly: "One might consider, you know, whether the controller and the writer——"

But Masterson interrupted. "Look here," he said, sitting up in obvious excitement, "how did you spot the unity of authorship business?"

"Similarity of style, I think." Anthony was reflective. "I've got quite an eye for style. Two or three times the fellow tried to disguise it. By doing that he gave the game away completely."

"Oh, but there was more than that!" cried the other, fumbling with shaking hands at the sheaf of cuttings. "Wait till I find—ah! Now, look at this. 'The Minister of Imperial Finance, in his efforts for advancement of self, would do well to remember that hackneyed line of Pope: 'A little learning is a dangerous thing.' Did you see that?"

Anthony opened his eyes. "I did. And thought how refreshing it was to see the quotation given right. They nearly all get it wrong, though you'd think any one could see that Pope couldn't have been such a fool as to say a little knowledge was dangerous. Knowledge is always useful; learning isn't—until you've got plenty. But go on: what about it?"

Masterson was searching feverishly. "Tell you when I've found—here we are! Listen. Er-um Finance —policy—rumty-tumty—'when Greek joins Greek, then comes the tug-of-war!' There you are again. How many times d'you see that given right?"

"Never," said Anthony. "They all say 'meets.' "

"There you are, then. It all goes to prove what you felt and I'm certain about." He tapped the bundle of cuttings with a lean finger. "All these were written by the same man; there's not a doubt in my mind. Style—similarity in style, I mean—isn't proof; but this orgy of correctitude *plus* that similarity is. At least it's good enough for me. There are plenty more instances if you want them. There's one I remember well—a leader in *Vox Populi*. It was a more vicious attack on Hoode even than the others, and it was so damn' well done that it was almost convincing. It said, apropos of him: '*facilis descensus averno*. What about that?"

Anthony sat up. "'*Averno*' is very rare," he said slowly. "But it's a better reading. I saw it. I wondered. I wondered a lot."

There was a silence. The two looked at each other.

"Masterson," Anthony said at last, "you're very useful, you know. Most useful. Wish you weren't sick a-bed. Now here's another point. We've fixed the author of these articles as one man; but what about the motive force behind the author. I'm inclining to the view that as these papers differ so widely in everything else they are controlled by some one whose only interest in them was to do Hoode a bad turn. Agree?"

Masterson nodded emphatically.

"Right." Anthony leaned forward, speaking softly. "But did this motive force hire some one to write for it, or was its distaste for the unfortunate Robin Hoode so great that it wrote itself, being unwilling to forego the pleasure of, so to speak, giving birth to a new litter of scorpions three times a month or more? Briefly, are you with me in thinking that author and motive force are probably one and the same?"

"By God, I am!" Masterson said.

Anthony smiled. "Well, thank God I've found another lunatic! That's what we are, you know. Think of our theory! It is that some one had such a hatred of Hoode that the secret purchase of three newspapers was needed to assuage it. That's what we've said; we're thinking more. But we're frightened to say what it is because it'll sound so silly."

"I know. I know." Masterson's tone was almost fearful. "I say, we *can't* be right! It isn't sense! Now I come to think of it there are dozens of other theories that'd fit. There might be more than one person. The whole thing might be political. The——"

Anthony raised a hand for silence. "Fear not. Of course you can fit other theories. One always can; that's the devil of this bloodhound business. The only way to work is to pick a likely-looking path and go down it. I've chosen one to get on with. As you say, it's not sense; but then nothing else is. It's sad and bad and very mad and very far from sweet. But there it is. So we'll all go mad. I'm starting now." He got to his feet.

"Here, wait a minute!" Masterson cried. "Don't go. I—I might be able to help you."

"My dear fellow, you have already—immeasurably! For one thing you've crystallized my determination to go mad and stay mad——"

"Oh, I know all about that!" Masterson exhibited some irritation. "But I mean really help. I was just going to tell you. When I was with Hoode, before I told him about this business, I went to one of those filthy private inquiry agents. I was so absolutely certain, you see. I told this chap to find out, if he could, who the enemy was. Or rather I told him to find out who really owned the three newspapers. He thought I was mad, said he could do it in a day—but he didn't! I think he imagined he'd only got to look it up or get some one from Fleet Street to tell him. Of course, that didn't work, he only gave me the three figureheads that're shown to the trusting world. But when I laughed at him, and explained a little, I think he got his back up and really went for the job."

"D'you mean to say——" began Anthony.

"No, I don't! Before I heard any more I had the row with Hoode—I didn't tell *him* about the 'tec, of course; I was too angry—and dropped the whole business and paid this chap off. He was very fed up—kept trying to see me, and writing. Of course—well in the state I was in, I refused to see him and chucked his letters into the fire. But he was so very eager! He *might* know something, I think!"

Anthony was elated. "He might indeed. Masterson, you're a treasure! What's the name?"

"Pellet, he calls himself. Office is at 4, Grogan's Court, off Fleet Street, just past Chancery Lane."

"Excellent! Now I'm going." Anthony held out

his hand. "And thank you. Hope I've done you no harm."

"Not a bit. Feel better already. Let me know how you get on. Going to sleep now," said the invalid, and did, before Anthony had reached the door.

In the passage, Anthony hesitated. Should he go straight from the flat or should he tell Her first that he was going? Then, as he reached it, the door of the drawing-room opened.

The passage was dimly lit, and at first she did not see him. He moved toward her. There came a startled "Oh!" of surprise; then she straightened herself into a rigidity eloquent of protest. Anthony groaned. He had hoped the ruffled feathers smooth again.

"Your brother," he said, "is asleep. By the look of him he's in for a good twelve hours. He's none the worse and I'm even more full of information than I'd hoped to be. So everything in the garden is lovely!"

But Lucia was angry. Lucia was not to be put off by this light-and-airyness. When she spoke her voice was cold; cold and cruel. She meant to hurt—and succeeded.

"Is there nothing," she said, "that my brother and I can help you with further? Nothing that we can be *made* to do? A woman and a sick man! Oh, surely there is?"

For the second time that night Anthony lost his temper. One must, to a certain extent, forgive him. He was worried and tired and harassed and very much in love. He laughed, and peered down at her in the half-light. Lucia caught her breath. Like many lesser women she had, being angry, said far more than she had meant. And now she was sorry, and—well, yes, frightened.

"Before I go," Anthony said, "I will tell you a story. Once on a time there was a woman who had a big brother and a little sister. One night, she heard that her big brother, who was living in the great city, was sick with a chill. Good friends had taken him to their house and were caring for him. But the woman posted to the great city to make sure that her brother was indeed being well tended.

"But," he went on, "she left behind her in the country her little sister. Now, this maid was in great sorrow, for her lover had been seized by all the king's horses and all the king's men and thrust into a dungeon. Here he was to stay until the king's judges had decided whether or no to hang him for a misdeed of which he had not been guilty. So, left alone, the little sister grew more and more lonely and frightened, and became in danger of falling ill. She had nobody to comfort her, you see. But that, of course, did not matter, because big brother had his mustard plaster in the right place at last."

He walked to the front door; opened it. "Good night," he said, and shut it gently behind him.

Hands gleaming pale against her throat, Lucia leant against the wall of the passage.

Down in the street, Anthony jumped into his car; then for a moment sat staring before him. Like many lesser men, he had, being angry, said more than he had meant. And now he was frightened.

They had, it must be admitted, behaved like silly children. Very silly children. But then the best people so often do.

CHAPTER XIV

HAY-FEVER

I

AFTER that one moment of introspection, Anthony headed his car for Fleet Street. At twenty-five minutes past eleven he burst into the room of *The Owl's* editor.

The editor and his secretary were rather close together. The shining golden hair of the secretary was noticeably disordered.

"Er—hallo!" said Hastings.

Anthony said: "Get hold of private 'tec called Pellet; 4, Grogan's Court. Find out what he knows about the ownership of *The Searchlight, The St. Stephen's Gazette,* and *Vox Populi.* He was commissioned for same thing some time ago by J. Masterson. Never mind how much he costs. I'll pay. If Pellet doesn't know anything, find out yourself. In any case give me the answer as soon as is damn' well possible. Got that? Right. 'Night. 'Night, Miss Warren." The door banged behind him.

Margaret Warren snatched some papers from her table and followed. She caught him in the entrance hall.

"Mr. Gethryn!" she said, breathless. "Here's the report—asked—for—inquest.—Just finished—typed. You may—want it."

Anthony raised his hat. "Miss Warren, you're wonderful." He took the papers from her hand. "Many thanks. Hope I don't seem rude. Very busy. Good-night—and good luck." He shook her hand and was gone.

Slowly, Margaret went back to her editor. He was found pacing the room, scratching his head in bewilderment.

"Yes, darling, he was a bit strange, wasn't he?" Margaret said.

"He was." Hastings spoke with conviction. "I've known that man for fifteen years and I've never seen him all hot and bothered like that before. He's usually calmest when he's got most to do."

Margaret patted his cheek. "But, you silly baby, he wasn't like that because of the work he was doing. It was something much, much more important than that—or I'm a Dutchman!"

Hastings was alarmed. "Not that! Anything but that! What was it, then?"

"A woman, of course. *The* woman! Heaven, am I tied to an idiot?"

"Just you wait, wench, until I've seen Mr. Pellet!" said Hastings.

2

From Fleet Street, Anthony drove straight to the Regency, over whose great frontage flaring placards and violently winking electric signs announced that the great, the incomparable Vanda was gracing with her art this mecca of vaudeville. As he reached it the audience were streaming out from its great glass doors.

He anticipated difficulty, and approached the stage-door keeper with a five-pound note and broken English. He was, it seemed, Prince Nicolas Something-or-the-other-vitch. He was oh! so great a friend of the great, the incomparable Vanda—even a relation. He *must,* it was of an imperativeness, see her. Further, the good keeper of the door really must accept this so little piece of paper.

The good keeper did; then proceeded laboriously to explain that the Vanda was not in the theater. Hadn't been there at all that day. *And* there 'adn't been half a row about it, neither! She had wired to say she couldn't appear. Why? Gawd perhaps knew; certainly nobody else did. When would she reappear? The keeper of the door reely couldn't say. P'r'aps to-morrer. P'r'aps never. Good-night to *you,* sir.

Anthony went to his flat, surprised his man, and ordered a drink, a bath, fresh clothing, a drink, and supper.

At the meal, his hunger surprised him. Then he remembered that since the lightest of lunches he had eaten nothing. Having made up the deficiency, he lit a cigar, sat in a chair by the open window and read through, not once but many times, the typed report of the inquest.

Somewhere a clock struck two. Anthony put down the report, clasped his head with his hands, and plunged into thought. Presently he found his mind to be wandering, strictly against orders—wandering in a direction forbidden. He swore, got to his feet, and crossed to the writing-table. At this he employed himself with pen and paper for more than an hour.

At last he put down his pen and read through what he had written. The clock struck four. He finished his reading, said: "H'mm! Those blasted gaps!" and went to bed.

3

He had barely two hours' sleep, for by a quarter past six he was breaking his fast. At twenty minutes past seven he was driving his car slowly through London.

This morning he took the journey to Marling slowly: the pointer of his speedometer touched eighteen as he left the outskirts of town, and remained there. For Anthony was thinking.

For the first third of the journey his thoughts were incoherently redundant. They were of a certain scene in which A. R. Gethryn had lost his temper; had behaved, in short abominably, and this to the one person in the world for whose opinion he cared.

It cost him an effort greater than might be supposed to wrench his thoughts out of this gloomy train, but at last, he succeeded.

This puzzle of his—some of it, fitted now, only there were several idiotic pieces which, unfitted, made nonsense of the rest. He flogged his unwilling brain for the rest of the journey.

He backed the Mercedes into the garage of the Bear and Key at twenty-five minutes to ten. By five minutes to the hour he was walking with his long, lazy stride up the winding drive of Abbotshall.

Drawing near the house he saw that the great oaken door stood open letting a shaft of hot, clean, morning sunlight paint a golden track across the polished floor of the wide hall. He entered, flung his hat on to a chair, and turned in the direction of the stairs.

He had set foot upon the third step when from behind and below him came a noise—a rasping roar of a noise. To his overtired brain and overheated imagination it seemed a noise evil and inhuman. He swung round. The hall was as he had left it, empty of all save furniture. He descended the three steps; stood looking about him, then walked toward the front door. Before he could reach it, the noise came again, louder this time. The same roaring, rasping sound. But this time it had for a tail a snuffling choke which came, obviously, from the throat of a man.

Anthony laughed at himself. Noiselessly, he retraced his steps, passed the foot of the stairs, and halted outside the door opposite that of the study. It stood ajar, giving him a glimpse of the little room which he remembered as being the lair of the butler.

Anthony waited. In a moment came the roar again, now recognizable as half-cough, half-sneeze. Anthony pushed the door wide. Facing it, huddled in a chair, was the butler. His gray head was on a level with his knees. In one claw of a hand he clutched a bandanna handkerchief with which he dabbed every now and then at his streaming eyes.

Anthony stood unmoving in the doorway. Presently another spasm shook the old man.

"Bad cold, that," Anthony said loudly.

There was no answer. The coughing gasps went on; gradually grew less frequent. The thin shoulders ceased to shake.

"Bad cold, that," said Anthony again.

This time he got an effect. Poole leapt to his feet, fumbling hurriedly to hide in a tail pocket the capacious handkerchief.

"Your pardon, sir!" he gasped. "Did you want me, sir?"

"I only remarked that yours was a bad cold."

"Thank you, sir. Thank you. Not that it's a cold,

sir, exactly. It's this hay-fever. And very troublesome it is, sir, for an old fellow like me!"

"Must be." Anthony was sympathetic. "D'you have these attacks many times a day?"

"I used to, sir. But this summer it does seem to be improving, sir. Only takes me every now and then, as you might say." The old man's voice showed gratitude for this concern about his ailment.

But Anthony's interest in hay-fever was not yet abated. "This the first bad fit you've had for some time?" he asked.

"Yes, sir. Quite a while since I was so bad, sir. It didn't trouble me at all yesterday, sir."

Anthony drew nearer. "D'you happen to remember," he said slowly, "whether you—er—sneezed like that at all on the evening your master was killed?"

Poole exhibited agitation. "Whether I—the master——" the thin hands twisted about each other. "Forgive me, sir—I—I can't remember, sir. I'm a foolish old fellow—and any mention of—of that terrible night sort of seems to—to upset me, sir." He passed a hand across his forehead. "No, sir, I really can't remember. I'm an old man, sir. My memory's not what it was. Not what it was——"

But Anthony was listening no longer. He was, in fact, no longer there to listen. He had suddenly turned about and sprung into the hall. As Mr. Poole said later in the servants' hall: "I'd never of believed such a lazy-looking gentleman could of moved so quick. Like the leap of a cat, it was!"

Had he followed into the hall, he would have had more matter for gossip. For by the door of the verandah Anthony stood clutching, none too gently, the skinny shoulder of Robert Belford—the man-servant he had christened "Ferret-face."

"A word in your pointed ear, my friend," he said, and tightened his grip. "Now where shall we chat? The garden?" He pulled his trembling captive, whose face was a dirty gray with fear, out through the verandah and on to the terrace.

"Suppose," Anthony said, dropping his hand, "suppose you tell me why in hell you listen to my conversations with other people."

"I wasn't listening." The man's voice was sullen, yet at the same time shrill with fear.

"Why take the trouble?" Anthony asked plaintively. "Besides, it's wicked to tell stories, Belford. Wicked! Unhappy is the burden of a fib. We will, I think, get farther from our fellows and you shall tell me all about everything. I've been watching you, you know."

With these last words, true but intentionally misleading, a black shadow of hopelessness seemed to fall upon the prisoner.

"All right," he mumbled wearily, and followed meekly, but with dragging feet, while his captor led the way down the steps and across the lawn and into the little copse which faced the eastern end of the house.

As he walked, Anthony thought hard. He was something more than mystified. What in heaven, earth or hell was this little person going to tell him? Another old boot turning into a salmon, what? Father Gethryn, confessor! Well, every little helps.

When the house was hidden from them by the trees, he stopped. He sat on a log and waved Belford to another. Then he lit his pipe and waited. To his surprise, the little servant, after clearing his throat, began at once. Much of his nervousness seemed to drop from him, though he still looked like a man in fear.

"I'm rather glad this has happened, sir," he said, "because I was going to come to you anyway."

"You were, were you?" thought Anthony. "Now why?" But he went on smoking.

"I couldn't of stood it much longer, sir, reely I couldn't! And ever since you stopped that great brute of a sergeant from popping it across me, sir, I've been tryin' to make up me mind to tell you." He paused as if expecting an answer; but getting none, plunged on. "I wasn't upstairs *all* the time that night, like I said I was at the inquest!" Again he paused.

Anthony went on smoking. Here, if he wanted the story quickly, silence was best.

Belford swallowed hard. His face, as he went on speaking, turned from muddy gray to dead white.

"I—I come downstairs, sir, after I'd finished in the master's room. And when I got to the 'all I heard old Poole starting on one of them sneezin' fits. And—and, sir, I went into the study and I saw the master lyin' there on the rug—just like they found 'im! And—and I shut that door behind me quick—old Pooley was still coughin' and chokin' his head off—and I nipped back up the stairs, sir. It's God's truth, sir! It is——"

This time the pause was so long that Anthony knew speech necessary.

"Are you trying to explain," he said, "that though you did go into the study that night you didn't have anything to do with the murder?"

"Yes, sir, yes." The man's eagerness was pathetic. "That's just it, sir! I didn't have nothink to do with it, sir, ***nothink!*** So 'elp me God!"

"What did you go into the room for?" Anthony shot out the question. "Must've been for something you didn't want found out or Poole's hay-fever would not have been so important to you?" The logic, he knew, was faulty. But the thrust told.

Belford hung his head. "Yes, sir, it was what you say. I thought—one of the girls told me—the master was in the billiard room. And I knew as 'e always kept money somewhere in the study. I was goin' to pin—steal it if I could. I was desprit, sir. Desprit!"

Anthony was puzzled. "But if you came out without stealing anything, why didn't you rouse the house when you saw Mr. Hoode was dead?"

"I don't know, sir. Except that it all come as such a shock like—my sneaking in there while old Poole was sneezin'—and then finding—that, sir. You see, when I nipped out, the old man was still sneezin' with 'is 'ead on his knees. And I *knew* as he hadn't spotted me. And I bolted away to think. An' the more I thought, the more I feels as if I couldn't—hadn't better like—tell anybody.

"I can see, now, sir, 'ow blasted silly it were—me having done nothink wrong. But there it was, sir, I meant to tell, but as I'd gone in there to steal and 'ad sneaked in in the way I did—well, it made me feel as if they'd all jump on me immediate as the murderer. Specially as I never goes into the study in the ordinary way. You *do* see 'ow it was, don't you, sir?"

"I do," Anthony said. "But I also see that you're a fool. A fool for not rousing every one at once; a fool for not keeping quiet after you'd decided to say nothing about it."

Belford's little eyes opened wide. "But you—you

were on me, sir! You suspected me like—thought I was the murd'rer!"

Anthony shook his head. "Not really, Belford. You know, you looked too guilty to be true. I nabbed you just now because I don't like eavesdroppers. Also because anything fishy in this house interests me at present."

"I may be a fool," cried Belford in heavy tones not without humor, "but I feel better now I've got it off my chest like. Reely I do, sir! I kept sayin' to meself as how I wasn't guilty of anythink, and yet I 'ad the conscience awful! I've bin trying to tell you for twenty-four hours, sir, but when I 'eard you askin' Poole if 'e'd 'ad a 'tack of that hay-fever on the night the master was killed, I got frightened again and was goin' to bolt. Only you copped me." He was silent a moment, then burst out: "Mr. Deacon didn't do it, sir. He couldn't of! You know that, sir?"

Anthony did. But he wanted to turn this tragi-comic confession of nothing into evidence of importance, though he had but little hope of success.

"What time," he asked, with affected carelessness, "did you go into the study?"

"I was only just in and out like a flash, sir. But when I got back to the stairs, the clock there said five past eleven, sir—I remember it perfect. I wasn't lookin' for the time reely, only some'ow I saw it and couldn't forget it like."

Anthony repressed elation. "Thanks," he said, and got to his feet.

Belford jumped up. "Are you—going, sir?"

Anthony nodded.

"But what—what are you goin' to—to do about me? About what I told you, sir?"

Anthony looked down benignly. "Nothing."

Belford's mouth fell open. "Nothing! *Nothing?* But——"

"What I mean, Belford, is this. I'll keep you out of trouble. You've told me one thing that makes all your confession of nothing worth while. You may, later on, have to give evidence; but that's the worst you'll have to do as far as I'm concerned. And don't worry. And for the Lord's sake don't walk about as you've been doing lately, looking like Charles Peace with a belly-ache."

The little man smiled all over his wizened face. Anthony looked at him curiously. Somehow, when talking to him as a man and not a servant, one found something so far from being sly as to be almost lovable.

Anthony gave the narrow shoulders a reassuring pat and strolled away, making for the house. He had covered perhaps twenty yards when he stopped, turned on his heel, and walked back.

Belford was seated again on his log. His face was buried in his hands. Anthony stood looking down at him.

"What's the matter?" he asked.

The other dropped his hands with a cry, bounding to his feet.

"I—beg your pardon, sir. You—I——"

Anthony soothed him. "Steady, man, steady. Take your time. Lots of it."

Belford looked up at him, tried to speak, failed, and hung his head again.

"Just now," Anthony said, "you told me something about being desperate. What is it? Money?"

Belford nodded. "You're right, sir," he muttered. "It's—it's my wife, sir. Been very ill, she has. And is still. I was goin' to ask the master to 'elp me; but when it come to the point, I couldn't. That's why I was after pinchin', sir. I would 'ave asked 'im, I would reely, sir; but I knew he'd ask Miss Hoode about it, and that'd 'ave made it 'opeless. You see, sir, the missus was in service here before we was married—and, well, sir, she 'ad—'ad to leave in a hurry. And through me! You understand, sir—our nipper——" He broke off, looking up appealingly. "We're very fond of each other, sir," he finished. "And it's 'ard to see 'er so ill like!"

"How much d'you want?" Anthony felt for his note-case. "Here, you'd better have twenty now. And I'll fix you up properly to-morrow. Now, for God's sake, man, pull yourself together!" he added sharply.

For Belford's shrivelled, sharp-featured little face was working in a way which was not good to see. Gratitude is sometimes more terrible to watch than baser emotions.

Anthony thrust the notes into one limp hand and beat hurried retreat.

Belford stood where he was left. His lips moved soundlessly. The banknotes in his hand crackled as the stubby fingers clenched upon them. Presently he raised his head and looked with blurred vision along the path through the trees.

"Gawd!" he said, the refinement of the servants' hall now completely gone. "Gawd! What a bloke! What a *bloody* good bloke!"

Anthony took the terrace steps three at a time. He

was elated. The elation was short-lived; before he had reached the house, despair had taken its place. After all, this playing at detectives was foolery. Why such a day as this, with its hot, clean peace, its drowsiness, its little scented breeze—was it not a day for a lover to lie at the feet of his mistress? Was it not a day for hot, sun-warmed kisses?

He shook himself, laughing bitterly. "Affectioned ass!" he said to himself.

Sir Arthur came out of the house. "Lovely day, Gethryn. Early, aren't you?"

"It is and I am. I am also a detective of the greatest. Do I look it?"

Sir Arthur grew eager. "What d'you mean? Have you got anything? Found out anything important?"

Anthony nodded. "Yes, twice."

"But what, man? What?"

"One, the butler suffers from hay-fever. Two, the murder was committed at as near eleven o'clock as I am to you."

"Damn it all, Gethryn," said the elder man, "I don't think it's quite fair to pull my leg like that. Not about this. I don't really!"

"You're right, it isn't. I'm sorry." Anthony was contrite. "But you know, I'm not as silly as I sound. You must think I'm telling you things you knew before; but I'm not really. What I think these things mean, I'm not going to say just yet. Not to any one."

"I see. That's all right, Gethryn. You must forgive me if I seem touchy." Sir Arthur smiled forgivingly.

"Seen Deacon lately?" Anthony asked.

"This morning. In fact, I've just come back. He's wonderful, that boy!"

"He is," agreed Anthony. "I'm just going to see him now. Walk to the gate with me, will you? I want you to help me."

"My dear chap, with pleasure!" He put his arm through Anthony's as they walked.

"I want to know," said Anthony, as they reached the end of the house, "whether any one in any way connected with the household does any playing about with carpenter's tools. Amateurs, professionals, or both."

"Funny you should ask that, Gethryn? I've been thinking about that. But it's no help. You see, the place is full of 'em—carpenters, I mean. There's Diggle, the gardener, he's really an excellent rough-job man. Then there's the chauffeur, he made that shed over there—and a splendid bit of work it is. And John, well, it was his one hobby as it is mine. You know that set of three small tables in the drawing-room?"

"I did notice them. They puzzled me rather. Couldn't place 'em."

"John made those," said Sir Arthur, with a touch of pride, "nearly twenty years ago. I remember I was very jealous at the time. I couldn't ever have done anything so good, you see. I was a bit better than he at the finer sorts of work, though." He broke off, seeming to fall into reverie. After a while he added: "No, Gethryn, I'm afraid this line's no good to us. That wood-rasp doesn't belong to Abbotshall."

"You're sure?" Anthony asked.

"Well, it isn't mine, it didn't belong to John, it isn't Diggle's—he was questioned by the police, you know—and it certainly isn't the chauffeur's."

"Humph!" Anthony seemed annoyed.

They walked on to the gate in silence. Anthony nodded an adieu and set off down the white, dusty road with his long horseman's stride.

CHAPTER XV

ANTHONY'S BUSY DAY

I

HE covered the distance to the village in a time creditable for so hot a day. As he passed the Bear and Key, a knot of men stopped their conversation to eye him with thirsty interest. He smelt reporter and passed by, giving silent thanks to the efficiency of Boyd. Now that the case seemed, to the public at least, as good as over, there was no real danger; but had the news-hungry hordes been let loose at first to overrun Abbotshall, Heaven alone knew how impossible things could have been.

For the case of the murdered minister had seized violently on public imagination. It was so like, so very like, the books the public had read yesterday, were reading to-day, and would read to-morrow and to-morrow. Great Britain (and Ireland) was divided now into two camps—pro- and anti-Deacon. The antis had a vast majority. Many of them held that to waste time on a trial which would be purely formal was disgraceful. The wretch, they said, should be hanged at once. Not a few were convinced that hanging was too merciful. It was all very funny, really, thought Anthony, and wished he could laugh. But whenever he tried to realize how funny it was, he thought of Deacon, and then found that it wasn't funny at all, but rather terrible.

On this morning, though, he was at least on the road to high spirits, and walked on down the twisting, cobbled street toward the police-station, whistling beneath his breath. The whistle bewailed the cruel death of Cock Robin.

Still whistling, he ran up the steps of the police-station. As he passed through the doorway the whistling stopped, cut off in the middle of a bar. He stepped to one side, away from the door. Coming toward it were Lucia Lemesurier and her sister.

Neither at once saw Anthony. Then, with a gracious smile to officialdom, Lucia turned and looked full at him. He raised his hat and looked grim. He didn't mean to look grim; he was merely trying to behave well in a police-station to a lady he loved and had offended. Lucia flushed and bowed coldly and walked down the steps. She hadn't meant to do any of these things; but the man *did* look so forbidding. "Conceited idiot!" she said to herself, referring to Anthony and not meaning it in the least.

"Hell!" said Anthony under his breath, and went rather white.

Dora Masterson held out her hand. "Good-morning," she said, and looked curiously at him.

From somewhere he dragged out a smile.

" 'Morning. Feeling better?"

She beamed at him. "Oh, ever so much! Archie seems so—so exactly as if everything was the same as usual. He's wonderful! And I haven't forgotten what you said about miracles. You will do one, won't you?" With another smile she ran down the steps and after her sister. She had scented an intriguing mystery in the behavior of these two.

Anthony emerged from thought to find the inspector

looking at him with barely veiled curiosity. He essayed a cheerful manner. Perhaps the inspector would be so good as to let him see Mr. Deacon. If the inspector remembered, Superintendent Boyd——

In less than two minutes he was alone with the prisoner.

Deacon put down the book he was reading.

"Hallo-allo! More visitors for the condemned man. Good job you're early. I believe they're moving me to the county clink about eleven."

Anthony sat down upon the bed. "How are you?" he said. He said it to gain time. His thoughts, once so carefully ordered, had been thrown into much confusion. That bow had been so extremely distant.

"To tell you the truth," Deacon said slowly and heavily. "I feel absolutely rotten! It's beginning to get on my nerves—all this!" He made a sweeping gesture. "It—I feel——" He broke off and laughed. "Fan-tods won't do any good, will they? And it's only what I might have expected. Nurse always told me my middle name was Crippen."

Admiration and sympathy cleared Anthony's head. "When's the magistrate's court?" he asked abruptly.

"The balloon, I believe, goes up at 10 A. M. the day after to-morrow."

Anthony muttered: "Day after to-morrow, eh? Well, it may," and relapsed into silence.

Deacon half rose, then sat down again. "After you left me last night," he said, after a pause, "I had a visit from Crabbe—the solicitor Digby-Coates got. We had a long talk, and he's going to prime Marshall, who's going to come and see me to-morrow himself. So all the legal business is fixed up."

"Good," said Anthony. "What I came for this

morning was to ask you two questions. Are you ready?"

"Aye ready!"

"Have you any money? Besides the salary you got from Hoode, I mean."

"About two hundred and fifty a year," said Deacon. "When Cousin James dies of port it'll be about three thousand."

"That's good. You made that point with the solicitor, I hope. It tends to destroy that insane theft theory."

"I told the bloke all right. But it won't count much, I'm afraid. You see, I've been awfully broke for quite a time now. One thing and another, you know. However!" He shrugged.

Anthony said: "Now the second question. And it's really important! Think carefully before you answer. When recently—say within the last week—have you had in your hands *any* implement of *any* kind with a wooden handle four inches long and about three and a half round? Think, man, think!"

2

Ten minutes later, Anthony was running up the High Street toward his inn. Arrived there, he found a telegram. It read: "Authentic astounding revelations by Pellet what next Hastings."

Anthony wrote on a telegram form: "Wait with you afternoon office keep Pellet Gethryn." The form he gave to the barman with a ten-shilling note and instructions for immediate despatch, and then set off for Abbotshall at a fast walk.

As he entered the gates, a car—an unfamiliar green Daimler, a woman seated primly beside the chauffeur

—left them. In spite of the heat it was closed. Peering, Anthony saw the only occupant of the tonneau to be a woman. She was veiled. He deduced the flirtatious Mrs. Mainwaring and her Gallic maid. The sight appeared to amuse him. He walked on to the house humming beneath his breath.

Sir Arthur, he was told by a rejuvenated Belford, was believed to be in his own sitting-room.

Anthony mounted the stairs. He found Sir Arthur's door ajar; on it was pinned a notice in red ink; "Please do not disturb." From where he stood, all Anthony could see was the big arm-chair drawn up to the window, the top of an immaculate head above its back and some six inches of trouser and a boot-sole by each of its front legs.

Anthony chuckled, knocked, and entered. Sir Arthur rose, turning a frowning face toward the intruder. As he saw who it was, a smile replaced the frown.

"You looked," said Anthony, "like some weird animal, sitting like that. Hope I haven't disturbed you."

"Not a bit, my boy, not a bit. Very glad to see you." He picked up some sheets of paper from the chair. "As a matter of fact, I was just jotting down a few notes. I'd like you to read them—not now, but when they're finished." He hesitated; then added rather shyly: "They're just some ideas I've had about this awful business. Somehow, I can put them more clearly in writing. I want to give them to Marshall before the boy's tried, but I'd like you to see them first. There might possibly be some points which have escaped you, though I expect not."

"I'd like to look at 'em very much," Anthony said. "Get them done as quick as you can, won't you? Now, what I interrupted you for: is there in the house a good collection of reference books?"

"There is. Right-hand book-case in the study. You'll find anything you want from sawdust to Seringapatam. John got together the most comprehensive reference library *I've* ever seen."

"Good!" Anthony turned to the door. "No, don't trouble to come, I'll find 'em!"

It was, as Sir Arthur had said, a most comprehensive collection. Anthony locked the study door and sat at the big writing-table, now back in its old place, surrounded by the volumes of his choice. They were many and varied.

He worked for an hour, occasionally scribbling notes on a slip of paper. At last he rose, stretched himself, and returned the books to their shelves. Again sitting at the table, he studied his notes. They appeared to afford him satisfaction. He folded the paper and took out his note-case. As he opened it, the bunch of newspaper-cuttings fluttered down to rest upon the table.

He picked them up and slid them, with the notes he had scribbled, back into the case. As he did so a line of the topmost cutting caught his eye. It was the quotation from the *Æneid* which Masterson had referred to and which then had titillated some elusive memory. Now where, recently, had he seen this unusual and meticulous dative case?

His mind wrestled with forgetfulness; then, suddenly tired, refused to work longer on so arduous a task. As minds will, it switched abruptly off to the matter with which it most wished to be occupied. Before Anthony's eyes came a picture of a dark, proud face whose beauty was enhanced by its pallor. He thought of her as he had seen her that morning; as he had seen her that first time; as she had sat in her drawing-room that night—the night he had made her tell him all about it.

His mind, remorseful, perhaps, made a half-hearted attempt to get back to that tiresome business of the correct quotation from Virgil. Suddenly, it connected the work and the woman. The great light of recaptured memory burst upon him.

He jumped for the telephone; asked for Greyne 23; was put through at once; thought: "Wonder who'll answer?" then heard the "Hallo" of a servant.

"Miss Masterson in?" he asked.

"Yes, sir. What name shall I say?"

He told her. Waiting, he grew excited. If by any chance he was right, here was yet more confirmation of his theory.

Dora Masterson's voice came to his ears. "Hallo. Is that Mr. Gethryn? I——"

Anthony interrupted. "Yes. I wonder whether you can help me. The second time I was in your house I picked up a book. Little green book. Soft leather binding. Essays. Pleasantly written. One was called 'Love at First Sight.' Author's name on title-page was a woman's. D'you know the book I mean?"

"Is it one called *Here and There?*"

"Yes, now who wrote it? Was it really a woman? And is that her real name? I meant to ask at the time, but forgot."

3

At twenty minutes to two that afternoon, Anthony stopped his car outside *The Owl's* office. He had broken no record this time; his mind had been much occupied on the journey. The interviews he had held with Belford, Mabel Smith, and Elsie Syme before leaving Abbotshall had given him food for thought.

He found Hastings in his room, with him a little, dapper, sly-eyed man. "Discreet Inquiries. Divorces, Watching, etc.," thought Anthony.

"This," murmured Hastings, "is Mr. Pellet."

"Ah, yes." Anthony sat down heavily. He was tired and very hungry. He had not eaten since breakfast. Mr. Pellet displeased him.

"Mr. Pellet," said Hastings, "has some information which should interest you. I have paid him fifty pounds. He wants another two hundred."

"He would," Anthony said. "And if he's got what I want he shall have it."

"Thath right," said Mr. Pellet with a golden smile.

"It may be." Anthony fixed him with a glittering eye. "Let us hear you, Mr.—er—Pellet."

Mr. Pellet cleared his throat, produced a packet of papers, wiped his hands on a pink silk handkerchief and began.

"About theeth three newthpaperth," he said—and went on for one hour and fifty-seven minutes by the clock on Hastings's table.

He got his two hundred pounds.

4

There was a matinée at the Regency. At half-past four, Anthony was at the stage-door.

The stage-door keeper remembered that five-pound note and the foreign gent. He was civil. Yes, Madarm Vander was in the theater. She had, indeed, just finished her performance. He would see if the—the prince could be admitted. The prince scribbled on a card, placed the card in an envelope, and sealed the envelope. As balm for tender feelings, he gave the doorkeeper a flashing foreign smile and a pound-note.

He was kept waiting not more than three minutes. After four, he was ushered into the most sacred dressing-room in Europe.

From a silken couch in a silken corner a silken scented vision rose to meet him.

Anthony saw that they were alone. He bowed, kissing the imperious hand. He was regarded with approval by tawny, Slavonic eyes.

She peered at the card in her hand. "Who air you," she said, "that write to me of—of John?"

Anthony proceeded to make himself clear.

It was nearly six o'clock when he left the theater.

5

By half-past six Anthony was in his flat. At seven he bathed; at eight dined. From eight-thirty to nine he smoked—and thought. From nine until midnight he wrote, continuing his work of the night before. Save for occasional reference to notes, he wrote for those three hours without a pause. From midnight until one he considered what he had written. Then, after a long and powerful drink, he unearthed from its lair his typewriter.

It was lucky, he reflected, that two years ago he had wearied at last of professional typists and taken a machine unto himself.

From one-thirty in the morning until five—three whole hours and a half—he typed. There were two reasons why the work took him so long; the first, that he had not used the machine for six months; the second, that in copying what he had written he was constantly polishing, correcting, altering, improving.

At five he discarded the typewriter, took pen and paper and wrote a letter. This, altogether with the typewritten document, he placed in a large envelope. He stamped the envelope; was about to leave the flat and post it; then changed his mind. It should be sent by special messenger as early as one could be found awake.

He did not go to bed, feeling that if he did, nothing could wake him for at least twelve hours. He had another drink, another bath, and, when he had roused his man, a breakfast.

CHAPTER XVI

REVELATION AND THE SPARROW

I

HIS meal over, he left the flat, going first to a District Messengers' office and then back to the garage for his car.

He knew the road to Marling so well by this time that he could almost have driven blindfold, and he has said that on this morning he once or twice found himself to have been sleeping at the wheel. It is certain, anyhow, that he barely saw where he was going. Such thought as his tired brain could compass was not of murders and murderers, but of Love, a Lover and a Lady.

It was, if one is to believe him, at the cross-roads beyond Beachmere that he made up his mind to see Her, to drive straight to the house on the bank of the Marle.

He looked at his watch. The hands pointed to ten. He settled down in his seat. The needle on the speedometer jerked to twenty, to twenty-five; then gradually crept on till it hesitated between forty-five and fifty.

His spirits mounted with the speed. The car tore her way into Marling and down the cobbled slope of the High Street, swung to the left, took the little bridge at a bound, raced on, turned the corner next on the left after the river bank on two wheels, ploughed up the little lane, and pulled up at the gates of the house which was graced with Her presence.

Or should have been. For the parlor-maid informed him that her mistress and her mistress's sister were out. For the day, she thought. She was not sure, but she imagined the ladies to have gone to London.

Anthony, his fatigue heavy upon him, walked slowly back to his car. For a moment he sat idle in the driving-seat; then suddenly quickened into life. Though their ultimate destination might indeed be London, the women would surely stop on their way through Greyne. For in Greyne's jail was Deacon.

So to Greyne he drove at speed. He missed them by five minutes.

Had Anthony Gethryn been a man of common sense he would have returned at once to his Marling inn, fallen upon his bed, and let Sleep have her way with him. But he was not, so he stayed with Deacon. Deacon was obviously—in spite of his flippancy—delighted at this visit. Anthony stayed with him until two o'clock, when the great Sir Edward Marshall, K. C., arrived in person for consultation with his latest case, and then set out for Marling. This he did not reach for two hours, fatigue and preoccupation having cost him no fewer than three wrong turnings.

At the inn was waiting the reply to the letter he had sent by District Messenger that morning. It had come, this reply, in the form of a seemingly ordinary message over the inn's telephone. It was what he had expected, but nevertheless it made it necessary for him to think.

And think he did, sitting on the hot grass bank at the edge of the little bowling-green behind the inn, for as long as it takes to smoke one cigar and two pipes. Then he sought the bar, to slake a savage thirst.

He ordered a meal to be served at seven. To pass the hour that must elapse before this and to throw off the lassitude brought on by his fatigue and the oppression of the day's heavy, airless heat, he sought the bathroom and much cold water.

After the bath he felt better. He returned to his quarters whistling. Crossing his sitting-room to get to the bedroom which opened out of it, he saw something he had not noticed when going bath-wards. The whistling ceased abruptly. On the table in the center of the room lay an envelope. His name was on it, in hurried, penciled scrawl. The writing was feminine.

He ripped it open, read, and jumped for the door. The pink-cheeked chambermaid came runnning. She would not have believed this quiet gentleman could shout so loud, nor so angrily.

Anthony, his lank black hair disheveled, his long lean body swathed in a bath-gown, towered wrathfully above her.

"When did this note arrive?" He waved the envelope in her face.

The girl fingered her apron. "Oh, sir! It came this morning, please, sir. Lady left it, sir. Just after ten, it was. Mrs. Lermeesherer, sir."

"I know, I know!" Anthony snorted. "But why in Satan's name wasn't I told about it when I got back this evening?" He went back into his room, slamming the door and feeling not a little ashamed of himself.

The little chambermaid clattered downstairs to discuss with her colleagues the strange effect of a note upon a gentleman before so pleasant.

Anthony clad himself with speed; then ran downstairs to the telephone. The answer to his first call was disappointing. No, Mrs. Lemesurier was not back; would not be, probably, until eight.

He rang off, swore, bethought him of his work, made sure that the door of the telephone cabinet was closed, lifted the receiver and asked for another number.

It was ten minutes before he left the cabinet and went slowly to his dinner. He ate little, fatigue, preoccupation, and the stifling heat of the evening combining to deprive him of appetite. Over coffee he re-read his letter. It is a tribute to his self-restraint that he had delayed so long. It was a short letter, running thus:—

"DEAR MR. GETHRYN,—I am sorry you were out: I wanted to apologize for my unpardonable behavior. I can't think what made me so foolish; and quite see now that you had to talk to Jim and also that he was none the worse for the interview—in fact I hear from Mr. Hastings, who rang up early this morning, that he is ever so much better!

"If you are not too busy and would care to, do come and see us this evening. I would ask you to dinner, but we shall probably be late and have a very scrappy meal.

"Your gratefully,
"LUCIA LEMESURIER."

"P. S.—You were rather hard on me, weren't you? You see, I had asked Dot and she had urged me to go to town!"

There is a peculiar and subtle and quite indefinable pleasure that comes to a man when the woman he loves first writes to him. Soever curt, soever banal the letter, there is no matter. It is something from Her to him; something altogether private and secret; something She has set down for him to read; something not to be shared with a sordid world.

Anthony lost himself in this sea of subtle delight, varying joy with outbursts against himself for having exhibited such boorishness and for being so insanely, so youthfully in love. "For, after all," he told himself, "I haven't known her for a week yet. I've spoken with her not a dozen times. I am clearly a fool!"

Unpleasantly thoughts broke in upon him. He looked at his watch; then jumped to his feet and made his way upstairs to his rooms. He reached them mopping his forehead. He could not remember a day in England so oppressive.

He took his hat and turned to leave the room. As he did so a rush of wind swept in through the open window, and a long, low angry mutter of thunder came to his ears. Then, with a rush, came the rain; great sheets of it, glistening in the half-dusk.

Anthony put on a mackintosh, substituted a cap for the hat, and left the inn. He did not take his car. Even as he turned out of the yard into the cobbled street, the thunder changed from rumble to sharp, staccato reports, and three jagged swords of lightning tore the black of the sky.

Anthony strode on, hands thrust deep into pockets, chin burrowed into the upturned collar of the trench-coat. Incredibly almost, the volume of rain increased and increased.

2

Mr. Poole the butler—Anthony once said that he sounded like a game of Happy Families—was in a state of nervous agitation verging upon breakdown. The events of the past few days had shaken him, for some time an old man aged beyond his years, to such extent that he would not, he was sure, "ever be the same man again."

He sat in the little room opposite that which had been the master's study. He shivered with age, vague fears, and fervent distaste for the storm whose rain beat upon the windows, whose sudden furies of wind shook the old house, whose flashes of lightning played such havoc with the nerves.

Mr. Poole was alone. Miss Hoode had retired. Sir Arthur was reading in the billiard-room at the other end of the house. Belford was on three days' holiday, his wife, it seemed, being an invalid. The other servants were certainly either in bed or huddled together moaning as women will at the violence of the storm.

Mr. Poole was alone. All manner of lurking terrors preyed upon him. There were noises. Sounds which seemed like the master's voice. Sounds which seemed like the rustling of curtains, whispering and soft footsteps. Elusive sounds as of doors opening and shutting. Mr. Poole trembled. He knew his fears groundless; imaginings born of the roaring rattle of the Universe. But nevertheless he trembled.

Suddenly there came a knocking on the great front door. The knocking was not loud, yet it seemed to the old man the more terrible for that. For there is always something terrible about a knock upon a door.

For a full minute he strove to leave the shelter of the little, cheerful, glowing room. At last he succeeded, struggling through the beastly mysteries of the dimly lighted hall to open with trembling hands the great oak door.

Anthony stepped over the threshold; stripped off dripping cap and mackintosh.

"A dirty night, Poole," he said.

"It is indeed, sir! Indeed it is, sir!" The old man's voice was hysterical with relief.

Across the hall to them came Sir Arthur, sturdy, benign, hair as smoothly brushed as ever.

"Oh, it's you, is it, Gethryn?" he said. "I wondered who was knocking. You must have very pressing business to bring you up here on a night like this. Aren't you wet?"

"Nothing to speak of. I wanted to talk with you. It's important—and urgent."

Sir Arthur grew eager. "My dear boy, of course. Where shall we go? Billiard-room?"

"All right."

They turned, but before they had crossed the hall,

"Tell you what," Anthony said, "the study'd be better. Not so near the servants, you know."

"You're right," Sir Arthur agreed.

The study had that queer stillness which comes to a room at one time in constant use and then suddenly deserted save for the morning activities of a servant with duster and broom. It had an air of almost supernatural lifelessness, increased, perhaps, by the fact that now everything was in its accustomed place; the same pictures on the walls; the table; the chairs; the very curtains cutting off the alcove at the far end of the room hanging in the old slightly disordered folds.

A silence fell upon both men while they found chairs and drew them up to the table, under the light.

Sir Arthur spoke first. "Out with it, now, Gethryn. You've excited me, you know." He rubbed his hands.

"I've always thought you'd do something; go one better than those damn' fools of policemen!"

Anthony leant back in his chair. "This," he said, "is a most unusual business. I said so at the beginning, and, by God, I say so now! You might say that I have solved the mystery. After I've told you, that is. And in another way, as you'll see, it's more of a puzzle than ever."

Sir Arthur leant forward. "Go on, man, go on! Do you mean to say you actually know who killed John?"

"I do not." Anthony laid his head against the back of his chair and closed his leaden, burning eyes.

Sir Arthur started to his feet. A crash of thunder drowned his words. Followed a zig-zag of lightning so vivid as to seem more a stage-effect than an outburst of nature. Outside, the rain fell heavily, solidly—a veil of water. The furious blast of wind which had come hard on the heels of the great peal died away in a plaintive moan.

Anthony opened his eyes. "What did you say? Before that barrage, I mean."

Sir Arthur paced the room. "What did I say?" he exploded. "I said that if you hadn't found out who did it, I couldn't see the use of coming here and gabbling about mystery. Damn it, man, we're not in a two-shilling novel! We've got to get Deacon off, that's what we've got to do! *And* find the murderer! Not sit here and play at Holmes and Watson. It's *silly*, what we're doing! And I expected great things of you, Gethryn!"

"That," Anthony said placidly, "was surely foolish."

Sir Arthur made impatient sounds in his throat; but lessened the pace of his prowling. Under the graying hair his broad forehead was creased in a tremendous frown.

Anthony lit a cigarette. "But I may yet interest you," he went on. "You said, I think, that you wished to lay your hands on the murderer."

"I did. And by God I meant it!"

Anthony looked up at him. "Suppose you sit down and then I'll tell you all about it."

"Sit down!" Sir Arthur shouted. "Sit down! God above, you'll be telling me to keep calm next!" He flung himself into his chair. "Here I am then. Now get on!" He buried his face in his hands; then looked up to say: "You must forgive me, Gethryn; I'm not myself. I've been more on edge the last few days—a lot more—than I've let any one see. And to-night, somehow, my nerves have gone. And when you came with news I thought it meant that you'd caught the real murderer and that the boy would get off—and—and everything!"

"I was going to tell you," Anthony said, "that the murderer of John Hoode will never be caught. To get him is impossible. Please understand that when I say impossible I mean it."

"But why, man? Why?" cried Sir Arthur.

"Because," said Anthony slowly, "he doesn't exist."

"What?" Sir Arthur was on his feet again at a bound astonishing in its agility.

Anthony lay back in his chair. "I can't bear it! I can't bear it!" he said plaintively. "You know, you're very violent to-night. I can't talk if you will jump about so."

The elder man groaned apology and sat again in his chair. His eyes, bewildered, sought Anthony's.

Raising his voice to carry above the increasing roar

of the storm, Anthony said: "Sorry if I seem too mysterious. But you must let me elucidate in my own way. Here goes: I have said that the murderer of John Hoode doesn't exist. I don't mean that the murderer's dead or that Hoode committed suicide. I mean that John Hoode was never killed; is not, in fact, dead."

Sir Arthur's lips moved, but no sound came from them. His chair was outside the circle of light and it was by the vivid violet illumination of a quivering glare of lightning that Anthony saw the pallor the shock of his revelation had caused. Following that lightning came peal after peal of thunder.

As it died away, Anthony saw that the other was speaking. He had not moved in his chair, but his strong, square hands were twisting about each other to testify to the intensity of his emotion.

"What are you telling me?" he whispered. "Are you mad? John not dead! John not dead! Why, it's idiocy—stark idiocy to say what you have said!"

Anthony shook his head. "It isn't. Whatever it is, it isn't that. Wait till I have told you more. It's a long tale and strange."

Sir Arthur moistened his lips with his tongue but did not speak. Anthony's words had carried conviction; his words and a way he had of commanding attention.

The thunder, after the outburst of a moment before, seemed to have ceased entirely. No sudden furies of wind shook the house. The only sounds in the oppressive room were the tick-tick of the grandfather clock and the soft hish-hish of the rain against the closed windows.

Anthony drew a deep breath, and began:—

"My first impression of this affair, was as you know, that it was a straightforward murder, committed by some member of this household. Later, I had good reason to search this table here, and it was from the time of that search that I began to revise my theories. In this table I found—as I had expected—a drawer hidden from the casual eye. From that drawer I took some letters, a collection of newspaper-cuttings, a memorandum book, and other papers. You shall see them all in due course.

"The letters gave me my first inkling that there was something more obscure about the case than I had thought. So I went to the lady who had written those letters. From her I got the first pieces of the story, not without difficulty. I also went to see a man who had once been Hoode's secretary. He was obliging and clever. He had seen things, heard things, while he served Hoode, that had set him thinking. He thought so much that he employed, on his own initiative, a private detective. I have seen the detective. The detective, even after he was told to drop the business, went on detecting. You see, he had become interested. He is not a nice man. He smelt scandal and money. He, without knowing it, has helped me to piece together the whole amazing story—the story which shows how it was that John Hoode was not killed." Anthony paused, taking a last puff at his cigarette.

Sir Arthur, gray of face, hammered with his fists on the leather-padded arms of his chair.

"But the body!" he gasped. "The body! It was there!" He glanced wildly over his shoulder at the fireplace. "I saw it! I tell you I saw it!" His voice gathered strength. "And the inquest, the arrests, the identifications! And the funeral! Why, you fool!" he cried in a great voice, "the funeral is to-morrow. All England will be there! And you tell me this absurd story. What in God's name has come to you that you can play pranks of this sort? Haven't we all suffered enough without this?" The man was shaking.

Anthony sat up. "Wait!" he said. "And let me finish. I said that John Hoode had not been murdered. I did not say that no murder had been done. Murder was done. I know it. You know it. The world knows it. But what you and the world do not know is that the body upon which the inquest was held, the body which is to be buried to-morrow, is not the body of John Hoode!"

Sir Arthur glared at him. "What does this mean?" he said, and his lips trembled. "What is all this? I don't understand! I—I——"

Sleep was creeping insidiously upon Anthony. He wished that the storm had not ceased. Its violence had at least helped to keep one awake, helped to conquer this deadly fatigue which made talking so great an effort.

He began again: "The story is this. And though it's as mad as Hatta and the King's Messenger, it's true. John Hoode's mother, as you probably know, was, before marriage, a Miss Monteith. His father, as you must know also, was John Howard Beauleigh Hoode. Now, do you know that your John Hoode is very like—to look at, I mean—one of his parents and not the other?"

"Yes, yes. He and his father were—well like twin brothers almost."

"Exactly. John Howard Beauleigh Hoode had a way of passing on his features. John Howard

Beauleigh Hoode was married to Miss Adeline Rose Monteith in '73. In '72 John Howard Beauleigh Hoode's mistress, the daughter of Ian Dougal—he was a smith in Ardenross—gave birth to a son. That son, named also John, was maintained and educated at his father's expense; but he turned out as complete a waster as any man well could be. John Hoode—your John—didn't know of his half-brother's existence until John Howard Beauleigh Hoode's death. When he did find out—from his father's executors, I imagine—John—your John—was good to his bastard brother; and when first he saw him, he marvelled exceedingly at this bastard brother's likeness to him, for to look at his face was almost like looking into a mirror.

"The result of his kindness was the expected. Ingratitude, surliness, constant demands for money and yet more money; finally threats and blackmail——"

"No, no, no!" groaned Sir Arthur, his face in his hands. "It's all lies, lies! I knew John. He told me everything, everything!"

"Not he," Anthony said! "I've all the papers. Some of them here." He tapped his breast-pocket. "Birth certificates. Copy of John Howard Beauleigh Hoode's will, and so on. It's all by the book. Well, things went from bad to worse and from worse to intolerable for John—your John. These threats—I'll show you some letters later—wore his nerves, his health, to shreds. He tried every way of kindness—and failed." Anthony paused to moisten with his tongue his parched lips.

"Finally," he went on, "John—your John—found his work for the State to be suffering. He is, as I see him, an upright, conscientious, kindly man, but determined. He made up his mind. He would help once more, but once more only. He sent for the other John. He told him when and how to come, how to approach the house, to get into this room by that window, all without being seen.

"The other John came at the appointed time and knocked on the window. Your John helped him in. The other John, as always, was rotten with liquor. Your John told of the determination he had come to that this was to be the last time if the other John did not amend his ways. Then came trouble. Perhaps half-brother was more drunk than usual. Anyhow, he attacked your John. Sodden with drink though he was, he was the more powerful man. But John—your John—managed somehow to tear himself free. Not knowing what he did, he picked up the heavy poker and struck, not once, but many times——"

"But what—— Good God——!"

Anthony overrode the interruption. "Wait. Don't speak till I've finished. Appalled at what he had done, he stood looking down at his bastard half-brother's body. It sprawled there on the hearth in its untidy, shabby, mud-stained clothes. It was not, I conceive, a pretty sight. Then John—your John—did what better men had done before him. He lost his head. Completely he lost his head. And he thought at the time that he was clever!

"He locked the door, quietly, as the struggle had been quiet. Better for him had the struggle been noisy! He stripped to the skin. Then, naked as he was born, he stripped that sprawling thing which had been his brother. He donned the foul linen and musty cloths, the worn-out boots. More horrid still, he clad the body in his own good clothing. Carefully he did it, even to the tying of the black bow. And all the time, beneath his horror, was wonder for the amazing likeness of the thing's face and body to his own. For half-brother John was not one of those who carry the stamp of their dissipations.

"Then John—your John—hurried away. Through that window he went. As he crouched outside it, he heard the door of the room, which he had unlocked, open. He peered, and saw his sister. He saw her hand fly to her bosom. He saw her rush to the thing on the hearth. And he knew that his sister took that Thing for the brother she had known and loved and cherished all her life.

"He heard her scream. He saw her sway and fall. For an instant sanity returned, and he thought of going back to help her. Then fear got him by the throat again; fear of arrest; fear of publicity; fear of the hangman. He saw it all. And he drifted silently away through the darkness. And next morning, while the world read about his death, John Hoode lay in a Whitechapel doss-house. Later, an officious policeman found a carpenter's wood-rasp and on it some blood and some finger-prints. So Deacon was arrested for the murder of a man who was still alive. The blood on that wood-rasp was not the dead man's, nor were the finger-prints Deacon's. The explanation is long, but I will give it if you like." Anthony half closed his eyes and lay back in his chair.

A silence fell upon the room.

Sir Arthur shattered it. He leapt to his feet, his virility returned uncannily, a thousandfold. The light-blue eyes held fire in them.

"It's a lie!" he roared. "It's a lie!" He smashed his fist down upon the table. "A lie, I tell you!

What's that?" He turned sharply to face the end of the room.

"What?" Anthony rose to his feet.

"Nothing, nothing." He came close to Anthony. "What you tell me is lies! All lies! Lies and more lies, you——" His voice rose with each word.

Suddenly, amazingly, Anthony shouted too. "It's true, and you must believe it! Your help is wanted." He thrust his thin, dark face at the other's. "It's the truth! Truth! D'you understand? I know! I know because, because *Hoode told me himself—to-day! He's coming here to-night! Now!*"

Sir Arthur flung his arms above his head. "Lies, lies, lies!" His voice rose to a harsh, unnatural scream. "All lies! God rot him! Christ torture his soul in hell! He's dead! He's dead! You fool! *I* know, *I, I!* You know nothing!" His hands seemed to be reaching higher, clawing, as if they would tear holes in heaven. "You fool!" he screamed again. "He's dead. *I* know! *I killed him!* I climbed down and killed him——"

Anthony sat down on the edge of the table. "That'll be all, I think," he said.

The curtains over the alcove at the end of the room parted. From behind them came three men: the first tall and of middle-aged immaculateness, the second an obvious detective-inspector, the third negligible save for the pencil and notebook he carried.

Sir Arthur turned, crouching like an animal, to see the invasion. In a flash he whipped round and leapt at Anthony's throat, his arms outflung, his fingers crooked. Anthony, still sitting, had little time to avoid the rush. He raised a knee sharply. Sir Arthur fell to the floor, where for a time he rolled in agony.

The obvious detective-inspector bent over him. There was a click of handcuffs.

The immaculate man advanced to the table. "Very good indeed, Gethryn," he said.

"Thanks," Anthony said. "I suppose you're satisfied now, Lucas?"

"Eminently, Gethryn, eminently!" Mr. Lucas beamed.

"Then that's all right." Anthony's tone was heavy. "Now what about young Deacon? Can you unwind the red tape quickly?"

Mr. Lucas leant forward. "If you like," he whispered, "I can arrange for him to get away to-night. It's all very wrong and most unofficial; but I can manage it. Speak to the chief on the phone and all that sort of thing, you know."

Anthony's face relaxed into a smile. "Good for you. You might have Deacon told that if he likes I can arrange for the Bear and Key to fix him up for to-night."

"I'll tell him myself," said the other. "You're really rather a wonder, Gethryn! We ought to have you as a sort of super-superintendent. Or you might do well on the stage. At one time just now you almost took *me* in with that grisly tale and manner of yours. And what a yarn it was, too. Just enough to make that half-crazy devil think he'd killed the wrong man. Enough, I mean, to make him wonder whether you hadn't got half the tale right and had only gone astray about who actually did the bashing." Lucas chuckled reminiscently. "I say," he added, "it was a good thing nobody heard us getting in here through the window. It would've spoilt the whole thing. The storm effect helped everything along nicely, though, didn't it?"

"It did," Anthony said. "I didn't arrange that, you know."

Mr. Lucas smiled. "No, I suppose not; though I'm so full at the moment of wonder and admiration for the great Colonel Gethryn that if any one told me you had, I don't know that I should disbelieve 'em." He turned to look at the prisoner. "God!" he exclaimed. "Look at that!"

For Sir Arthur was sitting quietly at the feet of the plain-clothes man. And he was playing a little game with his manacled hands, tracing with both forefingers the intricate pattern of the carpet. Every now and again he would look up at his guard and laugh. It was not a pleasant sound, being childish and yet somehow evil.

Anthony looked, then turned away with a shiver. Lucas dropped a hand on his shoulder.

"Never mind, Gethryn," he said, after a moment. "It isn't your fault."

Anthony shook off the hand. "Damn it, I know that! Only the whole thing is so filthy. It might be said, I know, that I sent That mad. But it wouldn't be true. He did that himself. Hatred, ingrowing hatred of a better man: that's the cause."

Lucas was thoughtful. "It complicates things, this madness."

"It does. What'll happen?"

"Usual, I suppose. The case'll be tried. He'll be convicted—and sent to Broadmoor, where he'll die, or recover in a year and be let out to kill some one else. We're so humane, you know!" Lucas was bitter. "Anyhow, you won't be bothered any more, except for the trial, at which you'll figure prominently. Oh, yes! Great glory will be yours, Gethryn. Think what a press you'll have!"

Anthony grunted his disgust.

Lucas went on: "Lord! *What* a stir this is going to make. Millionaire M.P. arrested for murder of Cabinet Minister! It won't be nice for us at the Yard either. Not at all nice! Getting hold of an innocent man and all that. Police shown the way by amateur!" He groaned. "Never mind, *The Owl* shall be the first to publish anything. I arranged that before I came down. And then they'll have that report of yours to get out, too. What envy will tear Fleet Street! Of course, that report can't come out yet, you know. At least, I don't think so; not before the trial——"

Anthony started. "Lucas," he said, "there's something we've forgotten." He put a hand up to his hair.

"Gad! So we have. Let's see."

Together they stooped over the prisoner. He looked up at them and cackled.

"Rotten business!" Anthony grunted. "Seems almost indecent when the man's like this." He put his hand on Sir Arthur's head. His fingers groped for a moment; then came away. With them came that immaculate head of graying hair.

"Wonderful *toupé!*" Lucas stretched out his hands for it. "I'd never have noticed it. And I thought they were always obvious. Well, that's the last confirmation of your theory, Gethryn." He peered at Anthony. "Lord! You look worn out, man!"

Anthony said heavily: "I am. Think I'll get back to bed at my pub."

Lucas glanced at his watch. "Yes, do. Get off now: it's only ten past eleven. Shall——"

"What time did you say it was?"

"Eleven-ten."

"Gad! I thought I'd been here at least five hours. Only eleven-ten! And I'm sitting here!" Anthony made for the door.

Lucas grabbed at his arm. "Here, what's to do?"

"Got to go and pay a call." Anthony wrenched himself free and got to the door, paused to say over his shoulder: "Don't tell Deacon to come to my pub. Just let him go. He'll get where I want him," and was gone.

Lucas stared after him. "Fool ought to be in bed," he muttered. "Clever devil, though, but queer!" He turned to the business on hand.

Sir Arthur still sat on the floor, playing his game. His fingers wandered ceaselessly over the carpet. His head, bald save for a sand-colored tonsure, was sunk between his square shoulders. Every now and then he laughed that high-pitched laugh.

CHAPTER XVII

BY "THE OWL'S" COMMISSIONER

THE letter which Anthony had written in the early hours of that morning and dispatched by District Messenger, the letter which had brought so important a person as Mr. Egbert Lucas down to Abbotshall, had run as follows:—

"MY DEAR LUCAS,—As you know, I have been playing at detectives down at Marling. I have finished my game; the rest is up to you.

"What I have found, how I have found it, and my opinion of the meaning of what I have found you will discover set out in the enclosed document, typed by my very own fingers. You may—I cannot tell—think my conclusions wrong, and say that in real life, even as in fairy tales, a set of circumstances, a collection of clues, may equally lead to the innocent as to the guilty. For me, however, I am convinced. To put it in my own diffident way: I *know* that I am right!

"So please read the enclosed. If you agree with me, as I think you will, you will yet find that the evidence is insufficient: and you will be right. I will, therefore, endeavor to arrange for a confession by the guilty person to be given in the (unsuspected) presence of officers of your able department. In order for this to be done, will you give orders for some of your men—three, including a shorthand writer, would be enough—to meet me at the cross-roads on the London side of Marling at about nine to-night? I will then get them covertly into Abbotshall and dispose them in advantageous but secret positions. This may, I know, be irregular, but you can take it that I can manage things without any one in the house knowing until the business is over. Once your men are where I shall put them, I shall enter the house by a more orthodox way. The rest will follow.

"This is asking a lot of you, but, after all, you know me well enough to be reasonably certain that I am less of a fool than most. So, if you agree with my conclusions as set out in the report, please arrange this. Whether you agree or not, ring me up, before seven to-night, at my pub in Marling (Greyne 29). If I am not there leave a message: 'All right' or 'Nothing doing,' as the case may be. Whichever your answer is, I will ring you up when I have received it.

"My main reason—or one of my main reasons—for doing all this work was to do Hastings's little paper, *The Owl,* a good turn. The report is really for them, though I don't know when and to what extent you will allow them to publish it. But I rely on you to see that *The Owl* gets as much journalistic fat as it can digest. No other paper must hear a whisper until you've allowed Hastings to make a scoop out of the 'Dramatic New Developments.'

"Yours,

"A. R. Gethryn."

"P.S.—Don't forget that if you decide to let me try to arrange this confession, I may fail. I don't think I will; but I might. I shall rely to a great extent upon the fact that I am something of an actor."

Coming to the end of this letter, Mr. Egbert Lucas had whistled beneath his breath, instructed his secretary that on no account was he to be disturbed, and had settled down—he has the most comfortable chair in the Yard—to read the typewritten report.

Unfolding it, he murmured: "Unexpected chap, Gethryn. This ought to be interesting."

He read:—

"THE MURDER OF JOHN HOODE

"Upon the morning of the 20th of August, 192—, I drove to the village of Marling in Surrey. By 9.30 A. M. I had gained admission to the house Abbotshall.

"Owing to circumstances which need not be set down here, and also, in a great measure, to the courtesy and assistance of Superintendent Boyd of Scotland Yard, I was able from the beginning to pursue unhampered my own investigations. The result of these I give below.

"(For reasons which must, I think, be obvious, I have divided this report into four parts. Also, I would point out that, for reasons equally evident, the steps in my deduction, reasoning—call it what you will—are not necessarily given here in their chronological order.)

I

"Immediately upon my arrival at Abbotshall, I spoke at some length with Superintendent Boyd, who gave me the history of the affair as obtained by him through close questioning of the inmates. It appeared then that with the exception of the butler, these one and all had alibis, complete in some cases and in others as nearly so as could be expected of persons who had not known beforehand that they were likely to be accused of murder. (Later, of course, it was revealed—see reports of the inquest—that Mr. Archibald Deacon's alibi did not exist in fact.)

"Superintendent Boyd and I at once agreed that to suspect the alibiless Poole (the butler) was folly. He had been, obviously and by common report, devoted to his master. Moreover, he is physically incapable—even were he out of his mind—of dealing such blows as caused the death of the murdered man.

"After our conversation, Superintendent Boyd and I together made an examination of the study, the room in which the murder was done. Together we came to the following conclusions,[1] all of which were explained by the superintendent in his evidence at the inquest. Since, therefore, these points are by this common knowledge, I will not go into the processes by which they were arrived at, but will merely enumerate them as follows:—

"(i) That when Hoode was struck, either by the first or all the blows, he was seated at his table.

"(ii) That the appearance of the room had been carefully arranged to convey the impression that a struggle had taken place.

"(iii) That the murderer was well known to Hoode, and was, in all probability, an inmate of the house.

"(iv) That the murderer had worn gloves for most of the time during which he was in the study, there being no finger-prints anywhere except on the wood-rasp.

"(v) That the blows which killed Hoode must have had tremendous strength behind them.

[1] Colonel Gethryn is surely too modest here.

"(vi) That, in all probability, the murderer entered by the window. (I fully endorsed, at that stage of the inquiry, the opinion of the Police that Poole's evidence was reliable.)

"It will be seen that the cumulative implication of these six points tends to strengthen considerably the case against Deacon, which even without them is by no means weak circumstantially. It is now, therefore, that the keynote of my report must come.

"I met and spoke with Deacon for the first time on the afternoon of the day I arrived at Abbotshall. It needed but three minutes with him to convince me that here was a man who had not been, was not, and never could be a murderer. I cannot defend this statement with logic. It was simply conviction. Like this: In a party of, say twelve persons there will be eleven about none of whom I could say definitely: 'That one is incapable of stealing the baby's marmalade'; but in the twelfth I may find a man—perhaps unknown to me before—of whom I can swear before God or man: 'He *could* not have stolen the baby's marmalade—not even if he had tried to! He is incapable of carrying out such a crime.'

"Deacon was a twelfth man. Before I had seen him, my views were beginning to differ from those of Scotland Yard: after I had seen and spoken with him they became directly opposed. It became my business to prove, in spite of all difficulties, that this man, whatever the appearances, had had no hand in the death of John Hoode. In what follows, they who read will find, I hope, absolute proof of his innocence; or if not that, at least a battering-ram to shake the tower of their belief in his guilt.

"Knowing that Deacon was not the murderer, I nevertheless realized that his innocence—so strong was the case against him—could only be established by definite proof that some one else was. That is to say: a negative defense would be useless.

"It will be seen, then, that the divergence of my opinions from those of the Crown began almost at the outset of my investigation.

"Let us go back to the study at Abbotshall. On each of the numbered points I gave earlier, I agreed with Superintendent Boyd. Where I began to—had to—disagree was concerning their implication of Deacon. Points (i), (ii), (iii), and (iv) can be left alone; they will fit my murderer as well as, or better than, they fit Deacon. The remaining two, however, must be dealt with more fully.

"We will take (v) first. The obvious fact that strength far above the normal was behind the blows that killed Hoode was a perfect link in the chain of circumstantial evidence against the gigantic Deacon. But at the inquest, Dr. Fowler, the divisional surgeon, said: 'The wounds were inflicted so far as I can judge, either by a man three times stronger than the average or by a person of either sex who was insane and had the terrible strength of the insane.'

"Having to find an alternative to Deacon and having determined to cling to my theory that the murderer was an inhabitant—permanent or temporary—of the house, my choice of Dr. Fowler's alternative was a man or woman mentally unbalanced. This choice was not, as it might at first seem, a drawback; rather was it the reverse. For one of my first impressions had been that there was something of terrible senselessness about the whole affair, and this impression had increased a thousandfold when I saw the battered head of the dead man. Madness was my first thought then. Those blows—*four* of them, mark you! when the first had been obviously sufficient—surely spoke of madness; either the lust for blood and destruction of a confirmed homicidal maniac or *the consummation of a hatred so deadly, so complete in its possession of the hater, as to constitute of itself insanity.*

"The second was the theory I adopted. For, believing the murderer to be an inmate of the house, it was clear that I must look for one whose insanity was not of a type apparent to the world.

"Now for point (vi)—the entry by the window. As I have said, I agreed with the police that the murderer did enter by the window; but there our agreement ceased. It is a point in the crown's case against Deacon that his are the only legs in the house long enough to enable their owner to clear the flower-bed in stepping from the flagged path to the low sill of the study window. This, I am sure, is, as evidence against Deacon, more than useless. I have not taken measurements, but it is obvious that even for his long legs, a step right *into* the study would be impossible. This being so, the fact that he could step *on to* the window-sill is of no importance whatever. For one thing, it would have been extremely difficult for him to retain balance; for another, if he had retained his balance, the necessary scrabbling at the window and the twisting and turning he would have had to perform to get legs and then body into the room would have attracted Hoode's attention before he could see enough of the intruder to recognize him. And then the theory, agreed by the police, that Hoode did not rise from, or anyhow did not remain long out of, his chair, falls to the ground.

"Now let us get back to my murderer. Yes, he got in by the window; but he left the flower-bed unmarked. Now, as he is a member of the household we know that his legs cannot be as long as Deacon's. How, then, did he approach the window?

"He must have (*a*) jumped over the flower-bed and into the room; (*b*) stepped on the flower-bed, but, on leaving, repaired or disguised the damage he had done; or (*c*) *got his feet on to the sill and his whole self into the room without having crossed the flower-bed.*

"It is almost impossible that he should have done (*a*); (*b*) is unlikely, since after the murder the murderer had no time to spare. (This is proved later.) One is left, then, with the conviction that the real answer lies in (*c*). This means either that the murderer erupted through the floor or walls of the study or that *he descended the wall of the house and entered the open study window without ever reaching the earth in his journey.* (Entrance through the door is barred. Remember, we are taking Poole's evidence on that point as reliable.)

"As the murderer was presumably flesh and blood and there was no hole in walls or floor, I fastened on the 'descent' theory, which was subsequently confirmed by an examination of the wall outside and above the open study window. Over this wall—over the whole house, in fact—the commonest and creepiest of creepers creeps. I refer to *Ampelopsis Veitchii.* A large drainage-pipe runs to earth beside the study window in question, and for a space of perhaps half a foot on each side of it throughout its length the creeper has been cleared away. But half-way between the top of the window through which the murderer entered the study and the first-floor windows above it, a shoot of creeper has pushed its way out into the cleared space beside the pipe. This shoot drew my attention because it was black and shriveled.

"*Ampelopsis Veitchii,* though one of the commonest forms of creeper, is also one of the most tender. A sharp blow upon the main branch of a shoot means death to that shoot within a few hours. The dead piece of creeper I refer to was, I thought at first, at that point on the wall where it might have been struck by the feet of a man of middle height climbing out of either of the first-floor windows over the open one of the study at the moment when he was clutching the sill with one or both hands and hanging with arms bent.

"It was, I saw, clearly impossible for the murderer to have dropped from the upper window on to the sill of the open study window and so miraculously to have retained his balance that he did not fall on to the flower-bed. Also—in spite of the novelists—there are few drain-pipes which can be used to climb by. This drain-pipe is no exception. Fingers could not be clasped round it; neither would it support more than a five- or six-stone weight. It was clear, therefore, that the murderer, in descending the wall, had used something to climb down—probably a rope. (Descent of the wall was another confirmation of the theory that the murderer was of the house.)

"It will have been noticed that I have used the masculine personal pronoun to describe the murderer. Dr. Fowler's statement at the inquest, which I quoted earlier, would allow, given insanity, of equal rights to women. But I *felt,* from the beginning, that John

Hoode had been killed by a man, and I worked throughout on that assumption. At every turn little things told me that this was a man's work; and I was finally satisfied when I accepted the theory of descent by the wall.

"I will bring to an end here the first part of this report. But before starting upon the next, I will summarize the conclusions already shown, give them life with a touch of imagination, and let you see the picture.

"The murder was committed by a man who, if not completely mad, was at least insane in his hatred of Hoode and Hoode's. He sat at the time of the murder an inmate of Abbotshall. He effected entrance to the study that night by letting himself down from the more easterly of the first-floor windows over the most easterly of the study windows. He spoke to Hoode, jokingly explaining his unceremonious entry. By some pretext (it would, you know, be easy enough) he got behind Hoode as he sat at his big table. Then he struck.

"His object achieved, he carries out the plan he has been hatching for weeks. He sets the scene, overturning chairs, spilling papers, dragging the body to the hearth—and all as quietly as you please. He steps back, to regard with pleasure the result of his labors.

"He overturns the clock, having moved the sofa to rest it upon. He moves back the hands of the clock until they stand at 10.45. A quarter to eleven, mark you! Not ten to, not twenty to, not twenty-three and a half minutes to—but a quarter to!

"He gives a hasty glance round the room. Everything is in order. He thrusts his head cautiously from the window. All is as he had calculated: there is nobody about; the night is sufficiently dark. He goes up his rope again and through that first-floor window.

II

"Having established our criminal as at least a monomaniac and an inhabitant—permanent or temporary—of the house, let us go further into detail.

"First, as regards the finger-prints of which so much has been heard and so few have been seen.

"Every one is satisfied that the murderer wore gloves, because nowhere else in the study, where he must have handled one thing after another, were any finger-prints found. They are found, these important pieces of evidence, upon the one object where their presence is utterly damning—and there only!

"The spirals, whorls, and what-nots which compose these marks correspond exactly with those to be found in the skin and thumb and first two fingers of Archibald Deacon's right hand. *Ergo,* say Police and Public, Archibald Deacon is the murderer. But I say that these finger-prints go a long way to prove (even without the rest of my evidence) that Deacon *cannot* be the murderer.

"Here is the one really clever murder (of those discovered) committed within the last fifteen years. Yet, if one take the popular view, one has to believe that the murderer, who was wise enough to wear gloves during the greater part of the time he was in the study, actually removed one of them and carefully pressed his thumb and fingers upon the highly receptive surface of his weapon's handle before leaving that weapon in a nice easy place for the first policemen to find!

"Surely the fallacy of blindly accepting as the murderer the man who made those prints is obvious? Consider the *position* of the marks. They point down the handle, towards the blade! It is almost incredible that at any time would the murderer have held the weapon as a Regency buck dandled his tasselled cane.

"My difficulty was to reconcile with Deacon's innocence of the murder the presence of his finger-prints upon the tool with which it was committed. That the prints were his I had too much respect for the efficacy of the Scotland Yard system to doubt.

"A possible solution came to me from memory of a detective story [1] I once read, in which the murderer, something of a practical scientist, made, by means of an ingenious and practicable photographical process, a die of another's man's thumb-print. This he used to incriminate the innocent owner of the thumb.

"For a while I cherished this theory, so vivid was my recollection of the possibility of the method; but I was never really satisfied. Then, suddenly, I found the explanation which I was afterwards to prove true.

"Instead of going to the immense trouble of making a stamp or die, why not obtain beforehand upon the desired object the actual *finger-prints of the chosen scapegoat?*

"After consideration, I accepted this idea. It fitted well enough with my murderer—a fellow of infinite cunning. I proceeded with the work of reconstruction. Thus:—

"Since Deacon had no knowledge of the crime, the murderer must have induced him, in circumstances so ordinary or usual as to be likely to escape his memory, to take hold of the wood-rasp by its handle at some time before the murder; perhaps eight hours, probably

[1] *The Red Thumb Mark*, by R. Austin Freeman.

not more. For this clever murderer would realize the difficulty of retaining the finger-prints unspoiled.

"When, after obtaining the finger-prints, he had got rid of Deacon, he must have removed with gloved hands—taking care not to touch those parts of the handle where the prints must be—the handle he had loosened before Deacon had held it. Then that handle must have been packed (say in a small box with cork wedges) in such a way as to ensure that its carriage in the pocket for the descent of the wall and subsequent activities could be effected without those beautiful marks being spoiled. The reassembling of the tool must have been done after the murder; and the whole Deacon-damning bit of evidence then planted for the police to find.

"In the study, on a later visit, I found confirmation of the accuracy of my deductions. It will be remembered that when the wood-rasp was produced at the inquest, it was proved to the satisfaction of the court that it was indeed the weapon which had caused Hoode's death. This proof lay pre-eminently in the condition of the blade, which was far from nice. But it was also pointed out by the police, to make the jury's assurance doubly sure, that on a little rosewood table in the study there was a scar on the polish, known not to have existed before, which had obviously been made by the blade of just such a wood-rasp as this wood-rasp. Superintendent Boyd gave it as his opinion that the murderer had laid the wood-rasp on this table after he had killed Hoode, and while he was arranging the appearance of a struggle.

"I agree with the superintendent—but only up to a point. Where he was wrong was in assuming that the scar had been made by the murderer having put down on the table the *whole* wood-rasp.

"That scar is of exactly the same length as the *blade* of the rasp, and is in the center of the table, having on every side of it some six inches of unscarred table-top.

"Do you see? That scar *could not have been made by the complete tool!* The handle is two and a half to three inches in circumference, and if it had been joined to the blade would, by reason of its far greater thickness, *have allowed no more than an inch or so of the blade's tip to touch and scar the table.* Had the complete rasp been laid down at an edge of the table with the handle projecting into space, the full-length scar would have been possible. But the scar, as I have described, is in the middle of the table, and could therefore only have been made by the blade without its handle.

"Here, then, was the justification of my theory. Further proof came later. With full official permission I examined the wood-rasp. It was as it had been found. I held it in my hand. I shook it—and the blade flew off. Two small wooden wedges fell to the floor. I picked a shred of linen from the tang of the blade.

"Obviously, the use of the little wedges had been to hold the tang of the blade in the enlarged socket of the handle. And the fact that the socket had been enlarged, added to the inadequacy of the wedges, is surely proof enough that the blows which killed Hoode were struck with the blade alone. There is, however, yet more—the shred of linen. It came, I should say, from a handkerchief, the use of which had been, I take it, to get a better grip of the thin tang when striking. The glove the murderer was undoubtedly wearing probably proved insufficient to insure against a slipping grip. So he wrapped a handkerchief about his gloved hand. An inequality in the surface of the steel caught some loose thread. This he did not notice when hastily ramming handle and blade together after the kill.

"The wedges and the shred of linen are in the keeping of Superintendent Boyd, to whom I gave them at the time of my discovery. I could not, my case being incomplete, explain then their significance.

"My next step was to question Deacon. To my surprise and consternation I found that although he was a man for whom tools had neither interest nor meaning and for whom therefore the handling of any such implement might be so much out of the ordinary as to impress itself upon his memory, he had no recollection of ever seeing, before the inquest, any wood-rasp. He even suggested that until now he had not known such a tool to exist.

"I will not deny that Deacon's emphatic assertion that he had never even seen the rasp until it was exhibited at the inquest gave me a shaking. It did, and a bad one. I tested all the links in my chain, only to find each sound and the whole most obviously right—until this blind alley.

"Then it struck me, and I laughed at myself as those who read are probably already laughing at me. I saw that I was committing the grave error of underrating my man. I saw that so far from having received a check I had really been advanced.

"The finger-prints were on the handle of the rasp, and the handle—had I not been at much pains to prove it?—had been separated from the blade by the murderer—being an intelligent murderer—would certainly never have been such a fool as to let the fearsome and so-likely-to-be-remembered blade within Deacon's sight. No, it was far more likely that he had disguised the handle as the handle of something else.

"Having got thus far, I progressed at speed. As what could he have disguised the handle? With efficacy, only as that of another tool. But he probably knew Deacon as a man who had no truck with tools. How, then, did he get the so-ordinary surroundings necessary to prevent awkward memories arising afterwards in the mind of Deacon? The answer is that they were there, ready-made, to his hand. In order to avoid obscurity, I will elucidate this.

"The indication all through had been that the murderer was a man accustomed to the use of carpenter's tools. The murderer was an inmate of the house. Put one and two together and you will see that he would very possibly be known to the household as one who was 'always messing about at that there carpent'ring.' Deacon was also of the household, and would therefore see nothing unusual in, say, being asked to 'hold this chisel (or gouge, or anything else you like) for just half a second.' If this seem farfetched, remember that from the beginning I felt the murderer as one who had been preparing his work for some long time.

"It was almost at the moment when I reached this stage of thought that a number of hitherto insufficiently substantiated suspicions which had been steadily massing in my mind suddenly rearranged themselves in such a manner as to become extra links in my chain of reasoning rather than the wild plungings of a mind tired of logic. This merging of reason with intuition (they are twins, those two) left me certain that I should know who I was trying to prove guilty if Deacon gave me the name of the man against whom these suspicions of mine had been directed in answer to the question: 'Who, at any time within the last twenty-four hours preceding the murder, induced you to hold in your right hand an implement with a short, thick wooden handle of the same appearance as the handle you have seen in the wood-rasp?'

"You see, I had already learned that of the Abbotshall *ménage* four men frequently used, and had consequent access to, carpenter's tools. These were the gardener, the chauffeur, the murdered man, and the guest from whom I had the information.

"Hoode, the gardener, and the chauffeur I disregarded. The first because he was not his own murderer; the second because at the time of the murder he was in bed at the Cottage Hospital in Marling; and the third because he has respectable and trustworthy friends to swear that he spent the evening of the crime in their company.

"Remained the guest—that enthusiastic amateur Dædalus—and he the man that from the beginning had excited those nebulous suspicions I have mentioned. He was living in the house at the time when the murder was committed. He was, by his own showing, an amateur carpenter of experience and enthusiasm. (Early he simulated ignorance as to the name of a wood-rasp. Later, by his voluntary statement, he showed that he could not have been ignorant of it. This was the only slip he made when talking with me.)

"Before I took opportunity to ask Deacon the all-important question, I did much and thought more. With one exception, these thoughts and actions are proper to the next part of this report, and accordingly are dealt with there. The exception is this:—

"I became aware that of the two first-floor windows of Abbotshall which (see Part I) are over the window through which the murderer entered the study, the more easterly must have been the one used by the murderer. For I saw what I had not seen at first, that it would be almost an impossibility for a man descending by a rope from the other window to swing his legs, at the end of the descent, on to the sill of the study window, since that window is not exactly, as one would find in a house younger and less altered than Abbotshall, between the two first-floor windows above it but has most of its length beneath the more easterly. Moreover, although a man descending from the less easterly window might possibly have struck with his foot that one shoot of creeper in the cleared space beside the drain-pipe (see Part I), he would also be bound to do damage to the main body of the creeper —and that is uninjured.

"It was, in fact, obvious that the murderer had come out of the room with the more easterly window. (I was annoyed with myself for not having seen this sooner.)

"That window is to the room occupied as a sitting-room by Sir Arthur Digby-Coates.

"My suspect amateur carpenter was Sir Arthur Digby-Coates.

"When at last I put to Deacon my question of who had given him any implement with a wooden handle to hold, the answer was: 'Sir Arthur Digby-Coates.'

"(*Note.*—Before going on to Part III, it might be well to explain briefly the circumstances in which Deacon was induced to leave the prints of his fingers on the handle. It is not essential, but may be of interest. Deacon, when I asked him my question, explained that on the morning of the day of the murder he passed by Digby-Coates's sitting-room. The door was open. Digby-Coates called to him to come in. He entered to find, *as on several previous occasions*, that Digby-Coates was amusing himself with the completing of an excellent carved cabinet he had been engaged on for many weeks. Digby-Coates was in difficulties, having, he explained, too few hands. Deacon was asked to stand by. He did so, and assisted the enthusiast by handing from the carpenter's bench near the window, one tool after the other. Among them was one, he just remembered, with a handle such as I had described and such as he remembered the wood-rasp handle to be now that he came to think of it.)

"So there you are. When I heard the story I felt, I confess, no little admiration for Digby-Coates. He is so thorough! You see, this was not the first time Deacon had given such assistance. And he knew Deacon thought little and cared less about the whole business of cabinet-making.

III

"It is evidence purely of trivialities which has put Deacon in a cell awaiting trial; yet I am convinced that did I attempt to establish his innocence merely by the means I have employed so far, the very people who already accept his guilt as certain would accuse me of having nothing but trivialities upon which to base my version of the affair. Further, it could be said—and would be—that I have read between the lines writing which was not there; that I have so ingeniously twisted the interpretation of what are, in fact, merely ordinarily meaningless signs as to make them appear a grim and coherent indictment against another man; that I have seen an anarchist bomb in a schoolboy's snowball and a Bolshevik outrage in a varsity rag.

"So I must strengthen my case; for the truth is that this evidence of trivialities is good, but not nearly good enough. It must have a backing to it.

"Now, there is, if you look at it, a complete absence of any backing to the case against Deacon. 'What about the money?' you say. 'What about that hundred pounds belonging to Hoode? There's motive for you!' 'Nonsense!' say I. Deacon was paid six hundred pounds a year. He had also an allowance from his only living relative. He had been, it is true, a little shorter of money than usual lately; but to suggest that he would commit a murder for a hundred pounds is absurd. A man in his position could have raised the money in a thousand safer and less energetic ways. No, Deacon's story that the money was a birthday gift from Hoode is, besides being more likely, true. Further, it is easy of proof that Deacon and Hoode were on the best of terms: for corroboration apply to the Ministry of Imperial Finance and the households of Abbotshall and 12 Seymour Square. Further still, look at Deacon's record and see how rash it is to condemn him murderer with nothing more to go upon than those too-beautiful finger-prints and a few ragged pieces of circumstantial evidence, *the two best of which were supplied—oh! so ingeniously—by Sir Arthur Digby-Coates*. For it was from him that the police first learnt that Hoode had drawn a hundred pounds in notes from his bank. And it was through him that it became known that Deacon had asked him the time at ten forty-five on the night of the murder—the time to which the hands of the clock in the study had been moved by the murderer.

"There being no backing to the case of the Crown against Deacon, I saw that if I could find a stout one for mine against Digby-Coates I should score heavily.

"The first thing to be found was motive. What, I asked myself, could it be? Money? No. Digby-Coates is a wealthier man by far than ever was Hoode. Revenge for some particular ill turn? Hardly that, since Hoode, though a politician, bore all his life the stamp of honesty and straight dealing. A woman? I was not prepared to accept one as the sole cause. She might, of course, be contributory, but I wanted something more likely. Middle-aged men of the social and intellectual standing of these two do not often, in this age of decrees nisi and cold love, go about killing each other over a woman if she is only the first blot upon the fair sea of their friendship.

"I was forced back, in this search for motive, upon the deductions I had made from those little material signs, and remembered that I had determined, before ever I thought of putting a name to the murderer, that John Hoode was killed by a man insane; not mad in the gibbering, straws-in-the-hair sense, but mentally unbalanced by a kind of ingrowing, self-nourishing hatred.

"I took this as my starting point and asked myself how I could find corroboration of and reason for this hatred having existed in the heart of a man ostensibly the closest friend of its object. The answer was: look at their past history; as much of it as is available in books of record. I did so, using Hoode's own books.

"I found soon enough reason for the hatred. Look

as I looked. You will see that always, always, always was Digby-Coates beaten by the man he killed. Were the race one of scholarship, sport, politics, social advancement, honors, the result was the same. Hoode first; Digby-Coates second. Look in the *Who's Who*, *Hansard*, the records of Upchester School and Magdalen, the Honors Lists. Look in the minds of the men's colleagues and contemporaries. Always will you find the same story. Look at this, the slightest extract from the list:—

John Hoode.	*Arthur Digby-Coates.*
Captain of Upchester (last three years at school).	Senior Monitor (same three years).
Won John Halket scholarship to Magdalen.	Second on list.
Rowed 2 in Oxford boat (third year).	Rowed 6 in trials (third year).
Gaisford (fourth year).	Newdigate (fourth year).
Minor office (Admiralty) after three years in Parliament.	Still merely M.P. after six months longer in Parliament.
President of Board of Trade.	Still M.P. (He was, I believe, offered at this time a minor Parliamentary Secretaryship; but refused.)
K.C.M.G., C.V.O., etc.	K.B.E.
Minister of Imperial Finance (from the date of the forming of the Ministry in 1919.)	Almost at same time accepted Parliamentary Secretaryship to Board of Conciliation.

"One could go on for pages, for ever telling this story of races won by a stride—Hoode the winner,

Digby-Coates his follower-up—and that stride getting longer and longer as time went on.

"But at last came the race for the Woman—the race whose loss snapped the last cord of sanity in the mind of the loser.

"I discovered the existence of the Woman in this way: I searched Hoode's desk in suspicion of a hidden drawer. I found one and in it a diary (of no use save to corroborate the fact of some of those races), and a bunch of newspaper-cuttings. But I knew—how is no matter—that something was missing from that drawer.

"What that something was I did not know. I only knew that it was most probably of importance. So I searched the house—and found it. A packet of letters from the Woman. As I was by then up to the neck in the unspeakable nasty work of the Private Inquiry Agent, I read them. Who the woman is will not be set down here. It is my hope that not even in court shall I have to give her name.

"I sought her and talked with her. But briefly and brutally her replies were that I was correct in assuming that she had been Hoode's mistress, and that I was also right (this was a shot in black dark) in assuming that she knew Sir Arthur Digby-Coates. She did not, it seemed, have any affection for the gentleman. She made it plain to me, under some pressure, that Sir Arthur had wished her to stand in the relation to him that she subsequently did to John Hoode. But (a shrug of distaste) Sir Arthur had been sent packing—and quickly.

"Is not that enough, when added to those other and perpetual defeats of the past five-and-thirty years, to show the reason for hatred in the mind of the egoist?

Consider the history of the matter. First, boyish jealousy and a determination to win next time; then the gradual process of realization that strive as he would he would never reach a common goal before his rival; then the slow at first but increasingly fast transition from healthy jealousy to dislike, from dislike to utter hatred. Then, at last, with the crowning loss of the Woman, the monomania—for this is what the hatred is grown—takes a firmer hold and becomes a fire so fierce that only the complete elimination of the hated man will quench it.

"So much for reasons why Digby-Coates should have hated Hoode. Now for corroboration that such hatred actually existed.

"I wrote just now of certain newspaper-cuttings which I found in the hidden drawer of Hoode's desk. These were a bunch of twenty-four, taken from various issues (all bearing dates within the last two years) of *The Searchlight*, *The St. Stephen's Gazette*, and *Vox Populi*. Every one of the cuttings was a leading or almost equally prominent article attacking the Minister of Reconstruction in no half-hearted way.

"Being one who prefers news without sensationalism, I had never before read a line from any one of these three papers. I came to these extracts, therefore, with a mind not only open but blank, and was immediately struck by the strange unanimity of the three newspapers in regard to John Hoode. For, as all the world must know, whether they read them or not, the trio are of politics widely varying. Their attacks upon the murdered man were made upon different grounds, it is true, but the very fact that the attacks were made, and made so viciously, struck me as unusual. It seemed to me that in the ordinary way the fact of one attacking would be enough to make at least one of the others defend. Further, the grounds upon which the attacks were made appeared to my unbiased mind as flimsy compared with the whole-hearted virulence of the writing.

"From wondering and re-reading, I came upon a thing yet stranger: the unmistakable and mysterious similarity in the style of the composition. This similarity was to me, who have made something of a study of other men's methods, even more pronounced when attempts had been made to disguise or vary the manner of writing. After ten minutes' examination of those cuttings, I was prepared to swear that one man had been conducting the anti-Hoode campaign in three papers whose views on every other matter from vaccination to the Vatican are as wide apart as Stoke Poges, Seattle, and Sinbad the Sailor. I pictured a man of some scholastic attainment who was unable to write in fashion other than preciously correct and so set in his style as to be incapable of varying it, tried he never so hard.

"I took the cuttings and my conviction to Deacon. He could not help me, so I went to his predecessor as Hoode's private secretary (the real private secretary, like Deacon, not the departmental one). From him I obtained confirmation of my theory. He, too, had suspected that not only was one man behind these press attacks, but that this man was also the actual author. He showed me something I had only half-noticed till then; something which went further than mere similarity of style. Throughout the articles, he pointed out, quotations occurred. They were, some of them, unusual quotations. But usual or unusual, one and all were correct! They were correct in some cases to the point of pedantry—if correctness can be so described. And they were thus correct in these three widely differing and highly sensational papers, whose literary standards have always been a byword with those who hate journalese, *cliché,* and the dreadful mutilation, humiliation and weakening of the English language.

"It was when this former secretary of Hoode's pointed this out to me that I recollected having recently been puzzled by a memory which would not be remembered. In one of the cuttings I had come across a quotation from Virgil, in which a dative case had been used rather than the all-prevalent but less correct genitive, and had been haunted at the time of reading with a sense of having seen this same rarity only recently. Suddenly it came back to me. It had been in a book of essays I had dipped into—a book of essays which, on inquiry made later, turned out to be from the pen of Sir Arthur Digby-Coates, writing under a feminine nom de guerre.

"That, I admit, is not much to go upon. But more was to come. This forerunner of Deacon had—before he quarreled with Hoode and left him—on his own initiative employed a private detective and set him to unearth this enemy of Hoode's that seemed to command and write for three incendiary newspapers. You see, this secretary was sure that there was an enemy of some importance at work. At first he said nothing to Hoode, but at last told of his suspicions. He was laughed at. He returned to the charge—and they quarreled. He left Hoode's employment without having told him of the private detective. Being, with some excuse, not a little angry, he paid the detective, telling him to stop the work and go to hell.

"But, luckily, the private detective had smelt a Big

Thing, and consequently Big Money. He went on working. He finished his job. I got into touch with him. He has been paid, and the result of his labors has been forwarded to Scotland Yard.

"His proofs are more than adequate. He has established, mainly through the corruptibility of a disgruntled employee, that Digby-Coates was beyond doubt the hidden owner of those three newspapers and also the composer of all these elaborate pæans of hate which appeared in them from time to time, and were directed against the man who was his friend and whose friendship he so cleverly pretended to return. (One cannot but admire the ingenuity with which Digby-Coates foisted more or less respectable and quite foolish figureheads upon the world—including the rest of the Press—as owners of the papers upon the purchase and upkeep of which he must have spent nearly half his great fortune. He was truly a great Enemy!)

"But it was in himself writing the attacks with which he tried to bring Hoode to a fall that he overstepped himself and made a loophole through which curious persons could wriggle. Had he left the writing to different men and rested content with being the power behind the machine, he would have increased by a thousand his chances of remaining undiscovered. I suppose that his hate was so strong that to leave to others the forging of the weapons was beyond him.

"Before ending the third part of this report, I would draw attention to what has thus far been established—established, I hope, to the satisfaction of even the most rigorous anti-Deaconite.

"It has been shown that there is both reason for and corroboration of Digby-Coates's hatred of Hoode.

"It has been shown not only that all the evidence

against Deacon can be used equally well against Digby-Coates, but also that there is in fact more of this evidence of material signs against Digby-Coates than there is against Deacon.

"Above all, we have in the case against Digby-Coates two things (which might be called one thing) that there have never been against Deacon. The first is motive—although it is nothing more (nor less) than the crazy hatred of a half-madman. The second is reliable evidence that ill-will existed before the murder.

IV

"If I were delivering this report as a lecture, I am sure that there would be a little fat man in a corner bounding up and down with ill-suppressed irritation. At this stage he would be unable to restrain himself any longer and would ask passionately why the hell I was wasting my time and his by faking up a case against a man who had a chilled-steel alibi—the perfect, unassailable defense of a man who is seen by various people at such times and in such a place as to make it impossible for him to have committed the crime.

"I would assure the fat little man—as I assure those who read—that I would in due course deal with and demolish that alibi, pointing out at the same time that it was the very perfection of the thing which had bred some of my first suspicions of its owner. It was too good, too complete, in a household where every one else had only ordinary ones; it was a Sunday-go-to-meeting alibi; the alibi of a man who at least knew that a crime was going to be committed.

"But more of that later. For the moment I will

take two points which, though they might be considered proper to the first part of this document, I have seen fit to reserve until now.

"The first concerns a rope. I have explained that I found it necessary to search the house. During that search, which was not only for the missing letters from the drawer in Hoode's writing-table, I went into Deacon's bedroom. This is next to, and on the west side of, the room used by Digby-Coates as a sitting-room, study, and, occasionally, carpenter's shop. (He has had a bench fitted up there for him, as I mentioned earlier.)

"In the grate in Deacon's bedroom was a little pile of soot which at once attracted my attention, as being unusual in so scrupulously tended a house as Abbotshall. I investigated. On the ledge which runs round the interior of the chimney at the point where—on a level with the mantelpiece outside—it suddenly narrows, I found a coil of silk cord of roughly the thickness of a man's little finger. It was double-knotted at intervals of two inches throughout its length, which was sixteen feet. (By the time this report is read the rope will be in the hands of the authorities. They would have had it sooner, only I was not giving away information until my case was complete.)

"That pile of soot in the grate was not of long standing. The cord was new. I knew at once that I had found the rope by which my criminal had descended the wall. But how did it get where I found it?

"I saw that the only answer which would fit the rest of my case was that the rope had been put there by Digby-Coates. Since I knew Deacon to be innocent and I had nowhere found any evidence to show that

Digby-Coates had an accomplice, it could have been nobody else. And it was so easy for him, occupying as he did the room next to Deacon's.

"I am aware that here I am treading on dangerous ground—from the point of view, that is, of the logical anti-Deaconite—but I say nevertheless that this business of the rope strengthens my case and goes to give yet further indication of Digby-Coates's deliberate plan to fasten his guilt upon Deacon. Silk rope of so excellent a quality is not common, and I think that Scotland Yard should have little difficulty in tracing its purchase. So convinced am I that they will find Digby-Coates at the other end of the trail that, if I could be of any use, I would willingly help them. Without the rest of my investigations, the finding of that rope would only have hastened Deacon's journey to another and thicker one. But with them it has an effect most different.

"Now for the second matter which was to be dealt with before the alibi.

"It will be remembered that a great point against Deacon was that the hands of the overturned clock in the study stood at 10.45. The coroner, in reviewing the case at the end of the inquest, argued thus: At a quarter to eleven Deacon had entered the room of Sir Arthur Digby-Coates and inquired the time. That he had done so was apparent both from the evidence of Sir Arthur and of Deacon himself. All the other evidence pointed to Deacon. Was it not then only reasonable to assume that Deacon, after committing the murder and arranging the room to look as if a struggle had taken place, had pushed those hands back to 10.45, knowing that at that time he had been with so reputable a witness as Sir Arthur Digby-Coates? The whole thing was clear, said the coroner, answering his own question and practically directing the already willing jury to pass a verdict against Deacon.

"The coroner added that he could not say whether, if his assumption were correct, which he was sure it was, Deacon had asked the time of Sir Arthur Digby-Coates in order to be able, by moving the clock, to establish an alibi, or whether that request for the time had been an accident and the moving of the clock hands a subsequent idea brought about by memory of the 'time' incident. In any case, added this erudite official, the omission to make a corresponding alteration in the timing served to show how the cleverest criminal will always make some foolish mistake which will afterwards lead to his capture.

"How true! How trite! And, in this instance, how utterly wrong! Observe. Both Digby-Coates and Deacon are highly intelligent men. Suppose either of them wishing to show by moving back the hands of a clock that the clock stopped at a time earlier than it did in fact: would either make the ridiculous, childish mistake of forgetting the striking? I think not!

"Observe again. Two men know that one asked the other the time. Why, then, is the subsequent utilizing of that incident to be attributed to only one of them? Clearly it can apply equally to both!

"Here again the evidence which has been used against Deacon can be used at least equally well against Digby-Coates.

"This clock business, I say, is only further proof of the great ingenuity of Digby-Coates. It was the cleverest stroke of all. Deacon innocently, naturally, asks him the time. At once Digby-Coates, having already made up his mind that to-night was the night, is seized with an idea whose brilliance is surprising even to himself. Deacon, the man he has already chosen as scapegoat, is playing into his hands.

"Suppose (I can see his mind working) that he slew Hoode just on the hour, and then made sure, after the clock in the study had struck, that its works, though undamaged, would not go on working, and then moved the hands back till they stood at 10.45. This disorder of the striking when the clock was set going again would reveal to investigators the fact that the hands had been moved and that the clock had stopped not before the hour but after it. Why, these investigators, would ask, had the hands been moved to that particular place—10.45? Soon they would find out—he, clever fellow! helping them without seeming to—that at this moment on the night of the crime Deacon had asked him the time. 'Ah-ha!' would say the investigators, 'Mr. Deacon, to whom so much else points, has been trying to make alibis for himself!'

"But how, he thinks, can he carry out this great, this wonderful scheme? Ah, yes! Let him put himself in Deacon's place; let him think what Deacon would do if he was killing Hoode. If he stopped the clock, he wouldn't draw too much attention to it, so—so—ah, yes!—he would try to make it look as if there had been a struggle and would derange the tidy room accordingly!

"That, I am convinced, is the way Digby-Coates reasoned. To put it briefly, he had to arrange the study to look, not as if a struggle had really taken place, but as if some one had tried their best to *make it look like that*. That is to say, while giving the air of a genuine attempt to mislead, he must yet make sure that investigators were not, in fact, misled; the first thing, for instance, that he had to do was to insure that attention was drawn to the clock, but in such a way as to make it seem that endeavors had been made to draw attention *from* it.

"Clever, you must admit. Clever as hell! And successful, as those who have followed the case must know. He got the effect he wanted—that of a man who had tried to mislead. The police know that 'struggle' scene for a fake. But I hope I have shown that it was a double fake. If you think I have imbued my criminal with more ingenuity than any murderer would possess, remember that I, too, am a man, and therefore a potential murderer. Remember also something of which I have given more tangible proof—the finger-print game he played on Deacon. Remember that it was through him that the police first learnt of the money Hoode had drawn from his bank, and the fact that at 10.45 on the night of the murder Deacon had asked him the time! Remember that this business of the clock and the 'struggle' is like that of the silk cord—nothing without what I have described in the earlier parts of this report, but with it a great deal.

"And now for that alibi.

"That the murderer was in the study after the clock there—which, by the way, was correct by the other clocks in the house, had struck eleven, is proved by the fact of the striking of that clock being one hour behind.

"Miss Hoode entered the study and found the body at about ten minutes past eleven.

"The murderer, then, left the study at some time between two minutes past the hour at the earliest and ten minutes past.

"So soon as I was certain that the murderer was

Digby-Coates, I saw that before my case against him was complete I must disprove his alibi; also I realized that this could best be done by ascertaining much more definitely at what time he left the study to climb back up the wall and into his room. That eight minutes between eleven-two and eleven-ten was too wide a margin to work in.

"The more I pondered this task the more removed from possibility seemed its completion. Then, by the grace of God, there emerged, in circumstances which need not be set down here, a new witness whose evidence put me in possession of exactly the information I needed.

"This witness is Robert Belford, a man-servant, and therefore a permanent member of the Hoode household. He is a highly-strung little man, and refrained at first from telling what he knew through very natural fear of being himself suspected of the murder of his master.

"Before Belford's emergence I had come to the conclusion—though I could not see then how this was going to help—that the acceptance of the old butler—Poole—as a perfect trustworthy witness had been a mistake. I discovered, you see, that he suffers from that inconvenient disorder hay-fever.

"When in the throes of a seizure he can neither see, hear nor speak; is conscious, in fact, of nothing save discomfort. That these seizures last sometimes for as long as a minute and a half I can swear to from having watched the old man struggle with one.

"Immediately after my discovery of the existence in him of this ailment, I questioned Poole; with the result that at last he remembered having suffered a paroxysm on the night of the murder at some time during that part of the evening before the murder when his master was in the study and the rest of the house was quiet. He had not remembered the incident until I asked him. His memory, as he says, is not what it was, and in any case the event was not sufficiently out of the ordinary to have stayed in his head after all the emotions of that crowded night.

"But it was during, or rather at the beginning, of that minute and a half or two minutes during which the old man could do nothing but cough and sneeze and choke and gasp with his head between his knees, that Belford—the new witness—had entered the study —by the door!

"When he got into the room he saw immediately the body of his master. In one horrified second (I have said that he is an intensely nervous, highly-strung little man) he took it all in; corpse, disorder, and all the other details of that brilliant and messy crime. *And there was, he swears, no one else in the room.* The only place in which a man could have hidden would have been the alcove at the far end of the room, but the curtains which, as a rule, cut that off from view, were on that night drawn aside.

"Belford, after that one great second of horror, fled. As he closed the door behind him, he noticed that Poole, in his little room across the hall, was still wrestling with his paroxysm. Belford retreated. He was terrified that this dreadful crime he had seen might be laid at his door were he seen coming from the room. It was, to say the least, unusual that he should enter the study when his master was working there. Nobody, he felt, would believe him if he told them that he had gone there to ask a favor of the dead man. He crept up the dark hall and crouched on the stairs.

"His position was directly under the clock which

hangs there; and here you have the reason for what has possibly seemed meticulousness on my part in describing this minor incident. He became aware, without thinking, of what that clock said. He stared up at it blankly. But, as often happens, this mechanical action impresses itself on his memory. He swears—nothing will shake his evidence—that the time was *five minutes past eleven.*

"There you have it. Digby-Coates, as I have shown, cannot have left the study before eleven-two. At some point between eleven-four and eleven-five Belford finds the study empty of life.

"I split the difference and took eleven-three as the time at which Digby-Coates left the study—by the window. He must have been, I argued, snugly back in his room by four minutes past at the latest. He is still an active and very powerful man, and the climb could not have taken him long.

"Having, after hearing what Belford had to tell me, thus been enabled to know at least a part of the time which must prove a weak spot in the alibi, I reviewed that itself. Before I do so, here, however, there is one more point which I must settle. It concerns the hay-fever of the aged Mr. Poole. As the attack of this malady which let Belford into the study unobserved failed to stay in his memory, it might be thought that he may have had another attack, enabling another man to enter the study without being seen. That idea, which is sure to be entertained, is, I submit, of no value. One attack is ordinary enough; but the old man tells me that he has been 'better lately.' Two of those painful seizures would have stayed in his mind. Besides, there is the silk rope and other evidence to prove descent by the wall. Also, the crime was obviously premeditated, and no murderer of such skill as Hoode's would rely upon the hay-fever of an aged butler, even if he knew of its existence.

"Now for the facts of the alibi. It will be remembered that Digby-Coates had, on the night of the murder, retired to his own sitting-room at a few minutes after ten. The night was hot. He opened the window to its fullest extent; also flung the door open. This was (I use his own words, spoken at the inquest) 'in order to get the benefit of any breeze there might be.' Further, since he 'wished to be alone in order to go through some important papers,' he pinned upon that open door a notice: 'Busy—do not disturb.'

"After he had gone to his room, the first incident with which we need concern ourselves occurred at 10.45, when Deacon made that famous request for the time. At that moment Digby-Coates was pacing the room, and Deacon, disregarding or not seeing the notice on the door, put his question from the passage.

"About seven minutes later, Belford, walking down the passage, saw Digby-Coates standing in the doorway.

"The next we hear is from Elsie Syme, one of the housemaids, who 'saw Sir Arthur sitting in his big chair by the window' as she passed his door. (The quotation is from her reply to a question of Superintendent Boyd's.) So far as can be ascertained, this was not more than five minutes after Belford had passed by—making the time about 10.57.

"Next comes another housemaid, Mabel Smith, who had been working in the linen-closet, which is opposite the door of Deacon's room. She said that returning from the journey she had made downstairs (and by forgetting which she had furnished Deacon with that false alibi which he rather foolishly tried to make use of) she had noticed Sir Arthur 'sitting in his room.' The time then, as guessed at by the girl and more definitely confirmed by Elsie Syme, who knew what time she had left the servant's hall, was between eleven and one minute past.

"Next comes Belford again. You remember that he entered the study at a point between three and four minutes past eleven. On his way there from the upper part of the house he passed Digby-Coates's room and 'saw Sir Arthur by the window.' Since he went straight to the study, the time at which he passed Digby-Coates's door cannot have been earlier than 11.03.

"After this we have Elsie Syme again. This time she is on her way to bed. Passing along the passage she again 'saw Sir Arthur sitting by the window.' The time in this instance is a little harder to get at, but cannot have been more than six minutes past the hour.

"Last we have the evidence of old Poole, who, after entering the study on hearing Miss Hoode scream, immediately fled to fetch his dead master's friend. He found Sir Arthur sitting with a book, his arm-chair pulled close up to the open window. This, since Miss Hoode entered the study at approximately ten minutes past eleven, was probably at 11.13 or thereabouts.

"That is the alibi, and a very good one it is, too—too good. It was, of course, never recognized as being an alibi, since Digby-Coates was never suspected by police or public as being the murderer; but the very fact of its being there (it trickled out mixed up with unimportant and verbose evidence, and was very cleverly referred to by Digby-Coates himself on every possible occasion) must have its sub-conscious effect. (I should perhaps explain here that, as Digby-Coates was never suspected and the alibi was therefore the nebulous but effective thing I have described, the times I have given were not mentioned otherwise than generally: such exactitude as appears above is the result of Superintendent Boyd's and my own questioning, of which more came later.)

"I have shown that according to the witnesses, none of whom I could suspect of anything but honesty, Digby-Coates was seen there in his room at times which made it impossible that he should have done the murder. Yet I *knew* he was the murderer. Therefore some at least of these witnesses who had sworn to seeing him were mistaken.

"I had, then, to find out (*a*) which witnesses were thus in error, and (*b*) how they had been induced to make their common mistake.

"I got at (*a*) like this: (if the way seem long and roundabout, remember that it is far more difficult to find things out than to understand, when told, how they were so found out:—

"Digby-Coates, I reasoned, *must* have begun his preparations immediately after Belford saw him standing in the doorway of his room at eight minutes to eleven. To descend the wall; to enter the study; to hold Hoode in chaffing conversation for a moment to allay his curiosity regarding the unusual method of entry; to kill him; to reassemble the wood-rasp; to set the 'struggle' scene; arrange the clock; to climb back up the wall again; and all as noiseless as you please, cannot have taken him less than eight minutes at the very least. As I have shown, he was in all probability back in his room by four minutes past the hour (if not earlier) and it will be seen, therefore, that he must have begun descent of the wall by four minutes to at the latest.

"The witnesses I was after, therefore, were those who thought they had seen him between four minutes to and four minutes past the hour.

"Of these, as you can see from my statement of the alibi, Elsie Syme is the first, Mabel Smith the second, and Belford the third. (Elsie Syme, it is true, might be considered as barely coming within my rough-and-ready time-limit, but you must remember that all the times I fixed were calculations and not stop-watch records.)

"Separately, I questioned the three servants. It was not an easy task. I had to handle them gently, and I had to impress upon them the vital necessity to forget the conversation as soon as they had left me. I think I managed it.

"Their answers to my first important question were the same, though each was with me alone when I put it.

"I said: 'You say you saw Sir Arthur at such and such a time in his room on the night of the murder, and that he was sitting in his chair and that that chair was by the window. Are you certain of this?'

"They said: 'Yes, sir,' and said it emphatically.

"I played my trump card. I played it in some fear; if the answers were not what I expected, my case fell.

"I said: 'Now tell me: *exactly how much of Sir Arthur did you see?* What parts of him, I mean.'

"They goggled.

"I tried again: 'Was the chair that big arm-chair? And was it facing the window with its back to the door?'

" 'Yes, sir,' they said.

"I said: 'Then all you saw of Sir Arthur was——'

"They replied, after some further help but with conviction, that all they had seen was the top of his head, part of his trousers, and the soles of his shoes. Belford, who is an intelligent man, expanded his answer by saying: 'You see, sir, we're all so used-like to seein' Sir Arthur sittin' like that and in that chair as we just naturally thinks as how we'd seen all on 'im that night.' Which, I think, is as lucid an explanation of the mistake as could well be given.

"I must explain here how I came in possession of this trump card of mine. It was through two casual observations, which at first never struck me as bearing in any way upon the matter I was investigating. The first was the annoying, almost impossible tidiness of Digby-Coates's hair. It did not appear to be greased or pomaded in any way, and yet I never saw it other than as if he had just brushed it, and with care. The second was his curious trick of sitting on the edge of a chair with his feet thrust first backwards through the gateway formed by the front legs and then outwards until each instep is pressed against the back of each of those front legs. It is a trick most boys have, but it is unusual to find it persisting in a man of middle-age. Digby-Coates does not, of course, always sit like that, but frequently.

"What changed these two chance observations—the sort of thing one idly notices about any man of one's acquaintance without really thinking about them—into perhaps the most important minor step in my case was a glimpse I had of Digby-Coates from the very point from which the servants who made his alibi had seen him. He was sitting as they had seen him sit (though I did not know this until I questioned them) in the big arm-chair, which was facing the window. All I could see from the passage was the long, solid back of the chair, the top of the well-tended head, six inches of each trouser-leg, and the soles of two shoes. On the open door was a notice: 'Busy—Please do not disturb.'

"The scene was, in fact, a replica of what I had gathered it to be on the night of the murder. I fell to thinking, and suddenly the most annoying pieces of my jig-saw puzzle fell into place. I went in and spoke to him. I looked, more carefully than ever before, at his head, and came to the conclusion that he was bald, but wore the most skilfully made *toupé* I had ever seen. I remembered that he had told me that he never used a valet. I pictured him—he is the type—as one to whom the thought that any one else knew how unsavory he appeared minus hair was abhorrent.

"When I discovered the *toupé*, I knew that I could smash the alibi if only the unknowing alibi-makers gave me, honestly, the answers I wanted.

"As you know, they did. I consider the matter clear, but I know it. Perhaps I had better show what Digby-Coates did that night; how he set his stage and played out his one-act show.

"He retires to his room, knowing that Hoode is in his study, Deacon busy or, as often of late, out, Miss Hoode and Mrs. Mainwaring in their beds, and some of the servants, as he wishes them, moving about the house—he has studied their movements and knows that on this night of the week there is work to do which keeps them later than usual. Luckily for him, the night is hot. It gives the necessary excuse for leaving his door as well as his window open. Upon that open door—which is not back against the wall, but only half open—he places a notice: 'Busy—Please do not disturb.'

"(Observe the cunning of this notice. He had, I found from the servants, placed such a notice on the open door on two previous occasions. This, I am sure, he had done for a twofold reason: (i) to see whether it would really keep out intruders, and (ii) to insure, when eventually he placed it there on the night he chose for the killing of Hoode, that though the household were not become sufficiently accustomed to it to avoid a glance at it and subsequently into the room, the sight of the notice was yet familiar enough to insure that it was not remarkable as being without precedent. He had, you see, for the sake of his alibi, to make certain that people passing (i) would look into his room; (ii) would not come in; and (iii) would not think the notice anything out of the ordinary.)

"Having placed his notice he draws his arm-chair up to its *familiar* position facing the window. Then he has to wait. Sometimes he sits. Sometimes, the waiting too hard upon even such nerves as his, he paces the room.

"All goes well. Every one, everything, plays into his hands. The very man he has chosen to incriminate draws the noose, by that request for the time, tighter round his own neck. The leaden-footed minutes, what with this incident, that of Belford, and the increasing certainty of success, begin to pass more swiftly. People go their ways past his door but do not enter.

"At last it is time. He gets his knotted rope, secures it to the leg of the carpenter's bench Hoode has had fitted for him. The bench is clamped to the floor; no doubt but that it can stand the strain.

"Now, with a wary eye upon the door, he takes

from its hiding-place the replica of the *toupé* which is on his head, pads it out with a handkerchief, and sets it on top of a pile of books on the seat of the chair. The pile is just of the height to show the hair over the chair-back to one looking into the room from the passage. He knows, he has tested it many times. (He may, possibly, have used the half-wig from his head. But I think not. He must have had more than one; and he would not wish to have anything unusual in his appearance when he faced Hoode. The difficulty of explaining as a joke his entrance by the window would be sufficient.)

"A pair of dress trousers pinned to the chair, the lower ends of the legs slightly padded and twisted one round each of the chair's front legs, and a pair of patent-leather shoes set at the right angle, complete the picture.

"(So simple as to sound comic, isn't it? But if one thinks, one can see that in that simplicity lies that same touch of genius which characterizes the whole of the other arrangements of the crime. To utilize his own little tricks, such as that way he had of sitting on a chair like a nervous schoolboy, that is genius. He knew that all they could have seen of him from that doorway, if he had really sat in his favorite position in that chair, would have been the top of his head, the ends of his trousers, and his shoes. He knew also that they were so accustomed to seeing only hair, trousers, and shoes when he was really there, that if they saw hair, trousers, and shoes they would be prepared to swear they had seen *him*.)

"When the time comes, at last he drops his rope of silk from the window and descends, his heart beating high with exultation. The moment he has waited for, schemed for, gloated over, will be with him at the end of that short journey. . . . Some minutes later he returns by the same precarious stair.

. . . .

"It was the simplicity and sheer daring of the scheme that made this the well-nigh perfect crime it was. It was here that the maniac hatred he had of Hoode helped him greatly. I cannot conceive any but a man insane running the tremendous risk of discovery which he took with such equanimity. Nor would any but one with the great clarity of mind only attained by the mad have even dreamed of carrying out a crime so adult by means of the schoolboy trick of the dummy. It was an application of the bolster-in-the-dormitory-bed idea which nearly succeeded by virtue of its very unlikelihood.

"I have little more to say, though it would, of course, be possible to go much further in endeavoring to show the subtler shades of motive for each separate link of Digby-Coates's plot, and to go into such questions as whether he chose Deacon as scapegoat merely for convenience in drawing suspicion away from himself or whether he had some darker reason; but the time for that sort of thing is not yet.

One more word. I wish to make it plain that as a case I know this report to be less complete than is desirable. I know that it might be impossible to hang Digby-Coates simply upon the strength of what I have set down. I know that in all probability the Crown would say, that, unless the case were strengthened, it could not be regarded as enough even to try him on. I know the later stages of the report are mainly conjecture—guess-work if you like.

"I know all this, I say, but I also know that if there is any justice in England to-day I have shown enough of the true history of John Hoode's death to bring about the immediate release of Archibald Deacon.

"*I* know that Arthur Digby-Coates is guilty of the murder of John Hoode, and, having gone so far towards proving this beyond doubt, I intend to see him brought to trial.

"The only way to bring this about is to give my work the substantial backing of a confession by the murderer. This I intend to obtain.

"I cannot but think that, if I succeed, my work is finished and the agreement of even the most sceptical assured.

"A. R. GETHRYN."

CHAPTER XVIII

ENTER FAIRY GODMOTHER

I

DINNER that night had been a melancholy business for the sisters. During the day the anodyne of action had brought them at times almost to cheerfulness; but from the moment when they had left the chambers of the great Marshall's junior, their spirits had begun steadily to evaporate.

Of the two, perhaps Lucia suffered the most. She was older. She had not the ingenuousness which enabled Dora to take at their face value the reassurance of barristers and the like. And she suffered, though she would barely admit it to herself, from a complication of anxieties.

As the evening grew old so she grew angry and more angry—and always with Lucia Lemesurier. She felt something of contempt for herself. Surely a woman of thirty—Heavens, what age!—should have more feeling, more decency, when her little sister was in trouble so grave, than to offer only half her mind for the duty of consolation? Surely it was hardly—hardly seemly for this middle-aged woman to be—well, worrying, at such a time as this, over a petty quarrel with a man she barely knew? Yet, yet—well, he might have *answered* that note if he couldn't come.

Lucia took herself in hand. This must stop! She

looked across the pretty room to where Dora lay coiled upon a sofa, a book held before her face.

Lucia conceived suspicions of that book. She investigated, to find them well-founded. The book was upside down; the face behind it was disfigured by tear-laden, swollen eyes.

Contrite, Lucia attempted consolation, and was in a measure successful. For an hour—perhaps two—Dora lay with her head on her sister's breast.

"Feeling better, dear?" Lucia said at last.

Dora nodded. "I do. Really I do. Sorry I'm such a little idiot. Only it's—it's—I can't help thinking, wondering—oh, what's the good? Everything's going to be all right. It's got to be! It *must* be!"

"Of course it will." Lucia stroked the red-gold hair.

Dora sat upright, hands pressed to flushed cheeks. "Don't know why I'm behaving in such a *damn'* silly way!" she burst out. "You ought to shake me, darling, instead of being so sweet. Look at Archie. He's wonderful! And he'd hate it if he knew I was slobbering here like a nasty schoolgirl. He says it'll be all right. And so does Colonel Gethryn."

Lucia drew away; then silently reviled herself. Why, why in Heaven's name, should mention of this man affect her?

But Dora went on. Dora was no fool, and Dora was interested. A good thing for Dora; for a moment it lifted from her that black pall of brooding fear.

"Weren't you surprised, Loo, when Archie told us this morning about Mr. Gethryn really being Colonel Gethryn? And all those wonderful things he did in the war with the Secret What-d'you-call-it?"

"No," said Lucia absently. Then hurried mendaciously to correct herself. "Yes, I mean. I was surprised. Very much!" She felt a hot flush mount to her cheeks. This did not lessen her annoyance with Lucia Lemesurier.

Came a silence, broken at last by the younger sister.

"I," she said, with a gallant attempt at frivolity, "am going to repair to my chamber, there to remove traces of these ignoble tears." And she hurried from the room.

Lucia stared a moment at the closed door; then sank back into the softness of the couch. Her thoughts cannot be described with any clarity. They were, as may be imagined, again a jumble. One moment she would smile at some secret thought; another would find her tense, pale, vivid imagination of horrors to come to her sister and her sister's lover possessing her.

Would everything, as she had so confidently said, be "all right?" Would miracles indeed be worked by this—by Colonel Gethryn? How absurd the "Colonel" sounded! Colonels surely, were purple, fat, and white-moustached, not tall, lean, "hawky" persons with disturbing eyes.

She was startled from her reverie. Had she heard anything? Yes, there it was again—a tapping on the window. The thunder had stopped now, and the sound came sharply through the soft hissing of the rain.

There is always something sinister in a knocking upon a window. With a jump one exchanges the dull safety of ordinary life for the uncomfortable excitement of the sensational novel. Lucia, her nerves wrecked by the emotions of the past week and further jarred by the noise of the storm, sprang to her feet and stood straining her eyes, wide, startled and black as velvet shadows, towards the French windows.

The tapping came again, insistent. She took hold of her courage, crossed the room, and flung them open.

Anthony stepped across the sill. He was, as he had left Mr. Lucas ten minutes before, without hat or mackintosh. He seemed, as indeed he was, serenely unconscious of his appearance. But the pallor of fatigue, the blazing eyes, the laboring breath, the hatless head shining with wet, the half-sodden clothes, all had their effect upon Lucia. It had been for her an evening of horror. Now, surely, here was news of worse.

Her eyes questioned him. Her heart hammered at her breast. Speech she found impossible.

Anthony bowed. "Enter Fairy Godmother," he said. "Preserve absolute calm. The large Mr. Deacon is a free man. Repentant policemen are busy scouring his 'scutcheon. I think it not unlikely that he will be here within an hour or so."

Lucia was left without breath. "Oh—why—what——" she gasped.

He smiled at her. "Please preserve absolute calm. My nerves aren't what they were. What do we do next? Tell little sister, I imagine."

"You—I—I——" she stammered, and rushed from the room.

Anthony, having first covered the seat with a convenient newspaper, sank into a chair.

He communed with himself. "Lord, I'm wet! How is it that I can be so melodramatic as well? I must curb this passion for effect. Still, it kept her off any expressions of gratitude and the like. Good God! Gratitude! It's not that I want. And what do I want?

All. Yes, all! But I must go softly. One must wait." He shook himself. "And anyhow, you blasted idiot, what chance *can* you have?" He grew depressed.

The door burst open. There was a flurry of skirts. Dora, transfigured, rushed at him as he rose, words pouring from her. Anthony was dazed.

He waved his hands to stem the flood. Arms were thrown about his neck. Warm lips were pressed to his cheek. Another flurry—and she was gone.

Anthony looked after. "If you were your sister, my dear," said he to himself, "escape would've been more difficult."

The door opened again. This time it is Lucia, composed now and more mistress of herself than for days past. With relief, her sense of humor had returned in full strength; there is nothing more steadying than one's full sense of humor.

Anthony was still on his feet. She looked first at him and then at the damp pages of the *Telegraph* covering the chair. She began to laugh. He was well content; the most seductive, the most pleasant sound within his experience.

He stood smiling at her. The laughter grew. Then, with an effort, she controlled it.

"I'm sorry. Only I couldn't help it. Really I couldn't!" Her tone was contrite.

"And why should you?" Anthony asked. "But I hope you appreciate my tender care of your cushions."

She seated herself, waving him back to his chair. "Oh, I do! I think it was wonderful of you to—to think about my furniture at a time like this. But then you're by the way of being rather a wonderful person, aren't you?"

"You deceive yourself if you mean that," said

Anthony. "A matter of common sense plus imagination; that's all. The mixture's rare, I admit, but there's no food for wonder in it." He hardly heard his own words. He found clear thought an effort. He wanted only to be left in peace to look at her and look and look again. He found himself glad, somehow, that to-night she was not in an evening gown. The simplicity of her clothes, perfect though they were, seemed to make her, paradoxically, less remote.

She smiled at him. "Now, please, you must tell me all about everything."

Anthony groaned.

"Please."

"Must I?" He raised feeble hands.

"Of course, you silly person, I don't really mean 'everything.' How could I when you're tired, so awfully tired! But you come here all strange and mysterious and dramatic and simply tell us that Archie's all right. How *can* one help being curious? Why is he all right? Have you only persuaded them that he didn't do it? Or have you shown them the person that really did?"

"The second," Anthony said, covertly feasting his eyes.

"Who? Who?" She had risen in her excitement.

Anthony looked up at her, and looking, forgot the question.

She stamped her foot. "Oh, you irritating man!" she cried, and shook him by the shoulder. "Tell me at once!"

"It was—Digby-Coates," said Anthony slowly, fearing the news might affect her deeply.

She took that in silence. Whether astonishment or

other emotions had affected her he could not at the moment discern. Her next words told him.

"I suppose"—her tone was thoughtful—"that I ought to be surprised. And horrified. But somehow I'm not. I don't mean, you know, that I ever suspected him or anything like that. But I'm just not awfully surprised, that's all."

It dawned upon Anthony that if he were not to seem a boor he must make an effort at intelligence. He strove to quiet the exuberant agility his heart had exhibited since her hand had touched his shoulder.

He did his best. "You didn't like him, I gather," he said.

She shook her head. "No. Not that I really disliked him. I just wasn't quite comfortable whenever he was with me. You know. I always had to be nice, of course. Before my husband died they were always together. You see, they had the same tastes. They were about the same age, too." She relapsed into silence.

"So they were much of an age, were they?" Anthony said to himself. "Now, that's illuminating. Coates is over fifty." He was about to speak aloud, but was forestalled.

"What on earth must you think of me?" Lucia cried. "Here are you, that've done all these miracles for us, all tired and wet, and I'm sitting here as if this was afternoon tea at the Vicar's." She ran to the bell. "First, you must have a drink. Whisky? That's the second time I've forgotten my hospitality when you've been here."

Anthony got his drink. When he had finished the second,

"You," she said, "must go back to your inn. And

you'll have to walk, poor thing. My little car's been out of action for a fortnight and I've sent away the one we hired for to-day. But the walk may do you good. You'll get warm."

Anthony set down his tumbler. "Exit Fairy Godmother."

The great eyes burned him with their reproach.

"That's not fair," she said, and Anthony could have kicked himself. "You know it isn't! What I *want* to do is offer you a bed here. Well, there's a bed, but nothing else. No razor. No pyjamas even. You'd be uncomfortable. And you've simply *got* to take care of yourself to-night!"

Anthony rose. "Forgive me. It seems my fate always to be rude to you. And you're quite right." He moved towards the door.

She followed him. With his fingers on the handle, he paused. "Damn it!" he thought. "She's hard enough to resist when one's in full command of oneself. But now! Oh, Jupiter, aid me!"

He prepared to make his adieux. She touched him on the arm.

"One more question before you go." She smiled at him, and Anthony caught his breath. "Was I—am I—oh! I mean, is my evidence part of your case? You know, about my being outside the window that night—what I saw——"

"Two of my main objects," Anthony said, "have been to get Deacon off and to keep you and your brother out. I think I've done both. I thought at one time that I couldn't round off the business without dragging you in. But the gods were good and dropped into my hands a little man who knew as much and a deal more than you. I exulted. I still exult. Like

Stalky, I gloat!" He thumped his chest with an air. "I know everything; but I shan't tell. I know so much that I could tell you almost to a minute what time it was when you looked through the window of Hoode's study—and that's more than you know yourself. But I won't tell. Your secret, lady, is safe with me!"

She laughed; but there was something more than laughter in the sound.

"I think," she said slowly, "that you are a very perfect—Fairy Godmother! And now you must go, or you'll have pneumonia. And if you did you might never hear those thanks I'm going to give you"—she smiled, and he saw with wonder that the dark eyes were glistening with tears—"*after* I've apologized for behaving as I did the other night." She paused; then burst out: "And, please, will you shake hands?"

Anthony looked at the white fingers held out toward him. The last shreds of self-control went flying.

"No, by God, I won't!" he shouted.

Lucia, amazed, was caught in long arms. Kisses were rained upon her mouth, her eyes, her hair, her throat. She strove with hands against his chest.

The great eyes blazed dark fire into his above them. "Let go! Let go, I say! *Will* you let me go!" The words came between her teeth.

Some measure of sanity returned to him. His arms dropped to his sides. Lucia, released, fell back against the wall. There she remained, hands behind her and pressed her to the panelling. Her eyes ("God! what eyes!" thought poor Anthony) never left his face.

He said very heavily: "I suppose—I suppose I've been presumptuous. Oh! I'll grant you it was unpardonable. But, Lord, there's reason enough for my madness. I know I'm ridiculous. I feel, believe me, sufficient dislike of myself. But I make this excuse for the inexcusable." He paused and moistened his lips. They were parched, dry.

The woman stayed half-leaning, half-crouching, against the wall. Still those eyes were fixed upon his.

Anthony went on: "I offer this excuse, I say. It is that I love you. Oh, I know I'm laughable! You can tell me I've only known you for—what is it?—three days. You can tell me that I have only been in your company for a few—a very few—hours of those days. You can tell me all this and more. You can tell me that I know nothing of you nor you of me. And to it all I answer: Days? Time? Hours? Friendship? What have all these to do with me? I love you."

The diffidence born of contrition for his treatment of her was fading fast. He came a step nearer.

"D'you hear what I say? I love you. I love you. I love you! From the first moment I saw you—in this room here—when I had come to make you tell me what you knew, from that moment, in that moment, I loved you." He straightened himself and flung out both hands in a gesture almost Latin. "And, by God, can I be blamed? Can I be blamed for what I did just now, I say? For a hundred hours that were a hundred years I have been obsessed by you. Your hair—that black net of beautiful magic; your eyes—those great dark windows of your heart—they have been with me all those hundred hours that were a lifetime. I have drowned my soul in those eyes of yours, Madonna Lucia. I have——"

"Oh, stop, stop! What are you saying? This is all madness! Madness!" She was erect now, hands pressed to flaming cheeks.

But he would not stop. "Oh, I haven't finished!" He laughed—a wild sound. "Not yet. You say this is madness. What is it that has made me mad? It is you, you, you! You—your face, your body, all the unbelievable wonder of you! You say that I am mad. I say that I am sane. What could be saner than a man who tells you, as I have told you, that he loves you? For how could any man help loving you? Madness, the real madness, would have lain in not telling you." He came close and caught her hands and carried them to his lips. Fingers, palms, wrists, he covered with kisses.

He straightened himself and released her. "And that," he said wearily, "is that. I'm afraid I've grown dramatic. Forgive me."

She did not speak. Anthony looked down; he could not trust himself to meet those eyes.

"And so now," he said, "I'll go." He turned to the door.

There came a voice from behind him.

"But—but"—it stammered deliciously—"but please, I don't *want* you to go. Please will you come back."

2

"On Saturday," said Anthony in his lady's ear—one chair held them both—"on Saturday we leave this England. Before I'm wanted at this unpleasant trial a fortnight or three weeks will elapse, if I know anything of English justice. In that time, lady, we will paint a girdle of color about the earth—or some of it at least." His clasp tightened about her shoulders. "Shall we? Shall we? I want to take you away, right away! I want to show you places you've never seen before though you may have been in them many times. Where shall it be? Paris? Brittany? Sicily? Madrid? Any'll be a better heaven than is really possible."

To their ears came the hum of a car. As they listened, it grew louder; and yet louder. The car swept up the drive; halted. Down the stairs and past the door of the drawing-room came flying feet—Dora's.

"Archie. It's Archie!" Lucia struggled to free herself.

Anthony held her closer. "Never mind Archibald. Answer me, woman! Do we leave England on Saturday?"

They heard the heavy front door flung open; then a cry of delight; then silence.

"Let me down! Oh, do let me down!" Lucia begged. "Tony, pleeease! They'll be in here in a minute."

He released her, only to snatch her to him again when both were on their feet.

He held her close. "You've got to answer, you know. Do we leave England——"

"Oh, yes. All right, all right! but haven't you forgotten something?" He felt laughter shake her body.

"Forgotten something?" he said. "No, don't think so."

She drew his face down to hers. "Don't we get married at all?" she whispered.

"Hell!" said Anthony. "I'd forgotten that. Damn it! That means we can't go until Monday."

They heard footsteps outside. Lucia wriggled free, her face flaming.

The door burst open. "Here we are!" said Deacon, enormous in the doorway. "The return of Crippen. Most affectin'!" He advanced into the room. "First:

Gethryn, thank you." He stretched out a big hand and crushed Anthony's.

Dora, entering in a rush, fell upon her sister. "Loo! Loo!" she cried, "we're going to be married! Soon!"

Lucia clutched at her and began to laugh. "Why, darling," she said, "I believe I am too."

3

In town, Spencer Hastings and his betrothed were discussing details.

"Of course," said Hastings, "A. R. Gethryn for best man?"

Margaret patted his cheek. "It wouldn't surprise me, little man," she said, "if we found he wasn't eligible."

A CATALOGUE OF SELECTED DOVER BOOKS IN ALL FIELDS OF INTEREST

THE EARLY WORK OF AUBREY BEARDSLEY, Aubrey Beardsley. 157 plates, 2 in color: *Manon Lescaut, Madame Bovary, Morte Darthur, Salome,* other. Introduction by H. Marillier. 182pp. 8⅛ x 11. 21816-3 Pa. $4.50

THE LATER WORK OF AUBREY BEARDSLEY, Aubrey Beardsley. Exotic masterpieces of full maturity: *Venus and Tannhauser, Lysistrata, Rape of the Lock, Volpone,* Savoy material, etc. 174 plates, 2 in color. 186pp. 8⅛ x 11. 21817-1 Pa. $4.50

THOMAS NAST'S CHRISTMAS DRAWINGS, Thomas Nast. Almost all Christmas drawings by creator of image of Santa Claus as we know it, and one of America's foremost illustrators and political cartoonists. 66 illustrations. 3 illustrations in color on covers. 96pp. 8⅜ x 11¼. 23660-9 Pa. $3.50

THE DORÉ ILLUSTRATIONS FOR DANTE'S DIVINE COMEDY, Gustave Doré. All 135 plates from Inferno, Purgatory, Paradise; fantastic tortures, infernal landscapes, celestial wonders. Each plate with appropriate (translated) verses. 141pp. 9 x 12. 23231-X Pa. $4.50

DORÉ'S ILLUSTRATIONS FOR RABELAIS, Gustave Doré. 252 striking illustrations of *Gargantua and Pantagruel* books by foremost 19th-century illustrator. Including 60 plates, 192 delightful smaller illustrations. 153pp. 9 x 12. 23656-0 Pa. $5.00

LONDON: A PILGRIMAGE, Gustave Doré, Blanchard Jerrold. Squalor, riches, misery, beauty of mid-Victorian metropolis; 55 wonderful plates, 125 other illustrations, full social, cultural text by Jerrold. 191pp. of text. 9⅜ x 12¼. 22306-X Pa. $6.00

THE RIME OF THE ANCIENT MARINER, Gustave Doré, S. T. Coleridge. Dore's finest work, 34 plates capture moods, subtleties of poem. Full text. Introduction by Millicent Rose. 77pp. 9¼ x 12. 22305-1 Pa. $3.00

THE DORE BIBLE ILLUSTRATIONS, Gustave Doré. All wonderful, detailed plates: Adam and Eve, Flood, Babylon, Life of Jesus, etc. Brief King James text with each plate. Introduction by Millicent Rose. 241 plates. 241pp. 9 x 12. 23004-X Pa. $5.00

THE COMPLETE ENGRAVINGS, ETCHINGS AND DRYPOINTS OF ALBRECHT DURER. "Knight, Death and Devil"; "Melencolia," and more—all Dürer's known works in all three media, including 6 works formerly attributed to him. 120 plates. 235pp. 8⅜ x 11¼. 22851-7 Pa. $6.50

MAXIMILIAN'S TRIUMPHAL ARCH, Albrecht Dürer and others. Incredible monument of woodcut art: 8 foot high elaborate arch—heraldic figures, humans, battle scenes, fantastic elements—that you can assemble yourself. Printed on one side, layout for assembly. 143pp. 11 x 16. 21451-6 Pa. $5.00

THE COMPLETE WOODCUTS OF ALBRECHT DURER, edited by Dr. W. Kurth. 346 in all: "Old Testament," "St. Jerome," "Passion," "Life of Virgin," Apocalypse," many others. Introduction by Campbell Dodgson. 285pp. 8½ x 12¼. 21097-9 Pa. $6.95

DRAWINGS OF ALBRECHT DURER, edited by Heinrich Wolfflin. 81 plates show development from youth to full style. Many favorites; many new. Introduction by Alfred Werner. 96pp. 8⅛ x 11. 22352-3 Pa. $4.00

THE HUMAN FIGURE, Albrecht Dürer. Experiments in various techniques—stereometric, progressive proportional, and others. Also life studies that rank among finest ever done. Complete reprinting of *Dresden Sketchbook.* 170 plates. 355pp. 8⅜ x 11¼. 21042-1 Pa. $6.95

OF THE JUST SHAPING OF LETTERS, Albrecht Dürer. Renaissance artist explains design of Roman majuscules by geometry, also Gothic lower and capitals. Grolier Club edition. 43pp. 7⅞ x 10¾ 21306-4 Pa. $2.50

TEN BOOKS ON ARCHITECTURE, Vitruvius. The most important book ever written on architecture. Early Roman aesthetics, technology, classical orders, site selection, all other aspects. Stands behind everything since. Morgan translation. 331pp. 5⅜ x 8½. 20645-9 Pa. $3.75

THE FOUR BOOKS OF ARCHITECTURE, Andrea Palladio. 16th-century classic responsible for Palladian movement and style. Covers classical architectural remains, Renaissance revivals, classical orders, etc. 1738 Ware English edition. Introduction by A. Placzek. 216 plates. 110pp. of text. 9½ x 12¾. 21308-0 Pa. $7.50

HORIZONS, Norman Bel Geddes. Great industrialist stage designer, "father of streamlining," on application of aesthetics to transportation, amusement, architecture, etc. 1932 prophetic account; function, theory, specific projects. 222 illustrations. 312pp. 7⅞ x 10¾. 23514-9 Pa. $6.95

FRANK LLOYD WRIGHT'S FALLINGWATER, Donald Hoffmann. Full, illustrated story of conception and building of Wright's masterwork at Bear Run, Pa. 100 photographs of site, construction, and details of completed structure. 112pp. 9¼ x 10. 23671-4 Pa. $5.00

THE ELEMENTS OF DRAWING, John Ruskin. Timeless classic by great Viltorian; starts with basic ideas, works through more difficult. Many practical exercises. 48 illustrations. Introduction by Lawrence Campbell. 228pp. 5⅜ x 8½. 22730-8 Pa. $2.75

GIST OF ART, John Sloan. Greatest modern American teacher, Art Students League, offers innumerable hints, instructions, guided comments to help you in painting. Not a formal course. 46 illustrations. Introduction by Helen Sloan. 200pp. 5⅜ x 8½. 23435-5 Pa. $3.50

THE ANATOMY OF THE HORSE, George Stubbs. Often considered the great masterpiece of animal anatomy. Full reproduction of 1766 edition, plus prospectus; original text and modernized text. 36 plates. Introduction by Eleanor Garvey. 121pp. 11 x 14¾. 23402-9 Pa. $6.00

BRIDGMAN'S LIFE DRAWING, George B. Bridgman. More than 500 illustrative drawings and text teach you to abstract the body into its major masses, use light and shade, proportion; as well as specific areas of anatomy, of which Bridgman is master. 192pp. 6½ x 9¼. (Available in U.S. only) 22710-3 Pa. $2.50

ART NOUVEAU DESIGNS IN COLOR, Alphonse Mucha, Maurice Verneuil, Georges Auriol. Full-color reproduction of *Combinaisons ornementales* (c. 1900) by Art Nouveau masters. Floral, animal, geometric, interlacings, swashes—borders, frames, spots—all incredibly beautiful. 60 plates, hundreds of designs. 9⅜ x 8-1/16. 22885-1 Pa. $4.00

FULL-COLOR FLORAL DESIGNS IN THE ART NOUVEAU STYLE, E. A. Seguy. 166 motifs, on 40 plates, from *Les fleurs et leurs applications decoratives* (1902): borders, circular designs, repeats, allovers, "spots." All in authentic Art Nouveau colors. 48pp. 9⅜ x 12¼. 23439-8 Pa. $5.00

A DIDEROT PICTORIAL ENCYCLOPEDIA OF TRADES AND INDUSTRY, edited by Charles C. Gillispie. 485 most interesting plates from the great French Encyclopedia of the 18th century show hundreds of working figures, artifacts, process, land and cityscapes; glassmaking, papermaking, metal extraction, construction, weaving, making furniture, clothing, wigs, dozens of other activities. Plates fully explained. 920pp. 9 x 12. 22284-5, 22285-3 Clothbd., Two-vol. set $40.00

HANDBOOK OF EARLY ADVERTISING ART, Clarence P. Hornung. Largest collection of copyright-free early and antique advertising art ever compiled. Over 6,000 illustrations, from Franklin's time to the 1890's for special effects, novelty. Valuable source, almost inexhaustible.
Pictorial Volume. Agriculture, the zodiac, animals, autos, birds, Christmas, fire engines, flowers, trees, musical instruments, ships, games and sports, much more. Arranged by subject matter and use. 237 plates. 288pp. 9 x 12. 20122-8 Clothbd. $13.50

Typographical Volume. Roman and Gothic faces ranging from 10 point to 300 point, "Barnum," German and Old English faces, script, logotypes, scrolls and flourishes, 1115 ornamental initials, 67 complete alphabets, more. 310 plates. 320pp. 9 x 12. 20123-6 Clothbd. $13.50

CALLIGRAPHY (CALLIGRAPHIA LATINA), J. G. Schwandner. High point of 18th-century ornamental calligraphy. Very ornate initials, scrolls, borders, cherubs, birds, lettered examples. 172pp. 9 x 13. 20475-8 Pa. $6.00

ART FORMS IN NATURE, Ernst Haeckel. Multitude of strangely beautiful natural forms: Radiolaria, Foraminifera, jellyfishes, fungi, turtles, bats, etc. All 100 plates of the 19th-century evolutionist's *Kunstformen der Natur* (1904). 100pp. 9⅜ x 12¼. 22987-4 Pa. $4.50

CHILDREN: A PICTORIAL ARCHIVE FROM NINETEENTH-CENTURY SOURCES, edited by Carol Belanger Grafton. 242 rare, copyright-free wood engravings for artists and designers. Widest such selection available. All illustrations in line. 119pp. 8⅜ x 11¼. 23694-3 Pa. $3.50

WOMEN: A PICTORIAL ARCHIVE FROM NINETEENTH-CENTURY SOURCES, edited by Jim Harter. 391 copyright-free wood engravings for artists and designers selected from rare periodicals. Most extensive such collection available. All illustrations in line. 128pp. 9 x 12. 23703-6 Pa. $4.00

ARABIC ART IN COLOR, Prisse d'Avennes. From the greatest ornamentalists of all time—50 plates in color, rarely seen outside the Near East, rich in suggestion and stimulus. Includes 4 plates on covers. 46pp. 9⅜ x 12¼. 23658-7 Pa. $6.00

AUTHENTIC ALGERIAN CARPET DESIGNS AND MOTIFS, edited by June Beveridge. Algerian carpets are world famous. Dozens of geometrical motifs are charted on grids, color-coded, for weavers, needleworkers, craftsmen, designers. 53 illustrations plus 4 in color. 48pp. 8¼ x 11. (Available in U.S. only) 23650-1 Pa. $1.75

DICTIONARY OF AMERICAN PORTRAITS, edited by Hayward and Blanche Cirker. 4000 important Americans, earliest times to 1905, mostly in clear line. Politicians, writers, soldiers, scientists, inventors, industrialists, Indians, Blacks, women, outlaws, etc. Identificatory information. 756pp. 9¼ x 12¾. 21823-6 Clothbd. $40.00

HOW THE OTHER HALF LIVES, Jacob A. Riis. Journalistic record of filth, degradation, upward drive in New York immigrant slums, shops, around 1900. New edition includes 100 original Riis photos, monuments of early photography. 233pp. 10 x 7⅞. 22012-5 Pa. $6.00

NEW YORK IN THE THIRTIES, Berenice Abbott. Noted photographer's fascinating study of city shows new buildings that have become famous and old sights that have disappeared forever. Insightful commentary. 97 photographs. 97pp. 11⅜ x 10. 22967-X Pa. $4.50

MEN AT WORK, Lewis W. Hine. Famous photographic studies of construction workers, railroad men, factory workers and coal miners. New supplement of 18 photos on Empire State building construction. New introduction by Jonathan L. Doherty. Total of 69 photos. 63pp. 8 x 10¾. 23475-4 Pa. $3.00

THE DEPRESSION YEARS AS PHOTOGRAPHED BY ARTHUR ROTHSTEIN, Arthur Rothstein. First collection devoted entirely to the work of outstanding 1930s photographer: famous dust storm photo, ragged children, unemployed, etc. 120 photographs. Captions. 119pp. 9¼ x 10¾.
23590-4 Pa. $5.00

CAMERA WORK: A PICTORIAL GUIDE, Alfred Stieglitz. All 559 illustrations and plates from the most important periodical in the history of art photography, *Camera Work* (1903-17). Presented four to a page, reduced in size but still clear, in strict chronological order, with complete captions. Three indexes. Glossary. Bibliography. 176pp. 8⅜ x 11¼.
23591-2 Pa. $6.95

ALVIN LANGDON COBURN, PHOTOGRAPHER, Alvin L. Coburn. Revealing autobiography by one of greatest photographers of 20th century gives insider's version of Photo-Secession, plus comments on his own work. 77 photographs by Coburn. Edited by Helmut and Alison Gernsheim. 160pp. 8⅛ x 11. 23685-4 Pa. $6.00

NEW YORK IN THE FORTIES, Andreas Feininger. 162 brilliant photographs by the well-known photographer, formerly with *Life* magazine, show commuters, shoppers, Times Square at night, Harlem nightclub, Lower East Side, etc. Introduction and full captions by John von Hartz. 181pp. 9¼ x 10¾. 23585-8 Pa. $6.00

GREAT NEWS PHOTOS AND THE STORIES BEHIND THEM, John Faber. Dramatic volume of 140 great news photos, 1855 through 1976, and revealing stories behind them, with both historical and technical information. Hindenburg disaster, shooting of Oswald, nomination of Jimmy Carter, etc. 160pp. 8¼ x 11. 23667-6 Pa. $5.00

THE ART OF THE CINEMATOGRAPHER, Leonard Maltin. Survey of American cinematography history and anecdotal interviews with 5 masters—Arthur Miller, Hal Mohr, Hal Rosson, Lucien Ballard, and Conrad Hall. Very large selection of behind-the-scenes production photos. 105 photographs. Filmographies. Index. Originally *Behind the Camera.* 144pp. 8¼ x 11. 23686-2 Pa. $5.00

DESIGNS FOR THE THREE-CORNERED HAT (LE TRICORNE), Pablo Picasso. 32 fabulously rare drawings—including 31 color illustrations of costumes and accessories—for 1919 production of famous ballet. Edited by Parmenia Migel, who has written new introduction. 48pp. 9⅜ x 12¼. (Available in U.S. only) 23709-5 Pa. $5.00

NOTES OF A FILM DIRECTOR, Sergei Eisenstein. Greatest Russian filmmaker explains montage, making of *Alexander Nevsky,* aesthetics; comments on self, associates, great rivals (Chaplin), similar material. 78 illustrations. 240pp. 5⅜ x 8½. 22392-2 Pa. $4.50

PRINCIPLES OF ORCHESTRATION, Nikolay Rimsky-Korsakov. Great classical orchestrator provides fundamentals of tonal resonance, progression of parts, voice and orchestra, tutti effects, much else in major document. 330pp. of musical excerpts. 489pp. 6½ x 9¼. 21266-1 Pa. $6.00

TRISTAN UND ISOLDE, Richard Wagner. Full orchestral score with complete instrumentation. Do not confuse with piano reduction. Commentary by Felix Mottl, great Wagnerian conductor and scholar. Study score. 655pp. 8⅛ x 11. 22915-7 Pa. $12.50

REQUIEM IN FULL SCORE, Giuseppe Verdi. Immensely popular with choral groups and music lovers. Republication of edition published by C. F. Peters, Leipzig, n. d. German frontmaker in English translation. Glossary. Text in Latin. Study score. 204pp. 9⅜ x 12¼.
23682-X Pa. $6.00

COMPLETE CHAMBER MUSIC FOR STRINGS, Felix Mendelssohn. All of Mendelssohn's chamber music: Octet, 2 Quintets, 6 Quartets, and Four Pieces for String Quartet. (Nothing with piano is included). Complete works edition (1874-7). Study score. 283 pp. 9⅜ x 12¼.
23679-X Pa. $6.95

POPULAR SONGS OF NINETEENTH-CENTURY AMERICA, edited by Richard Jackson. 64 most important songs: "Old Oaken Bucket," "Arkansas Traveler," "Yellow Rose of Texas," etc. Authentic original sheet music, full introduction and commentaries. 290pp. 9 x 12. 23270-0 Pa. $6.00

COLLECTED PIANO WORKS, Scott Joplin. Edited by Vera Brodsky Lawrence. Practically all of Joplin's piano works—rags, two-steps, marches, waltzes, etc., 51 works in all. Extensive introduction by Rudi Blesh. Total of 345pp. 9 x 12. 23106-2 Pa. $13.50

BASIC PRINCIPLES OF CLASSICAL BALLET, Agrippina Vaganova. Great Russian theoretician, teacher explains methods for teaching classical ballet; incorporates best from French, Italian, Russian schools. 118 illustrations. 175pp. 5⅜ x 8½. 22036-2 Pa. $2.00

CHINESE CHARACTERS, L. Wieger. Rich analysis of 2300 characters according to traditional systems into primitives. Historical-semantic analysis to phonetics (Classical Mandarin) and radicals. 820pp. 6⅛ x 9¼.
21321-8 Pa. $8.95

EGYPTIAN LANGUAGE: EASY LESSONS IN EGYPTIAN HIEROGLYPHICS, E. A. Wallis Budge. Foremost Egyptologist offers Egyptian grammar, explanation of hieroglyphics, many reading texts, dictionary of symbols. 246pp. 5 x 7½. (Available in U.S. only)
21394-3 Clothbd. $7.50

AN ETYMOLOGICAL DICTIONARY OF MODERN ENGLISH, Ernest Weekley. Richest, fullest work, by foremost British lexicographer. Detailed word histories. Inexhaustible. Do not confuse this with *Concise Etymological Dictionary*, which is abridged. Total of 856pp. 6½ x 9¼.
21873-2, 21874-0 Pa., Two-vol. set $10.00

A MAYA GRAMMAR, Alfred M. Tozzer. Practical, useful English-language grammar by the Harvard anthropologist who was one of the three greatest American scholars in the area of Maya culture. Phonetics, grammatical processes, syntax, more. 301pp. 5⅜ x 8½. 23465-7 Pa. $4.00

THE JOURNAL OF HENRY D. THOREAU, edited by Bradford Torrey, F. H. Allen. Complete reprinting of 14 volumes, 1837-61, over two million words; the sourcebooks for *Walden*, etc. Definitive. All original sketches, plus 75 photographs. Introduction by Walter Harding. Total of 1804pp. 8½ x 12¼. 20312-3, 20313-1 Clothbd., Two-vol. set $50.00

CLASSIC GHOST STORIES, Charles Dickens and others. 18 wonderful stories you've wanted to reread: "The Monkey's Paw," "The House and the Brain," "The Upper Berth," "The Signalman," "Dracula's Guest," "The Tapestried Chamber," etc. Dickens, Scott, Mary Shelley, Stoker, etc. 330pp. 5⅜ x 8½. 20735-8 Pa. $3.50

SEVEN SCIENCE FICTION NOVELS, H. G. Wells. Full novels. *First Men in the Moon, Island of Dr. Moreau, War of the Worlds, Food of the Gods, Invisible Man, Time Machine, In the Days of the Comet.* A basic science-fiction library. 1015pp. 5⅜ x 8½. (Available in U.S. only) 20264-X Clothbd. $8.95

ARMADALE, Wilkie Collins. Third great mystery novel by the author of *The Woman in White* and *The Moonstone.* Ingeniously plotted narrative shows an exceptional command of character, incident and mood. Original magazine version with 40 illustrations. 597pp. 5⅜ x 8½. 23429-0 Pa. $5.00

MASTERS OF MYSTERY, H. Douglas Thomson. The first book in English (1931) devoted to history and aesthetics of detective story. Poe, Doyle, LeFanu, Dickens, many others, up to 1930. New introduction and notes by E. F. Bleiler. 288pp. 5⅜ x 8½. (Available in U.S. only) 23606-4 Pa. $4.00

FLATLAND, E. A. Abbott. Science-fiction classic explores life of 2-D being in 3-D world. Read also as introduction to thought about hyperspace. Introduction by Banesh Hoffmann. 16 illustrations. 103pp. 5⅜ x 8½. 20001-9 Pa. $1.50

THREE SUPERNATURAL NOVELS OF THE VICTORIAN PERIOD, edited, with an introduction, by E. F. Bleiler. Reprinted complete and unabridged, three great classics of the supernatural: *The Haunted Hotel* by Wilkie Collins, *The Haunted House at Latchford* by Mrs. J. H. Riddell, and *The Lost Stradivarious* by J. Meade Falkner. 325pp. 5⅜ x 8½. 22571-2 Pa. $4.00

AYESHA: THE RETURN OF "SHE," H. Rider Haggard. Virtuoso sequel featuring the great mythic creation, Ayesha, in an adventure that is fully as good as the first book, *She*. Original magazine version, with 47 original illustrations by Maurice Greiffenhagen. 189pp. 6½ x 9¼. 23649-8 Pa. $3.00

UNCLE SILAS, J. Sheridan LeFanu. Victorian Gothic mystery novel, considered by many best of period, even better than Collins or Dickens. Wonderful psychological terror. Introduction by Frederick Shroyer. 436pp. 5⅜ x 8½. 21715-9 Pa. $4.00

JURGEN, James Branch Cabell. The great erotic fantasy of the 1920's that delighted thousands, shocked thousands more. Full final text, Lane edition with 13 plates by Frank Pape. 346pp. 5⅜ x 8½. 23507-6 Pa. $4.00

THE CLAVERINGS, Anthony Trollope. Major novel, chronicling aspects of British Victorian society, personalities. Reprint of Cornhill serialization, 16 plates by M. Edwards; first reprint of full text. Introduction by Norman Donaldson. 412pp. 5⅜ x 8½. 23464-9 Pa. $5.00

KEPT IN THE DARK, Anthony Trollope. Unusual short novel about Victorian morality and abnormal psychology by the great English author. Probably the first American publication. Frontispiece by Sir John Millais. 92pp. 6½ x 9¼. 23609-9 Pa. $2.50

RALPH THE HEIR, Anthony Trollope. Forgotten tale of illegitimacy, inheritance. Master novel of Trollope's later years. Victorian country estates, clubs, Parliament, fox hunting, world of fully realized characters. Reprint of 1871 edition. 12 illustrations by F. A. Faser. 434pp. of text. 5⅜ x 8½. 23642-0 Pa. $4.50

YEKL and THE IMPORTED BRIDEGROOM AND OTHER STORIES OF THE NEW YORK GHETTO, Abraham Cahan. Film *Hester Street* based on *Yekl* (1896). Novel, other stories among first about Jewish immigrants of N.Y.'s East Side. Highly praised by W. D. Howells—Cahan "a new star of realism." New introduction by Bernard G. Richards. 240pp. 5⅜ x 8½. 22427-9 Pa. $3.50

THE HIGH PLACE, James Branch Cabell. Great fantasy writer's enchanting comedy of disenchantment set in 18th-century France. Considered by some critics to be even better than his famous *Jurgen*. 10 illustrations and numerous vignettes by noted fantasy artist Frank C. Pape. 320pp. 5⅜ x 8½. 23670-6 Pa. $4.00

ALICE'S ADVENTURES UNDER GROUND, Lewis Carroll. Facsimile of ms. Carroll gave Alice Liddell in 1864. Different in many ways from final Alice. Handlettered, illustrated by Carroll. Introduction by Martin Gardner. 128pp. 5⅜ x 8½. 21482-6 Pa. $2.00

FAVORITE ANDREW LANG FAIRY TALE BOOKS IN MANY COLORS, Andrew Lang. The four Lang favorites in a boxed set—the complete *Red, Green, Yellow* and *Blue* Fairy Books. 164 stories; 439 illustrations by Lancelot Speed, Henry Ford and G. P. Jacomb Hood. Total of about 1500pp. 5⅜ x 8½. 23407-X Boxed set, Pa. $14.00

HOUSEHOLD STORIES BY THE BROTHERS GRIMM. All the great Grimm stories: "Rumpelstiltskin," "Snow White," "Hansel and Gretel," etc., with 114 illustrations by Walter Crane. 269pp. 5⅜ x 8½.
21080-4 Pa. $3.00

SLEEPING BEAUTY, illustrated by Arthur Rackham. Perhaps the fullest, most delightful version ever, told by C. S. Evans. Rackham's best work. 49 illustrations. 110pp. 7⅞ x 10¾. 22756-1 Pa. $2.00

AMERICAN FAIRY TALES, L. Frank Baum. Young cowboy lassoes Father Time; dummy in Mr. Floman's department store window comes to life; and 10 other fairy tales. 41 illustrations by N. P. Hall, Harry Kennedy, Ike Morgan, and Ralph Gardner. 209pp. 5⅜ x 8½. 23643-9 Pa. $3.00

THE WONDERFUL WIZARD OF OZ, L. Frank Baum. Facsimile in full color of America's finest children's classic. Introduction by Martin Gardner. 143 illustrations by W. W. Denslow. 267pp. 5⅜ x 8½.
20691-2 Pa. $3.50

THE TALE OF PETER RABBIT, Beatrix Potter. The inimitable Peter's terrifying adventure in Mr. McGregor's garden, with all 27 wonderful, full-color Potter illustrations. 55pp. 4¼ x 5½. (Available in U.S. only)
22827-4 Pa. $1.10

THE STORY OF KING ARTHUR AND HIS KNIGHTS, Howard Pyle. Finest children's version of life of King Arthur. 48 illustrations by Pyle. 131pp. 6⅛ x 9¼. 21445-1 Pa. $4.00

CARUSO'S CARICATURES, Enrico Caruso. Great tenor's remarkable caricatures of self, fellow musicians, composers, others. Toscanini, Puccini, Farrar, etc. Impish, cutting, insightful. 473 illustrations. Preface by M. Sisca. 217pp. 8⅜ x 11¼. 23528-9 Pa. $6.00

PERSONAL NARRATIVE OF A PILGRIMAGE TO ALMADINAH AND MECCAH, Richard Burton. Great travel classic by remarkably colorful personality. Burton, disguised as a Moroccan, visited sacred shrines of Islam, narrowly escaping death. Wonderful observations of Islamic life, customs, personalities. 47 illustrations. Total of 959pp. 5⅜ x 8½.
21217-3, 21218-1 Pa., Two-vol. set $10.00

INCIDENTS OF TRAVEL IN YUCATAN, John L. Stephens. Classic (1843) exploration of jungles of Yucatan, looking for evidences of Maya civilization. Travel adventures, Mexican and Indian culture, etc. Total of 669pp. 5⅜ x 8½. 20926-1, 20927-X Pa., Two-vol. set $6.50

AMERICAN LITERARY AUTOGRAPHS FROM WASHINGTON IRVING TO HENRY JAMES, Herbert Cahoon, et al. Letters, poems, manuscripts of Hawthorne, Thoreau, Twain, Alcott, Whitman, 67 other prominent American authors. Reproductions, full transcripts and commentary. Plus checklist of all American Literary Autographs in The Pierpont Morgan Library. Printed on exceptionally high-quality paper. 136 illustrations. 212pp. 9⅛ x 12¼. 23548-3 Pa. $7.95

CATALOGUE OF DOVER BOOKS

GEOMETRY, RELATIVITY AND THE FOURTH DIMENSION, Rudolf Rucker. Exposition of fourth dimension, means of visualization, concepts of relativity as Flatland characters continue adventures. Popular, easily followed yet accurate, profound. 141 illustrations. 133pp. 5⅜ x 8½.
23400-2 Pa. $2.75

THE ORIGIN OF LIFE, A. I. Oparin. Modern classic in biochemistry, the first rigorous examination of possible evolution of life from nitrocarbon compounds. Non-technical, easily followed. Total of 295pp. 5⅜ x 8½.
60213-3 Pa. $4.00

THE CURVES OF LIFE, Theodore A. Cook. Examination of shells, leaves, horns, human body, art, etc., in "*the* classic reference on how the golden ratio applies to spirals and helices in nature . . . ."—Martin Gardner. 426 illustrations. Total of 512pp. 5⅜ x 8½. 23701-X Pa. $5.95

PLANETS, STARS AND GALAXIES, A. E. Fanning. Comprehensive introductory survey: the sun, solar system, stars, galaxies, universe, cosmology; quasars, radio stars, etc. 24pp. of photographs. 189pp. 5⅜ x 8½. (Available in U.S. only) 21680-2 Pa. $3.00

THE THIRTEEN BOOKS OF EUCLID'S ELEMENTS, translated with introduction and commentary by Sir Thomas L. Heath. Definitive edition. Textual and linguistic notes, mathematical analysis, 2500 years of critical commentary. Do not confuse with abridged school editions. Total of 1414pp. 5⅜ x 8½. 60088-2, 60089-0, 60090-4 Pa., Three-vol. set $18.00

DIALOGUES CONCERNING TWO NEW SCIENCES, Galileo Galilei. Encompassing 30 years of experiment and thought, these dialogues deal with geometric demonstrations of fracture of solid bodies, cohesion, leverage, speed of light and sound, pendulums, falling bodies, accelerated motion, etc. 300pp. 5⅜ x 8½. 60099-8 Pa. $4.00

Prices subject to change without notice.

Available at your book dealer or write for free catalogue to Dept. GI, Dover Publications, Inc., 180 Varick St., N.Y., N.Y. 10014. Dover publishes more than 175 books each year on science, elementary and advanced mathematics, biology, music, art, literary history, social sciences and other areas.